Praise for Stardust

"Carla Stewart writes with incredible heart and warmth. Her stories manage to challenge and comfort me all the while keeping me glued to the page. She's an amazing talent."

—Gina Holmes, bestselling author of
Crossing Oceans and *Dry as Rain*

"With beautiful imagery that engages all the senses, Carla Stewart swept me right into the world of the bayou in the 1950s. Her latest novel, *Stardust*, is told with heart and skill and obvious love for her characters. A gripping storyline that is inspiring and unforgettable."

—Julie L. Cannon, bestselling author of
I'll Be Home for Christmas, 2010, and *Twang,*
coming September 2012

"Carla Stewart is a talented writer who has proven that again with *Stardust*. I was hooked from the first sentence and am anxious to share this engaging story with our She Reads readers."

—Marybeth Whalen, founder and codirector of She Reads
(www.shereads.org), the fiction division of Proverbs 31 Ministries,
and author of *She Makes It Look Easy* and *The Mailbox*

"A reverence for the past and a keen eye for interesting characters make *Stardust* as bright and magical as a twinkling neon sign on a dark, lonely two-lane. You'll love the journey as much as the final destination. Another winner from an author with a uniquely beautiful talent!"

—Lisa Wingate, national bestselling and award-winning
author of *Dandelion Summer* and *Blue Moon Bay*

"Carla Stewart is one of the best at slicing out a piece of Americana and serving it to the reader in a delicious story. *Stardust* is a smooth, inviting, well told story that will stick with you long after you read the last line and close the book. A worthy read."

—Rachel Hauck, award-winning author of *Dining with Joy*

"Carla Stewart writes from the heart about a hard subject. As a polio survivor, I understand the fear and worry that the polio epidemics of the twentieth century evoked. Carla transcends that fear with compassion and achingly beautiful prose. *Stardust* is a winner."

—Linda S. Clare, author of *The Fence My Father Built*

Praise for Broken Wings

"Stewart skillfully entertains and engages the reader with each character's private pain and survival skills." —*Romantic Times*, 4 stars

"Carla Stewart writes powerful, beautiful, emotionally evocative stories that touch my heart. *Broken Wings* is no exception. I couldn't put it down."

—Susan May Warren, award-winning bestselling author of *Nightingale*

"I smiled through my tears as I read *Broken Wings*. Those of us who have been abused can cheer for Brooke, who stands up and fights with what she has: friendship and the love of God. Keep writing, Carla. We need the voice of hope."

—Shelley Adina, author of the All About Us series

"A relevant story that explores the beauty of friendship as well as the heartache of abuse. Carla Stewart is an engaging storyteller."

—Susan Meissner, author of *The Shape of Mercy*

"With apt descriptions and artful prose, Stewart delves into the vibrant, jazzy 1940s, at the same time creating a true-to-life present. Moving between the two time periods, readers discover what everlasting love is, and how strong a woman must be to recognize it."

—Christina Berry, award-winning author of
The Familiar Stranger

Praise for Chasing Lilacs

"Stewart writes about powerful and basic emotions with a restraint that suggests depth and authenticity; the relationship between Sammie and her mother Rita, the engine that drives the plot, is beautifully and delicately rendered. Coming-of-age stories are a fiction staple, but well-done ones much rarer. This emotionally acute novel is one of the rare ones."

—*Publishers Weekly*, starred review

"This first-person narrative contains resolute characters and vivid descriptions of a small Texas community in the 1950s. If her debut is any indication, Stewart has a promising future."

—*Romantic Times*, 4½ stars

"A warm, compelling tale with characters who will stay with you for quite a while...Those who lived during the 1950s will have delightful flashbacks, and those who didn't will get a true glimpse into that era. All will identify with Sammie and the friends and family who deeply influence her search for the truth about her family—and herself."

—*BookPage*

"Carla Stewart's book, *Chasing Lilacs*, was a delightful read. The perfect book for a snowy afternoon. It'll warm your heart."

—Jodi Thomas, *New York Times*
bestselling author

Stardust

More Heartfelt Fiction from Carla Stewart:

Broken Wings

Chasing Lilacs

Available from FaithWords
wherever books are sold.

Stardust

a novel

Carla Stewart

New York   Boston   Nashville

FaithWords
Hachette Book Group
237 Park Avenue
New York, NY 10017

www.faithwords.com

Printed in the United States of America

First Edition: May 2012

10 9 8 7 6 5 4 3 2 1

RRD-C

FaithWords is a division of Hachette Book Group, Inc.
The FaithWords name and logo are trademarks of Hachette Book Group, Inc.

The Hachette Speakers Bureau provides a wide range of authors for speaking
events. To find out more, go to www.hachettespeakersbureau.com or call
(866) 376-6591.

The publisher is not responsible for websites (or their content)
that are not owned by the publisher.

Library of Congress Cataloging-in-Publication Data

Stewart, Carla.
     Stardust / Carla Stewart.—1st ed.
         p. cm.
     ISBN 978-1-4555-0428-2
     1. Widows—Texas—Fiction.   2. Motel management—Fiction.
3. Mistresses—Fiction.   4. Family secrets—Fiction.   5. Forgiveness—
Fiction.   6. Texas—Fiction.   I. Title.
     PS3619.T4937S73 2012
     813'.6—dc22

                                                                2011029396

To my four sons—Andy, Brett, Scott, and James.
You've filled my life with joy.

[ACKNOWLEDGMENTS]

The inspiration and journey of each of my books has been so different that it's difficult to know where to start in paying homage to those who've influenced me along the way.

I'm thankful and grateful for the constants in my life—Max, for sure, who bears the brunt by being married to a writer. Thank you for your unwavering love and being willing to suspend disbelief and accept that life is normal when meals come in takeaway bags and soggy boxes. Andy, Amy, Brett, Cindy, Scott, Denice, James, and Allison—what a joy to have such an amazing group of kids to enrich my life. Drake, Nash, Seth, Davyn, Jorgen, and Jeremy—you make me smile and remember what is important in life.

Camille, Courtney, and Myra—your friendship is precious to me. So are your virtual red pencils that have made the prose better, the sentences stronger. Kellie, thank you for sharing a great weekend in East Texas and brainstorming until the wee hours.

The FaithWords team—you all have my deepest gratitude. Special thanks to Christina Boys and Lauren Rohrig, whose insights and encouragement made this a better book. A nod, also, to Laini Brown, Sarah Reck, Shanon Stowe, Jody Waldrup, and the design team. It is a joy to work with you.

Sandra Bishop. My agent and friend. Your insights and encouragement go above and beyond. Thank you.

Jeane Wynn, you astound me and bless me with your support on my behalf.

To those in the town of Jefferson, Texas. You opened your arms with Southern hospitality and shared your anecdotes. I don't even know all your names, but you helped shape the fictional town of Mayhaw. Thanks to Bob and Pam at Delta Street Inn, Kathy Patrick at Beauty and the Book, Tiajuana, Allison, and the ladies from the First Methodist Church and the *Books Alive!* weekend. A handshake to the riverboat guide who showed me the ways of the bayou, and the folks at the Jefferson Museum. I hope I've done justice to your neck of the woods. Any mistakes are mine alone.

A special note of gratitude to Kathryn Black, who bravely told her story, *In the Shadow of Polio* (Perseus Publishing, 1996). Her writings about the polio epidemic in the first half of the twentieth century, the work of the March of Dimes, and the eventual development of the vaccine that would stop this crippling disease were invaluable to me in my research. Her vivid descriptions and compassion gave me great insight and reminded me of two of my own relatives who were childhood victims of polio and bore the physical manifestations their entire lives.

Thanks to my dad, Mike Brune, and my sisters, Donna and Marsha, for your willingness to listen and for the cherished memories you've given me. You are loved.

To those who've taken time from their busy lives to read my books and share them with others, I'm so grateful. Your letters have brought me great joy and a few tears as you've told me your own stories. You make it all worthwhile.

For Jesus, I thank you for loving me in my weakness and allowing me the opportunity to write stories. I pray they will be used for your eternal glory.

Stardust

CHAPTER I

April 1952. Mayhaw, Texas.

My marriage to O'Dell Peyton was already over when he washed up on the shores of Zion. Of course, no one knew it was O'Dell when the little boy came running from the bayou, bellowing to Cecil at the tire shop that he'd discovered a drowned body. Fact is, no one even knew O'Dell was missing. If someone had asked where he'd been keeping himself, I would've said, "Oh, you know O'Dell. He's got *The Book of Knowledge* encyclopedia route for all of East Texas. Wouldn't surprise me if he's sold to half the people in Tyler by now. Goes over to Kilgore some, too."

The truth was O'Dell left me and our two girls the second week in February. I found the note tucked in the sugar bowl, telling me he'd met a woman who appreciated him. I'd spent two months chewing on that, hot as a pistol one minute, crumpled in grief the next, trying to figure out where I'd gone wrong.

Aunt Cora said, "Georgia, there are plenty of men out there. You're lucky you found out now, while you're still young and have your looks." Aunt Cora, bless her, had yet to find a man in Mayhaw suitable—or willing—to marry her. And looks had nothing to do with it. She could still be a movie star pinup.

Which was totally immaterial in light of O'Dell's drowning. I only mention it because you have a whole different knot on the inside from a husband who's unfaithful than you do from one who's dead.

We buried O'Dell on the second Friday in April. Mary Frances, his mother and a widow herself, clung to me like cellophane. Two bereft figures bobbing for air on the surface, entwined by grief at our roots. Still, it felt unnatural for me to plan the funeral in light of the circumstances. Mary Frances should have had the honor, but widowhood had not been kind to her, and her fragile constitution rendered her incapable. We all breathed a sigh of relief when she showed up in matching shoes and wearing a dress instead of her usual bathrobe.

A motley pair we made. The anguished mother and the betrayed wife sharing a pew, each wrapped in our own thoughts. If she knew O'Dell had deserted me, she'd not once let on. I still took the girls to see her on Sunday afternoons and had baked her an angel food cake for her birthday on St. Patrick's Day.

Aunt Cora told me the morning of the funeral, "Georgia, I didn't raise you to forget your manners. O'Dell might've been a two-timer, but you'll carry your head high and make me proud. His poor mother don't know up from sic 'em, and she needs you to lean on today. I'll take care of the girls."

So I sat with Mary Frances while Aunt Cora sat between Avril and Rosey and drew pictures of Peter Rabbit to keep them quiet during the service. Afterward, Aunt Cora shooed me into the Garvey's Funeral Home courtesy car with Mary Frances. She and the girls hitched a ride with someone else, and I heard later they stopped for ice cream at the Sweet Shoppe on the way home.

The cemetery sits on a rise outside of Mayhaw, inland from the bayou but nestled in its own sheltering grove of sweet gums. The funeral procession wound snake-like along the road, past the courthouse on the town square toward the outskirts. Cecil's Auto

Repair and Bait Shop on the right. The Stardust Tourist Cottages on the left. And beyond that, Mayhaw's backyard neighbor, Zion, huddled along the banks of the cypress swamp. Wavy pencils of smoke rose from Zion, thinning to nothing as they reached the sky. I squinted to see if I could get a peek, but dense pines cradled whatever lay inside, the undergrowth like swaddling clothes. My heart inched up a notch knowing the boy who found poor O'Dell lived in that tangle of forest. Must've darn near scared him out of his britches.

Beside me, Mary Frances sat rigid, hands folded across the handbag on her lap. Her face, stuporous with grief, mirrored my own unspoken turmoil. Did O'Dell call my name as he tumbled through the murky waters? Or that of his new lover? What he was doing in the rain-swollen bayou was a mystery in itself. Perhaps he'd come to his senses and gone out on his fishing boat to figure out a respectable way to come crawling back to me and the girls. It's easy to give a dead man the benefit of the doubt. Trickier, though, was the burning question: Were we still married in the eyes of God when O'Dell capsized?

Our courtesy car jerked to a stop inches from the hearse that carried O'Dell. A look of alarm flashed on Mary Frances's pasty face. "What's happening?"

I craned my neck. "Looks like a logging truck ahead of us. Creeping along like a box turtle. Guess it'll take awhile to get out to the cemetery. You want a mint?" I pulled a Starlight mint from my pocket and held it out.

She shook her head, sighed, and then snapped open her purse, took out a blue glass bottle with a milk of magnesia label, touched it to her lips, and took a swig. I was feeling dyspeptic myself, but I knew it wasn't milk of mag in the bottle. Mary Frances had her own kind of medicine. Pretending not to notice, I rolled down my window and looked at the Stardust.

Weeds had grown up over the winter. No travelers in front of the units, which were in dire need of freshening up. A feeling, akin to pity, twisted my gut. Guilt, too. I'd not been out to visit with Doreen and Paddy in a month of Sundays, Paddy being my uncle twice removed on the Tickle side. The *other* branch of the family, according to Aunt Cora. The way Paddy told it, he seized the opportunity when he saw it. Before the Depression, lots of folks passed through Mayhaw, needed a place to stay. I thought it was brilliant, and although he hadn't made a fortune, he'd done all right. Until he found out about the lung tumor.

My mind went back to the day when cherry-red paint outlined each window and washtubs full of geraniums greeted guests by their front doors. A magnificent neon sign pulsed red, blue, and yellow lights then, visible from one end of town to the other as it beckoned the weary travelers. The sign still rose to the heights, but now one point of the star had cracked, and no neon flickered.

My own heart sputtered. Cupping my chin in my hand, I crinkled my eyes, almost able to imagine when Mama and Daddy had first brought me to Mayhaw, and we stayed at the Stardust. We'd been in cottage number five, right in the middle. I ran my fingers over my cheek remembering the pattern the chenille bedspread left on my face while I was supposed to be taking a nap. Mama and Daddy were arguing, screaming at each other, so I kept my eyes shut tight until Daddy slammed out the door. Later we changed clothes, found Daddy out in the car smoking a cigar, and went to visit Aunt Cora.

I could still smell the smoke and closed my eyes, remembering how, later that day, Mama and Daddy left Mayhaw without me. Handed me over to Aunt Cora and never came back. The smell grew stronger, choking me, and I realized it wasn't Daddy's cigar at all, but Mary Frances puffing on a Pall Mall.

At least the funeral cars were moving again. I waved away the smoke and shivered, aware my mind had taken a trip back almost twenty years. Still, I couldn't take my eyes from the tourist court, each tiny building like a spectator of the funeral procession. And for the millionth time, I wondered why, after all this time, I still didn't know why my parents had left me. A wavy feeling passed over me. Clutching my white dress gloves in my fist, I glanced at Mary Frances, whose eyes now floated in their sockets.

Blinking, she tossed the cigarette butt out the window and unscrewed the lid from the blue bottle before hoisting it to her lips. She hiccupped and looked at me. "You and the girls are the only things left for me in this entire, whole wide world." She tilted sideways, resting her head on my shoulder.

A white-hot pang pierced my heart as I took her thin, pale fingers in mine and patted her hand. Clear liquid dribbled from the bottle, making a splotch the size of a fried egg on the upholstery, but Mary Frances didn't notice. Her soft snores filled the air inside the courtesy car.

✦

The next day, Sheriff Bolander knocked on the front door. All I could think was there must have been another disaster. I pasted on a smile and swung open the screen door. "Howdy, Sheriff. Something I can do for you?"

"Matter of fact." He jerked his head in the direction of the street. O'Dell's '46 Ford Coupe sat behind the sheriff's car, and in the morning sun, I couldn't make out who the driver was, but he had the same sturdy build, the same slicked-back hair, as O'Dell. I held on to the screen door for support, my knees as weak as if they'd been shot with Sheriff Bolander's pistol.

O'Dell? Alive? Then who in heaven's name did we bury next to O'Dell's daddy? My mind spun, a thousand thoughts jammed together, but I realized the sheriff was still speaking, and I hadn't heard him.

"I'm sorry. Come again?"

"As you can see, they found O'Dell's car. 'Twas over to Finney's Landing with the keys under the front seat. Finney thought it unusual to be there so many days running." He took a dingy handkerchief out of his back pocket and mopped his eyes. "Course, we drove it in and checked it over for evidence of foul play."

Instantly, I thought he must be fixin' to tell me O'Dell had been murdered by the angry husband of the woman from Tyler. Or Kilgore. Whichever it was. Maybe her dead body had been stuffed in the trunk. I shooed Rosey, who'd crept up behind me, away. A six-year-old shouldn't be privy to such gruesome news.

Stepping out on the front porch, I took a deep breath and said, "Well? What did you find?"

I got a one-sided smirk from the sheriff. "Nothin' incriminating, Georgia. A couple boxes of them there books he was peddling. A briefcase. Nothing to indicate O'Dell had done more than play hooky from work and spent a day fishin'. Only mystery to me is what caused him to capsize unless he'd been in the bayou since that rain week before last. One thing's for certain: O'Dell knew the ways of the bayou."

Contemplating how long he'd been there might've been important to the sheriff, but not a thought I wished to dwell on. "Did you find the boat?"

"No, ma'am. Even if it washes up somewhere, I wouldn't count on it being much."

"I'm sure you're right."

He shoved a clipboard toward me. "I need you to sign for the car." He motioned for the driver, who I now saw was Deputy Sam Beggs, to come to the porch.

I signed the paper and took the keys from Sam. Up close, he

didn't look a thing like O'Dell. Sam's belly hung over his belt, and he had a gap in his grin where his two bottom teeth used to be. I thanked him. And the sheriff, who tipped his hat.

"Don't know as I ever told you how sorry I am 'bout O'Dell. Crying shame to go so young."

"Thanks. Kind of you to drop by."

The girls had crept out on the porch during my conversation. I picked Avril up, licked my thumb, and wiped a dab of grape jelly from her cheek.

Rosey hugged my leg, her curly head hip-high to me. "That's Daddy's car." Her eyes, creamy brown, held a sparkle of what I could only think was hope. Hope that her daddy wasn't gone. That it had all been a mistake.

"Yes, it is. Isn't it swell someone found his car and brought it back to us?" I shifted Avril on my hip, took a step down, and lowered myself to the porch.

"I wish Daddy drove the car home, not that other man."

"Oh, sugar, I wish that, too. I'm sorry..."

I pulled the girls in tight, my gaze fixed on O'Dell's Ford. Not much to look at, and it probably had a million miles on it. But it was something. Some tiny glimmer that life goes on. At the moment, I had no idea what we'd do or how. I only knew that even though O'Dell Peyton had his flaws, it would be indecent to speak ill of him. His girls would grow up thinking he'd been on a long business trip and died before he got a chance to come home and read them a bedtime story.

The sun warmed my face, my armpits damp from the morning's dither, but I kept the girls close. Somehow we were going to be okay. Not just okay, but good. I kissed the top of Avril's head and got a taste of grape jelly. I licked my lips and said, "You know what? I'm starving. C'mon, girls, let's get you dolled up. We're going for ice cream."

⟡

CHAPTER 2

That evening I called to tell Aunt Cora about O'Dell's car.

"Yes. Sonny told me." Sonny Bolander, the sheriff. Aunt Cora's on-again, off-again beau since his wife died of cancer two years before.

"Sonny, huh?"

She sniffed the way she did when I irritated her. "Yes, he came by to bring the March of Dimes donations from the jars we put out downtown. Been doing that a few weeks now. You and the girls coming to lunch tomorrow?"

"If you're fixin' roast beef, we are."

"I'll set places for you."

Mara Lee, Aunt Cora's home, named after my great-grandmother, had been in the family since before the Civil War—one of the two dozen or so grand houses near downtown, but *grand* describes only the size. Bad investments gobbled up whatever fortunes Colonel Tickle, my great-grandfather, once had, and by the time of the Great Depression, Mara Lee stood tall, but in disgrace. Not unlike Aunt Cora, who was twenty-two years old when she'd inherited the crumbling mansion, the same week she inherited her six-year-old niece—me. I'd grown up in the rambling rooms, and now my girls loved to climb the curved staircase and explore the nooks and crannies.

Which is what they were doing while I helped Aunt Cora make the roast beef gravy and carry the butter and jam to the dining room. Set in the turret, the dining room had tall ceilings with miles of plaster molding that had chipped and never been repaired. The wallpaper, once a delicate violet pattern, was now curled, faded, and worn at the edges of the six-on-six-paned windows that looked out to the heart of downtown Mayhaw.

Aunt Cora plopped the mashed potatoes into Grandma Tickle's china serving bowl, sending a dollop onto the counter. She had a nervous air about her—chatty but skittish. Perhaps she was sparing me talk of O'Dell and my current state of grief, but I didn't think so. "So, Georgia, what do you think? Sweet tea or lemonade? Sonny prefers tea, but if you think the girls would rather have lemonade—"

"Milk for the girls. And it doesn't matter to me. Here, let me help." I scooped the remaining potatoes from the pan and piled them onto the others in the bowl. "Should we take the hot dishes in or wait until the sheriff gets here?"

"If he's late, he's late. Don'tcha think the man could try to get here on time? He knows I like to eat by one at the latest, and here it is, ten after, and he hasn't arrived."

"If it bothers you, why do you keep inviting him over?"

"Where else would he eat? Gracious, he eats the most horrid stuff on his own. Sardines in that nasty mustard. Peanuts. Gallons of RC Cola. The only vegetables he eats are what I put on the table."

"Then why don't you get married? He's going to quit asking you one of these days."

"Phfft. Feeding a man and living with him are hardly the same thing. Besides, I've been thinking." She rearranged the sweet lime pickles in a relish dish, adding a sprig of parsley. "That cracker-box you call home has got to be awfully cramped..." She set her mouth in a tight line when she saw me shaking my head. "Now let me finish before you start telling me all the reasons you and the girls shouldn't move in here with me. Why O'Dell didn't provide you with a proper house while he was alive riles the ever-lovin' daylights out of me."

"We have . . . had money set aside for a down payment for something more *proper*—"

"Had? You mean O'Dell took your savings when he left you?"

"No, I've been dipping into it for groceries, things for the girls. And now there's the funeral to consider. But it's not like I'm destitute or anything. I'll find a job."

"I would've thought O'Dell's mother would offer to pay for the funeral, knowing how he ran out on you and the girls."

"It's not a topic I've discussed with her. She's in too much of a state."

Aunt Cora pointed a tablespoon at me. "And we all know what state that is. Think of the girls. We could fix up the place here. Lord knows it could use a coat of paint."

It wasn't that I cared about the shabbiness of Mara Lee. It hadn't bothered me growing up and wouldn't now. It was more than that, but I couldn't tell Aunt Cora.

"My savings should cover the funeral. I'm not the first person who's lost a husband and found herself in tight straits." I wasn't sure the money in savings would be enough for the funeral and the fancy casket I'd picked out to please Mary Frances. But even O'Dell deserved a decent burial. "And I'm sure it won't be hard to find a job."

"Which will be what? It's not as if you're trained to be an assistant in an attorney's office or work at the courthouse. And heaven forbid you'd wait tables down at Ruby's Café. You'll need a stable environment for the girls while you pursue something befitting. Living here in the meantime only makes sense."

"For one thing, I see nothing wrong with waiting tables. But you're using us as an excuse not to marry Sonny."

The back door slammed, and Sonny came sailing into the kitchen, removing his hat. "My ears was burning. What're you two lovely ladies saying about me?" He pecked Aunt Cora on the cheek, but she ignored the affection and said, "You're late, Sonny."

I couldn't imagine Sonny and Aunt Cora married any more than I could picture the girls and me moving into Mara Lee. Aunt Cora and I had been butting heads since the day I landed on her doorstep. I had no reason to believe things would be different now. And I didn't necessarily blame her. It wasn't her fault she'd been straddled with an orphan niece, and she had put food in my stomach and clothes on my back.

A knot the size of Texas wedged into my belly. *Thank you kindly, Aunt Cora. I think I'll take a shot at raising my own girls.*

When he'd finished eating, Sonny folded his napkin and tucked it under the edge of Grandma's china. "Mayor Sheldon asked me if I had any suggestions for someone to head up the Mayhaw Festival this year. I told him you'd be just the ticket bein's what a jim-dandy job you've done with the March of Dimes campaign."

"You can't be serious. I wouldn't have the faintest idea where to start." She raised her penciled-on brows at me. "Georgia, this might be something to get your mind off your troubles. Give you a worthwhile project, and since you'd be in touch with all the merchants in town, you might keep an ear out for job opportunities."

"Actually, I hope to be employed before then. The festival's not until July, and the only part of the celebration I'm counting on is singing in the talent show. Bobby Carl Applegate's been playing a new song on the radio that's got a nice beat."

"If Bobby Carl's playing it on KHAW, it's probably some honky-tonk horror."

"Yep. Hank Williams. But it's real catchy—"

Sonny burst out laughing. "Whatcha aimin' to sing? 'Your Cheatin' Heart'? That'd bring the bandstand down."

Aunt Cora's face splotched crimson. "Sonny Bolander. I told you"—she looked at the girls sitting wide-eyed at the table—"oh, never mind. It doesn't make any difference."

My mind was still back on what the sheriff said. What, exactly, had she told Sonny for him to make the cheatin' heart comment? Obviously, my efforts at keeping O'Dell's infidelity confidential hadn't been very effective. The whole town must've been laughing behind my back at the funeral. *Poor Georgia Peyton. Reckon she didn't have much chance, being raised the way she was. Too bad the cheat she married drowned in the bayou.*

"Maybe I can sing this year, Mommy." Rosey straightened in her seat. "I like Rosey Clooney on the radio."

"It's Rosemary, and yes, six is old enough to be in the talent show. We might even do a duet." I shrugged at Aunt Cora. "Guess the mayor will have to find someone else."

Aunt Cora laughed. "Where y'all get that penchant for singing is beyond me. None of the Tickles could carry a tune in a rain barrel. Now, who wants dessert? I made strawberry shortcake." That was the thing about Aunt Cora: she could shake off a disappointment as easy as flicking a crumb off the table.

By the time we'd polished off the dessert, Avril was rubbing her eyes, trying to stay awake.

"I'd better get the girls home and put Avril down for her nap."

Sonny leaned back. "I'll help Cora here with the dishes."

He winked at her, and I thought I caught a flirtatious look in her eye when she said, "Why, Sonny, that's the nicest offer I've had all day."

I asked Rosey to find Avril's shoes and the rag doll she toted around wherever she went while I helped clean off the table. A few minutes later, Rosey appeared with the shoes but not the doll.

"Avie's baby is up in the sky room, but the door's stuck. Come with me."

"What were you doing up there? Those stairs are too steep for Avril."

"It's okay. I carried her down, but we left her baby."

"It's a wonder you didn't drop her on her noggin." I did a playful knock-knock on Rosey's mane of outrageous curls. "You're the best big sister in the world watching after Avril, though. C'mon, I'll go with you."

The room Rosey called the sky room was the third story of the turret. I'd always called it the crow's nest, but Rosey thought sky room was better because it was like flying with the birds up high. We went to the doorway at the end of the second floor hall, which accessed a steep staircase in its own enclosed space—sort of a secret passageway. I had to give the door a hip shove to get it open. The old house sucked in humidity like a swamp-starved crawdad.

Rosey and I climbed the steps and entered, the brightness startling after the dark climb. The light also drew my attention to the dust and the cobwebs that had been there since I was a child and spent many an hour viewing the world of Mayhaw from my private perch. Mostly I'd kept an eye out for the return of Mama and Daddy. They would come from the Stardust, I knew, since in my child's mind that was the last place they'd been. I would stretch out on the window seat, propped up on my elbows so as not to miss anything going on below. Or sometimes, when Aunt Cora shooed me away, I sat cross-legged, one eye on whatever book I'd checked out from the library and the other eye on the walk. Her gentlemen callers always came to the side door of Mara Lee, and when I would ask Aunt Cora about them, she would laugh and tell me, "The most stimulating conversations are with men. Women don't know the art of talking about world events or good literature." Which to her was Shakespeare and Charles Dickens and William Faulkner, books she schooled me in with fervor. I ingested them like medicine, of course, and when shooed away for the evening I retreated to the crow's nest with my own beloved Jane Austen and Agatha Christie stories.

Grown up now, I shuddered at the memories and looked out across the world of Mayhaw. Not a lot had changed. I leaned into the glass and looked toward the Stardust. I could make out the postage-stamp roofs of the individual units, the office a slightly larger version of the cottages. Even from so far away, they had a flaky, dusty look, not a patina of something that had aged with grace. The split in the top of the star pierced me with sorrow. My throat grew thick. Letting my eyes relax, I stopped straining for the detail and rested my forearms on the window sash. The air around me stilled so all I heard was Rosey's soft breathing as her body pressed close to mine.

For several moments we stood there, mother and daughter, spitting images of each other according to everyone who saw us. "Two redheaded sprites," Aunt Cora said. Then I saw it. As if waiting for me to witness, the star and lettering of the Stardust Tourist Cottages sign sputtered and shone, the neon pulsing, beckoning. I knew the sun had merely taken that moment to glint off the frame around the sign, but I watched in awe, afraid to take a breath.

Longing wrapped itself around me while hunger gnawed its way through my insides. The rhythm of my heart pounded in my ears, and like the flicker of the Stardust sign, I felt a surge of knowing this moment had a purpose. Something tangible.

And strong. And at the same time as elusive as the parents who'd dumped me in Mayhaw.

"Mommy. Did you see that? The star winked at us."

I slumped onto the window seat, drew Rosey into my arms, and kissed an errant curl. "Yes, it did, sugar. Yes, indeed."

I pulled Rosey in tighter. A visit to Doreen and Paddy at the Stardust was long overdue. Funny how God draws your attention to things like that. Yes, indeed.

CHAPTER 3

I'm not a big believer in signs and premonitions. Obviously, if I were more attuned, O'Dell's straying from me might have caught my attention sooner. But the more I tried to shove the incident in the sky room from my mind, the more it invaded my thoughts. I'll admit the Stardust did have a grip on me as a child, like when having a pulled tooth, I couldn't keep my tongue from running over the hole it left behind. Like the hole in my life Mama and Daddy once filled. The truth was, even at six years old, I knew it was odd we had stayed at the Stardust when we came for Grandfather's funeral. Odder than odd. There was a world of room at Mara Lee, and a perfectly decent hotel downtown a stone's throw away. Being the Stardust's owner's distant relatives hardly seemed a logical reason.

That knowing only fed my imagination, giving birth to a dozen scenarios throughout my childhood. No matter which theory I entertained, it always ended with me dreaming of Mama and Daddy's magical reappearance at the Stardust.

If pressed, Aunt Cora would laugh and wave away my questions with, "The past is like the color of your eyes. You can't change it so you might as well get used to it." Which was ludicrous in light of the fact most folks in Mayhaw lived in the past and revered statues of Confederate generals and waved Southern Cross flags in the Founder's Day parade.

To her credit, Aunt Cora did lavish me with the best she could. New shoes for Easter and the first day of school. And she put forth valiant efforts to turn me into a lady. To her utter dismay, my fiery hair matched my temperament, and I balked at every turn. All I wanted was to climb trees and wear britches like the boys. Which gave Aunt Cora the vapors more often than not.

My only consolation was the beat-up bicycle Mr. Wardlaw from the newspaper let me ride if I would deliver the weekly *Mayhaw Messenger* to the far end of town. Would I? I hiked my dress up and off I went. My favorite destination was the Stardust. I spent hours with Doreen, who let me count the change in the cash register while she knitted from her rocking chair behind the desk. And when I told her Aunt Cora would have a hissy fit if she caught me at the Stardust, Doreen would put a finger to her lips. "It'll be our secret."

I outgrew my days of Doreen and Paddy when I got interested in boys, but on the occasions we ran into each other in town, they were always warm and asked about Aunt Cora or my girls or how O'Dell was doing. Sadly, I'd not been to visit in a long time and vowed to remedy that the following day.

That evening, I bathed the girls, tucked them in, and settled into going through the things that I'd brought in earlier from the trunk of the car. Two complete sets of *The Book of Knowledge*. O'Dell's hard-sided briefcase, which I knew held sales brochures and a tattered copy of his treasured five-point sales pitch. A duffel bag with a change of clothes, a toothbrush, and assorted toiletries, including a bottle of aftershave that always reminded me of mosquito repellent. I unscrewed the lid and drank in the scent of O'Dell. It was pungent and yet had a sweetness I'd never noticed, and I expected to look up and see him standing there with his lopsided grin. I chewed on my bottom lip to·stop its quivering, screwed the lid back on the bottle, and tucked it in my drawer of underpants before I went back to sifting through O'Dell's things.

I took his briefcase to the kitchen table. No one from the regional sales office had attended the funeral or sent a bouquet, so I thought the least I could do was find their information and let them know about O'Dell. Like me, perhaps they didn't know he'd gone missing.

When a fruit fly buzzed near my head, I waved it away, impatient to finish the task I'd started. I clicked open the gold latches of the briefcase, only to be interrupted again. This time by the telephone.

Aunt Cora.

After dispensing with the pleasantries, she said, "We didn't get a chance to discuss when you and the girls could move in. I've decided to clear out your old room, and we'll go down to the lumberyard for paint—"

"Hold on. I don't recall agreeing to any such thing. It's nice of you to ask, but I thought I made it clear."

"It's for the girls. You can't expect them to deal with the tragedy of their daddy dying and having a mother who's off working or going to secretarial school…whatever it is you decide to do in light of your new circumstance. What do you intend to do with them? Avril's practically a baby."

"She's three years old, Aunt Cora. And it's not like I have to decide today. I'm considering my options. Maybe a change of scenery." I stretched the phone cord over to the table and leafed through the papers in the top of O'Dell's briefcase. Pretty much what I expected. E-Z payment plans, folded street maps of Tyler and Kilgore.

"Don't be daft, Georgia. Moving away from the only home and family you've ever known won't accomplish anything. That's why God made families. To take you into their bosom in times of trial and tribulation."

"Aunt Cora, it's a miracle we didn't kill each other when I was under your roof. Not that I didn't love you then…and now…but we're just not meant to—"

"One thing's for certain—you're as exasperating now as you were when you were a child."

"So there's your answer, and if it's any consolation, I'm not moving away."

"That's good."

The map of Kilgore stared up at me. *Was that where the other woman lived?*

"There's Mary Frances to consider, for one thing. She's having a tough time, and her cousin who came to the funeral is leaving in the morning. I'll have to check on her, take the girls by to visit their grandmother."

"She's a misery all right. 'Twouldn't surprise me if this pushes her plumb over the edge. But you can only do so much. Mercy, she could hardly stand up at the graveside, and I don't think it was grief wobbling her legs."

The fly buzz-bombed me again. I shooed it away with the street map, which only encouraged it as it circled around and lit on the table.

"Georgia, are you listening to me?"

"Yes, just thinking. I'm not ready to decide what the girls and I are going to do. Could we talk about this later?"

"Whatever suits you."

I hung up and then went back to sorting through O'Dell's business, half expecting the fruit fly to interrupt me again. When it didn't I picked up the next item on top—a small leather ledger with the telephone number of the sales office. Several pages of names followed, with check marks beside them in various columns that appeared to be the record of O'Dell's customers. Had I wanted to torture myself, I could've tried to guess which one of the customers was my replacement. The O'Dell knot tightened in my belly, and I realized I didn't want to know. Knowing would somehow burst the illusion I'd been weaving to keep O'Dell's reputation intact. For the girls. His swaggering mother. And oddly enough, for me.

I wrote down the name and number of the sales office and removed the last item in the briefcase—a trifolded document with a string clasp on it. It was the kind I'd seen on Aunt Cora's last will and testament where she bequeathed me the family mansion and all her worldly goods. Since she was only forty-two years old, I didn't expect to inherit anytime soon.

My fingers trembled as I unwound the string in the figure-eight way it was secured, took a deep breath, and leaned back in the kitchen chair. It was an official document, but not a will as I'd assumed it would be. Instead, it had the seal of the Harwell Insurance Company and in bold print gave the amount of life insurance due the benefactor in the event of the death of O'Dell Thomas Peyton. I gasped. *Ten thousand dollars.* Then I gasped again. The double indemnity clause for accidental death entitled me to twenty thousand dollars.

O'Dell might've been a skunk, but his fragrance had just gotten a whole lot sweeter. I speed-read through the rest of the document until my eyes landed on the benefactor line.

Fiona Callahan.

My mouth went dry. Fiona? Some Creole queen with a French-sounding name had stolen my husband? I stared until I was sure I'd burned the letters off the page.

What did Fiona have that I didn't? How could he? While I may not have been the most exotic woman on the planet, I'd been told I had a pretty smile and nice legs.

The familiar droning started near my ear, buzzing, drilling home the truth: my husband cheated on me.

Twenty. Thousand. Dollars.

I threw the document on the table and snatched the flyswatter from the hook by the back door, and when the light caught the iridescent-winged fly hovering over the Harwell insurance policy, I tensed my jaw, drew back my arm, and smashed it into a bloody smudge.

Right next to the name of Fiona Callahan.

CHAPTER 4

Southern manners and turning the other cheek be hanged. The name Fiona Callahan winked up at me from the insurance policy, mocking me in a way that felt like I'd been the one dragged through the swamp mud. Who was I kidding? O'Dell's infidelity left a hole as big as a moon crater in my heart, and I'd allowed the crater to be lined with the saccharine taste of denial. If I had a grain of sense, I would've packed up the girls at once and moved to Dallas. Or Shreveport. Or Nashville. Maybe I could get a job waiting tables at a Western bar and start my life over. And I'm as certain as my name is Georgia Lee Peyton, if O'Dell had walked through the door that night, I would have personally dragged him down to the bayou and drowned him myself.

By three in the morning, I'd riffled through every drawer, shoe box, and place I could think of searching for an insurance policy with *my* name as the benefactor. Nothing. I had a house, bought and paid for—thirty-two hundred dollars, completely furnished, thank you. A savings account with three hundred and forty-six dollars that had to pay for a funeral and our living expenses until I could find a job or move in with Aunt Cora.

Other assets: two girls who depended on me. A 1946 Ford

Coupe that was six years old and needed new tires. A gold wedding band from the Mercantile in Jefferson. And a mother-in-law who clung to me like Spanish moss on a cypress tree.

Maybe I'd been living my entire life in a dreamworld where I thought people came back and loved you and would hang the moon if you asked them to. You'd think by now it would have sunk in that people are not necessarily who you think they are. Parents leave their children. Husbands have affairs. Mothers-in-law drink themselves into oblivion, and the one person who wanted to take us to her bosom was an aunt who could've been a kissing cousin of Rahab the harlot.

I shuddered and pushed it out of my mind. I'd been down that path so many times I knew every crack in the sidewalk. Tomorrow I would call on Mary Frances and see if she knew anything about O'Dell leaving any life insurance policies lying around. That did give me a glimmer of hope since O'Dell's daddy had been an independent insurance salesman and had left Mary Frances with a tidy sum when he died. I also needed to check on her. Just because her son didn't give a fig about me didn't mean I could abandon her.

※

Rosey dawdled over her cornflakes while I fortified myself with a second cup of coffee and found her schoolbag, then adjusted the clip in her hair, which flew in more directions than my thoughts.

"All right, time for school. Don't want you to be late."

She opened her mouth to protest, then clamped her lips together. We'd already been over it a dozen times. Yes, she had to go to school. No, she didn't have to talk about her daddy dying. Yes, Mommy would pick her up. And yes, I crossed my heart and hoped to die I would never leave her. Thank goodness, her six-year-old brain didn't see the irony in that promise.

The air was heavy with bayou smells—rotted earth and mud turtles and boggy pools—smells that tickled the back of my throat, clung to my skin, and reminded me it was God's way of dust to dust in the swamps. Our part of Mayhaw lay in the crescent of the bayou, and momentarily, I remembered that the other end of town had a completely different texture to the air. Pine needles. The smell of sawdust from the lumber mill up the road. Blue skies above the open meadows where cows grazed. The flashing neon of the Stardust.

After the two-block walk to Robert E. Lee Elementary and another round of hugs and kisses, Rosey shuffled into the front door of the school. As we headed back toward home, a car horn beeped, and I looked up to see my best friend, Sally Cotton, motioning for us to come over. She wore gypsy hoop earrings, sunglasses that covered half her face, and Japanese silk pajamas. "Time for coffee?" Her voice sparkled as always.

"Not today. Going to check on O'Dell's mom." Avril bounced up and down, yanking on my arm.

"Please, Mommy, I wanna play with Rae Rae." Avril couldn't say Nelda Rae, but she adored Sally's four-year-old, who sported skinned knees from falling out of trees and had a pair of six-shooters. Cowboys and Indians trumped MeMaw every time.

"Let Avie come, and you can swing by later to pick her up. We've a heap of catching up to do." Avril's pleading eyes looked up at me, so I opened the door, thanked Sally, and waved as Sally's Cadillac lurched forward.

Having decided to take advantage of the convenience of O'Dell's car, I went home, grabbed the keys, and ten minutes later pounded on Mary Frances's front door, waited a minute, and pounded again. When she didn't come, I let myself in. "Yoo-hoo! Mary Frances, it's me . . . Georgia."

Doing a quick survey of the living room, I found it wasn't too disorderly. Magazines scattered about. A cigarette burning in the ashtray, its long ash nearly to the filter. I stubbed it out and almost bumped into Mary Frances, who had apparently been in the bathroom. Her days with her cousin Bertha hadn't improved her personal hygiene. I'd seen bird's nests more organized than her salt-and-pepper hair, but she did have on lipstick, so maybe she was improving.

She blinked and said, "You scared me half to death. What are you up to, Georgia? Ever heard of the telephone?"

"I should have called. I'm sorry. I thought you might want some company."

"I've had all the company I can stand. Three days with my cousin Bertha could drive the governor himself out of office. Why, she went on forever and a day moaning about how horrible my life had turned out. You woulda thought it was her son that drowned the way she kept nursing my last bottle of gin. I'm on my way to Ralph's so I can get fortifications." Sure enough, she was half dressed, and I offered to zip the back of her dress, which still gaped open.

"Bertha? The cousin from Corsicana? I never knew she was a drinker."

"Neither did I. Not becoming for a mayor's wife, you know. And if she thinks I'm moving to Corsicana so she can mooch off me and the pittance I have left of Earl's life insurance money, she's nuttier than a hoot owl."

"What? She wants you to move in with her and the mayor?"

"No. Just to Corsicana. Thinks I should be near family in my time of need. I set her straight. I've got my own family to sustain me right here in Mayhaw."

When she saw my raised eyebrows, she added, "You, Georgia.

You and the girls. You're all the family I want. Or need." Her hands trembled as she fumbled with her silver lighter and Pall Mall. "So you didn't tell me what the occasion of your visit is."

"I came to check on you. And I have some questions."

"Could we discuss it on the way over to Ralph's?"

"He doesn't open until ten."

"Yes, my dear, I called ahead. He's meeting me at the Sweet Shoppe. He knows what I want."

And indeed he did. And since we were there, I bought Mary Frances a donut and a cup of coffee. Now that we had time to talk, bringing up the subject of life insurance felt mercenary. The dirt mound hadn't even settled over O'Dell's grave, and all I could think of was what provisions he left to the girls and me. Practicality won out.

"Mary Frances, I hate to bring it up, but I can't seem to find a life insurance policy at the house. Do you have any idea..."

Mary Frances twitched. Her shoulders first, then shaky hands. "You think we could cut this short? I need to get home."

"In a minute. I'm trying to figure out where we go from here. I have two girls who need clothes. And shoes. And food to eat. O'Dell didn't make a great deal of money...the truth is, I haven't seen any of his commission money in more than two months." I hated being so forthright, especially in public, but my lack of sleep and Mary Frances's twitching had taken their toll. Not to mention every time I took a breath, the name Fiona Callahan flashed through my head.

My mother-in-law sniffed. "I'm sure O'Dell had a good reason. Perhaps a slump in sales. And it's not that you can't get a job. I know it's early after O'Dell's passing to bring it up..." Her foot slipped off the bar at the counter, and she bumped her coffee cup, splashing it on the counter. I grabbed a napkin to mop up the mess and looked at her. Hard.

"Yes, I do plan on going to work. But in the meantime—"

"Hey, Georgia." A twangy voice on my left interrupted. I knew the voice without turning—Bobby Carl Applegate. I did a slow pivot on the counter stool to greet him.

"Hey, yourself."

"Sorry about O'Dell. Man, it gave me the willies when I was reading his obit on the radio." Bobby Carl. Local disc jockey, newsman, and the boy who gave me my first kiss. Age ten. I smacked him, but he'd acted like he had first rights to me ever since. Silly man.

"Thanks. It was a shock to all of us. We're still trying to make sense of it."

"Anything I can do?" He stood close enough I could smell the Aqua Velva he splashed on his fair, though somewhat doughy, face. He'd never outgrown the baby face, and his stature never caught up, either. In high school, I'd towered over him and still did.

"No, but thanks for asking."

"You aiming to stick around Mayhaw?"

"What else would I do?"

"You never know. A voice like yours, you could raise a few eyebrows at the Grand Ole Opry."

What a laugh. "I don't think so. Carrying a tune and being a real singer aren't in the same league. Besides, you have to be asked to appear on the show. Cut a record or something, which I've no intention of doing."

"Guess you'll be whuppin' up on all the other contestants in this year's talent show then?"

"Sure. If I have time. You never know what I'll be doing."

He craned his neck to look around me at Mary Frances, then winked and whispered, "If you need an escort to the dance, you know where to find me."

I rolled my eyes. "You're a mess, Bobby Carl."

With eyes narrowed, he said, "Well?"

Shaking my head, I told him to pick on some other poor defenseless widow. Then I paid for our coffee and took Mary Frances home. She remained quiet on the ride, her fingers curled around the paper sack holding her prescription for grief. And life.

I dropped her off, then gripped the wheel, determined not to make the same choices as Mary Frances. Even if I had to dance with Bobby Carl at the Mayhaw Festival, it was better than letting a bottle consume me.

And with a flick of my wrist, I wheeled the car toward Sally's, intending to take her up on her offer for coffee. Already, though, the morning had heated up, and when I got to the intersection at Main, I knew more coffee wasn't what I wanted. What I wanted was to go to the Stardust. To check on Doreen and Paddy. Perhaps Paddy had gone for another round of cobalt treatments and they'd closed the Stardust for a spell. There had to be an explanation for its ragged appearance. The least I could do was have a look. They were—in Cora's words—family. Of a sort.

The weeds had grown even more since O'Dell's funeral, tangling the ditch and threatening to choke the gravel drive beside the office. No cars in sight. I swung the Ford into the spot reserved for the manager and cranked the window open. To my surprise, a soft breeze filtered in, bringing with it a green, piney scent. Although the bayou veered off behind the Stardust, its presence seemed more remote here at the edge of town. A flutter came to my chest as I took a deep breath and turned off the Ford.

I slammed the car door and marched to the office. Cupped my hands and put my nose to the glass. Other than a dusty, stale look, the Stardust looked ready for business. Papers stacked neatly beside an adding machine. A coffee cup still on the counter. Brochures tucked in a wall rack, and on the far wall, cottage keys dangled from a board with numbers above the cup hooks. I jiggled the knob and found it, not surprisingly, locked. When I stepped back, the sagging wooden step creaked uncertainly. I studied the outside. The stucco could use a coat of whitewash, and some new shutters would work wonders.

It bothered me that there was no sign saying *Back after lunch* or *Gone Fishing*. It looked as if the Stardust had simply been abandoned. I had turned to go when I caught a movement of something or someone between two of the cottages. A blur of tan—a deer that had perhaps come to munch on the knee-high weeds. Curious, I crunched my way on the gravel path that led to the sidewalk connecting the cottages like a piece of seam binding. Up close they didn't look as worn and tired as I'd thought that day in the car. Some of the window boxes were missing, the remaining ones filled with weeds.

I slipped between the cottages where I'd seen the blur and jumped like a kangaroo rat when I nearly bumped into a child.

Taller than Rosey, with fuzzy black braids poking out in a dozen directions, the girl's eyes were as round as jawbreakers, the whites of her eyes so white they had a blue tinge, and in the center, they were inky black and staring at me like I was a swamp ghost.

"Oh, goodness. Looks like we 'bout scared each other plumb spitless." I smiled and extended my hand. "I'm Georgia. And who might you be?"

Course I knew she must've come up to the Stardust from Zion. The girl, eight or nine, I reckoned, said nothing, just bugged her eyes at me like she was frozen to the spot.

"Say now, you don't have to be afraid."

The eyes narrowed slightly as the girl bowed her head, studying pink palms, but not shying away from me. Then, as if her palms had given her the answer, she looked up and said, "My name is Merciful. And I ain't afraid."

"Merciful. What a beautiful name. Can you tell me where you live?"

Her head tilted toward Zion. "Yonder. In the trees." Then her face broke into a wide grin, her two front teeth on the top missing. A giggle started in her belly and shook her pudgy arms and body. "Not *in* the trees. In a house with Maw and Paw and my stinkbug brother. His name's Catfish, case you's wondering."

"Now that you mention it, maybe I was. So what brings you over to the tourist court today, Miss Merciful?"

Another giggle. "Y'ain't supposed to call me Miss. That's what we's supposed to call y'all white folk. Hey, you aimin' to be the new man here?"

"What do you mean? I'm a lady, for one thing, not a man."

"You know, the one who goin' to be running the place. The man. Your man. Like the other one and his lady that was here."

"Well, the ones who were here before seem to be gone right now, but I would guess they're coming back. You seem to know a lot more than I do. Care to tell me why it interests you?"

"No reason." For the first time, the wide-eyed child looked away, down at the grass.

"You surely don't mean that. Why else would you be leaving your maw and paw and coming up here?" The truth was, Merciful was quite an engaging child, and she was probably breaking every rule forty ways to sundown for even talking to a stranger, a white woman at that.

"Paw's gone on the lumber trailer with the others, and today is Maw's turn to take care of Mamey. She don't know I left." Then, as though the fact dawned on her for the first time, she backed away, looking toward the trees.

"It's all right. Your secret's safe with me. You come here often?"

"No, ma'am. Not no more. Maw says ain't no use crying over

spilt milk. The good Lord will provide." She studied her bare feet. Wide. Flat. And even though she was a mere child, they looked as tough as alligator skin.

Had the child ever owned a pair of shoes? Understanding crept upon me, a dim candle of knowing that warmed my face. The man—Paddy, I guessed—must've employed Merciful's momma to help clean the cottages. Sally, like every distinguished woman in Mayhaw, had a colored girl two days a week. Tansy. Or was it Fancy? A pleasant woman who busied herself with the dust mop and linseed oil.

Aunt Cora hadn't held to the tradition of hiring someone, burdened as she'd always been with raising a child on her paltry fortune, but I'd always had an unnatural curiosity about the folks who came in from Zion on colored day at the Mercantile. I would sneak downtown on my bicycle, pretending to be on an errand, and watch as they paraded into town, their mahogany faces glistening in the summer heat. Their voices, rich and peppered with laughter, filled my heart. Once I left my bicycle in the bushes and shimmied up close, walking along like I was one of them. I offered a pigtailed girl about my age a lemon drop and laughed along with her. By the time I got home, Aunt Cora had already caught wind of my escapade. She whipped the living daylights out of me with Grandma Tickle's wooden spoon.

The child before me stared at her feet, the dress she wore at least two sizes too big, the print of it faded to practically nothing. Such a respectful girl. Polite. Well-spoken. And whether she was aware or not…captivating.

"Merciful, did your momma used to work here?"

Her head shot up. "Yes, ma'am. And she let me help her collect the bedclothes and take them to the wash room. Over there." She pointed to a small building behind the office I'd not noticed before. "Ever' day, we came and did what the man asked. And on Saturday, he gave Maw her money and he'd give me a penny to put in the gumball machine."

"I bet you liked that."

Her wide, gap-toothed grin told me she did.

"I think I have a pack of gum in my car. You want a stick?"

Pigtails slapped all around her head when she shook it. "Cain't be seen on t'other side of the cottages. Maw would take a willow switch to me lickety-split if she was to hear of me talking to you."

"It's all right. I won't tell. And tell your momma I'm sure someone will be needing her help very soon. I'll be talking to the good Lord, too. Betcha it won't be long until the Stardust is back in business."

She nodded, the spark back in her eyes. I extended my hand and took her small, rough one in mine. "Happy to meet you, Merciful. You run on home now before your momma starts to worry."

CHAPTER 5

Merciful turned and ran toward Zion, her feet slapping the ground with a happy sound. She was just a speck on the horizon when she slipped into the trees, the pine branches swallowing her in an instant. My heart went out to her, but if what she said was true, Doreen and Paddy had shut the place up. Disappeared, it seemed, although I was sure there was an explanation. Still, it left a hollow spot in me, too, and I regretted not keeping up with their lives. I turned and started toward my car, then stopped when I saw Sonny Bolander pull up and hang his head out the window.

"Georgia, what the devil are you doing out here?"

I breezed up to him. "I could ask the same of you. But the truth is, I noticed all the weeds the day of O'Dell's funeral, and I realized I hadn't visited with Doreen and Paddy in a while. Any idea what's going on?"

"Matter of fact, I came out this way to check on the place. Make sure nothin's disturbed. The ol' feller passed last night."

"Paddy? He died?" My insides flipped, leaving me weak. I steadied myself with a hand on the sheriff's car.

"Cancer got him. He put up quite a fight. I heard this morning the funeral's Wednesday over to the Methodist church."

"Oh, gracious. I had no idea. He was my great-uncle, you know." And the *man,* according to Merciful in her tattered dress.

"Yes'm, reckon I forgot that. Been awhile since you been out here, then?"

"Too long. Aunt Cora used to have a fit when I sneaked over here as a child. Bad blood or something. Probably some long-forgotten feud like the Montagues and the Capulets."

"I don't know nothing about your Louisiana relations if that's what you're referring to, but I do know a thing or two about crossing your aunt Cora."

Inwardly, I smiled. Sheriff Bolander knew his job inside and out, but he didn't know Shakespeare from a poke in the eye. And part of his job was to know all the goings-on in Mayhaw, so I asked where I might find Doreen.

"They've been staying with her sister, Rue Ann Pitts. Over on Jefferson Street."

I thanked him and waited until he drove off before heading back toward Sally's to pick up Avril. Maybe the Stardust sign had beckoned me because Doreen needed my help. Being newly widowed, we certainly had plenty of grief to share, and helping her with the Stardust might be just the thing to keep me occupied until I sorted out my life.

Hazel Morton waved from her front porch where she was busy sweeping. I returned the wave and made a mental note to return her potato salad bowl—the one she brought to the house as part of the bereavement parade of food. While I was at it, I should bake an angel food cake for Doreen and her sister.

Two blocks from Main Street, I passed Dickie Mingo on his bicycle. He was eighty if he was a day and still peddling down to the Sweet Shoppe for a bacon and tomato sandwich every day at noon.

Noon already? I had no idea I'd been gone so long.

I pressed on the foot feed and sped over to State Street to Sally's home. She lived five houses down from Aunt Cora in a bright yellow plantation house—one that her in-laws' oil money had preserved and kept in grand style. From the day her in-laws moved to Houston and left her and Hudson in charge of the house, Sally had slipped into being Mayhaw's mistress of philanthropy as easy as pulling on a pair of kid gloves.

She met me at the front door and waved me back to the sun-room, where she'd fed lunch to Avril and Nelda Rae and set a place for the two of us.

"You must be parched. Want some mint tea? I was hoping you'd come along and try out this new chicken salad recipe I'm serving for the Magnolias next week."

I took the tea from her. "You're a lifesaver, and I'm glad to be the guinea pig for your garden club. Matter of fact, I'm starved." Avril slipped onto my lap and lifted her ketchup-smeared face to mine.

"Miss Sally let me put ketchup on my cheese sandwich."

"That was nice. Have you and Nelda Rae had a good time?"

"We watched *Howdy Doody.*"

"Cowabunga!" Nelda Rae shouted with a mouthful of apple-sauce, which dribbled down her chin.

Sally chided her. "Don't talk with your mouth full. And if you girls are finished, run out and play. Remember, stay in the shade. Don't want you catching any infantile paralysis, you hear?"

When the girls had gone, she settled into the wicker seat and raised her glass. "To summertime. Remember when our only concerns were catching crawdads and making our daily trip down to Marley's for an ice-cream cone? Now, every time you turn a corner, there's talk of a new case of polio."

"It is the season. Vigilance, Aunt Cora says. But how can you be vigilant about something that comes out of nowhere?"

She shuddered. "They're even showing those horrible clips at the movies. Kids on crutches. Spooky shadows that, I swan, have me looking over my shoulder and making the kids do the chin touch to see if their necks are still screwed on straight." She bobbed her head forward, touching it to her chest, her hoop earrings dancing against her olive complexion as she demonstrated.

"It's not like you to be such a worrier, Sally."

"Hud's cousin's girl down in Houston just came down with it. No earthly idea where it came from. One minute they think she has influenza. The next her legs have gone spastic, her neck is stiff, and she's lost her wits. It's scaring the tar out of me. Let's pray we don't get an outbreak here."

I raised my own glass. "Amen." The summer disease. The crippler. There were worse things than losing a husband. It could be one of my own girls.

Sally shuddered. "What am I thinking? You've got the world on your shoulders, and I'm carrying on about something that, Lord willing, we'll never see." She flicked a black curl away from her face. "So, tell me, how is Mary Frances?"

For a moment I had to think back. It seemed like days had passed since I'd seen her, but as Sally waited, waving a carrot stick at me, I shrugged. "You know Mary Frances. She'll be okay."

Sally snorted. "We both know Mary Frances will never be okay. So you've been over there all morning?"

I nibbled a corner of the chicken salad sandwich. "Mmmm. This is delicious. What did you do different? Is that pineapple I'm tasting?"

"No, it's not pineapple. Surely Mary Frances hasn't held you captive all this time? Trust me, Georgia, you are going to have to break gently from her. It's time for you both to move on."

"It's not as easy as you think. I feel I'm being pulled in too many directions at once. Mary Frances. The girls. And now Aunt Cora wants us to move in with her."

Sally's eyebrows arched like a cat's back. "You're not seriously considering it, are you?"

"No, but let's face it, I don't have many options. Get a job waiting tables at Ruby's. Move in with Aunt Cora. Or follow Bobby Carl Applegate's suggestion and sing at the Grand Ole Opry."

Sally burst out laughing. "Leave it to Bobby Carl. He's been pining for you forever. Has he asked you out yet?"

"Good grief. Even he's got brains enough to know how far that would get him."

"I'll give him a month."

I took another bite of my sandwich. "Are you sure there's no pineapple in here?"

"Yes, I'm sure. I put mandarin oranges in it. Do you think the Magnolias will like it?"

"I'm sure they will. It's delicious."

Sally lowered her head and placed her well-manicured hand over mine. "Forget the chicken salad. Tell me, how are *you*? The shock of O'Dell walking out, then him drowning—"

I held up my hand. "Hey, I'm through crying over O'Dell. Not only did he leave me without any means of support, but I found a life insurance policy in his briefcase with *her* name on it."

"*Her,* as in the woman he was stupid enough to leave you for? Was it someone you know?"

I shook my head. "Fiona Callahan. I can only imagine what kind of person she is. One with plenty of wiles, apparently, if he'd take out an insurance policy with her as the beneficiary." The self-pity

I'd told myself I wouldn't wallow in rose up like a phantom. I swallowed to keep it at bay, but tears sprang to my eyes.

Sally reached a bejeweled hand across the table to me. "Hey, you don't have to be brave on my account."

I drew my lips into a tight pose. "Thanks, Sal, but dang it, I'm sick of thinking about it day in and day out. I need to do something to get my mind off O'Dell, and crying all the time's pathetic and weak. I'm open to suggestions."

"Well, the Magnolias can always use your help."

"I'm not society material. Just because you and Hudson are swimming in dough—"

"Is that what you think? The Magnolias are a bunch of rich girls? Nu-uh-uh. Georgia, I love you more than all the china in my cupboards and half as much as your sweet girls, but I swear you jump to conclusions faster than a cricket with its tail on fire."

"I do not jump to conclusions. And crickets don't have tails... do they?"

We burst out laughing and spent the rest of the afternoon giggling like old times. It was medicine for my weary spirit, but when it was time to pick Rosey up from school, I wasn't an inch closer to knowing how I would take care of my girls. Or even where to start.

A phone call from Hugh Salazar, attorney-at-law, changed all that.

CHAPTER 6

I'd known Hugh Salazar for as long as I could remember. When he wasn't working on a case, he drank coffee and ate snickerdoodles at the counter of the Sweet Shoppe two doors down from his office. Not a lot of crimes are committed in Mayhaw, but Hugh was considered the best if you needed his services for a will, a contract, or a sticky divorce. He handled Aunt Cora's affairs, and I say that tongue in cheek as he was one of the most frequent of her gentlemen callers at Mara Lee on State Street. Dark and handsome, his ominous presence in my life scared the bejesus out of me. But he wasn't intimidating enough to keep me from showing up at his office every year on the anniversary of my grandfather's death to ask if he'd heard from my parents.

The year I was ten and had saved up twelve dollars from delivering the *Mayhaw Messenger* for Mr. Wardlaw, I went to him and asked him to hire a private investigator.

"My parents' names are Gordon and Justine Mackey, and the last place we lived was Truth or Consequences, New Mexico. I want you to have someone find them and give me an explanation of why they left me and when they're coming back to fetch me. A person should know, don'tcha think?"

"I know what their names were, Georgia. Justine was in my graduating class. I'll tell you one thing, you didn't get your pretty face from her." He stroked the dark shadow of whiskers on his chin and looked at me over the top of his wire spectacles. "And twelve dollars wouldn't be enough to get a private eye halfway across Texas. Your momma had her reasons, and you best give it up and concentrate on getting yourself out of the sixth grade."

"Fifth. I'm only in the fifth. Old enough to learn the truth, even if it ain't pretty."

"You best not let your aunt Cora hear you say *ain't,* or she'll be having you write 'I won't say ain't' five hundred times."

I remembered huffing up my shoulders and glaring at him. "If you know the reasons, then I'll give *you* the money and you can just tell me. 'Twould be the Christian thing for you to do, if you ask me."

He ruffled my hair and said, "You got the spunk, missy. Best be putting it to use on your schoolbooks." And then he ushered me out the door and slipped me a nickel. "Go have yourself some ice cream now."

Each year I dreamed up a new excuse to ask Mr. Salazar to help me find my parents, and sure as the sun sets over Hixon Bayou, he evaded me. The last time I'd asked him was two weeks before my marriage to O'Dell. And that time he'd called me into his office.

He set me down and lit up a cigar. "Georgia, I've been like a father to you, guiding you whenever I saw the opportunity—"

"All you've ever done is avoid my questions and pat me on the head. I could've used some fatherly advice now and then, but all my life I've wanted to know one thing and one thing only. Why did my parents leave me?"

He blew smoke in the air, and I knew then he was thinking up another excuse not to answer me. Instead, when the smoke thinned and my patience had gotten even thinner, he leaned over.

"I asked you here for two reasons. One: Why in the name of thunder are you marrying O'Dell Peyton? I thought you had better sense. You could go to secretary school or even the University of Texas if you wanted. Instead, you're marrying a boy with no more ambition than to run his daddy's fishing boat up and down the bayou—"

"What may seem like idle fishing to you is O'Dell's way of planning his future. He has his sights set on bigger things. You don't know him like I do."

"And how's that, Georgia?" He picked up the cigar and leaned back. "Please don't tell me you're in a family way."

The look on my face gave him the answer. I was eighteen years old and almost five months pregnant. I'd been dating O'Dell my senior year, and what I'd done was stupid, no doubt.

"He loves me and told me nothing would happen if it was my first time."

"I take back what I said earlier. O'Dell has two sterling qualities: fishing the bayou and he's a cockamamie salesman."

His tone dripped with sarcasm, but I leaned over and looked him in the eye. "You said you asked me here for two reasons. You've stated your dismay at my upcoming marriage. So be it. What was the other reason?"

"You didn't allow me to elaborate before you jumped in with your accusation of why I wouldn't tell you about your parents. If you're old enough to be married—and I have doubts, my dear— then perhaps it's time to tell you what I know of Justine and Gordon Mackey."

The oxygen in the room fled, swallowed up by the cigar smoke and the great hunks of it I'd inhaled, leaving me now with a head that swam with dizziness and a heart that galloped like a racehorse through my chest. My spine straightened, and I waited.

Mr. Salazar was no doubt amused as he waved his fingers

through the air and said, "By last count, Justine is wanted in three states for failure to appear after being charged with drunk driving. Her husband, Gordon, whom you call *Father,* has been divorced from Justine for twelve years. If my calculations are correct, that would put the demise of their marriage around the same time as your arrival in Mayhaw. His whereabouts are unknown."

The possibilities piled one upon another in my head. Alcohol, divorce, skipping from one state to another. The fairy tale of one day being reunited with them in a clapboard bungalow with a tire swing in the front yard had screeched to a terrible halt. Aunt Cora's declarations that my momma had done me a favor by dropping me off in Mayhaw settled over me like the final pounding of a judge's gavel. My destiny had never been mine to choose. Aside from getting myself in a *family way,* as Mr. Salazar put it.

And that was the thought uppermost in my mind the day Hugh Salazar's call came. Since O'Dell's family used Skaggs Whiting as their attorney, I discerned Hugh's call had nothing to do with O'Dell. When he asked me to come in at ten the following morning, I asked what was going on.

"Now, Georgia, I don't cotton to talking on the phone regarding legal matters. Get your pretty self down here in the morning."

Obviously, Aunt Cora was up to something. What, I couldn't imagine, but it would be like her to take matters into her own hands and ask Hugh to give me a job out of pity. Being the state typing champion my junior year hardly gave me credentials, but what else it could be escaped me.

Hugh jumped up and pumped my hand when I went into his office, then leaned across the desk and gave me a peck on the cheek. "Good to see you, Georgia. You know Mrs. Palmer, I believe." And in a grand gesture he held out his hand to Doreen Palmer.

Heat engulfed my face. Embarrassment over not calling on her in so long. And in the tizzy of worrying over being summoned to

Hugh's office, I'd not even baked the cake I meant to take to her in consolation over Paddy's passing. At least my manners took over, and I went to her and leaned over, gave her a kiss on her soft cheek.

"I'm so sorry about Paddy." Tears brimmed to the surface, but through the blur in my eyes, I could see her smile through deep lines of age and sorrow.

"He was a fighter, I'll give him that."

I tried to swallow, but shame and grief choked me. "You must think I'm awful. Not calling or bringing the girls by." My nose ran along with a new surge of tears.

"Don't you be fretting. Gracious, you've had your hands full, and losing your own husband to boot. I couldn't even make it to O'Dell's funeral. Tell me, how was it?"

I sniffed and blinked my eyes, trying to gain some control. Hugh handed me a handkerchief, and when I looked up to thank him, he nailed me with a look of stone.

"Thanks." I blew my nose and willed myself to calm down.

Hugh cleared his throat. "Why don't you have a seat?"

I scooted the empty chair closer to Doreen, took a deep breath, and dropped into the seat.

Hugh, however, remained standing, a document in his hand. "We're here today at Doreen's request. Paddy, as you are aware, passed away—rest his soul—and upon his being of sound mind and body when this instrument was established, this is his last will and testament."

My chest tightened as he read. At first I was curious. Intrigued. Then confused. Paddy had bequeathed *me* the Stardust Tourist Cottages. All of it except his and Doreen's personal belongings.

My heart sped up, and I was certain I'd misunderstood. While Hugh read on, Doreen reached over and took my shaking hand in her calloused, knobby one.

"There are a couple of provisions. The first is that Doreen

shall have access to one of the cottages for as long as she is alive or desires to occupy one. The second is you must continue the operation of the business for at least five years from the date of transfer of the property. You may assign a third party to run the day-to-day operations, but you may not lease or sell the property for the stated time."

As the news sunk in, the main question that surfaced was "Why? Why me?" And I asked it of Doreen, not Hugh.

"Simple, sweetie. Paddy always took a hankering to you as a child. Said you had the Tickle spirit. And I think you reminded him of a picture he has...*had* of his mother. She was a spitfire. Like you, Paddy said."

My insides churned with the gravity of it. What did I know about running a tourist court? What did I know about anything?

"I was crazy over him, too. But surely there were other nieces and nephews...or even you. Why wouldn't you want to continue to run the Stardust?"

She shook her head, her silver hair wispy and soft like a cloud. "The only other nieces and nephews are on my side of the family. Which is one of the reasons I'm anxious to finish the arrangements here. My family is from Oklahoma, and I'll be going there next week for an extended stay. Maybe permanently."

Done. Just like that. In the blink of an eye, I'd been handed the keys to my future. Unfathomable. Undeserved. And what it left me feeling was uncertain.

Hugh ruffled the papers. "I can draw up the document to transfer title. It shouldn't take more than a day or two."

Doreen stood. "Thank you. I hate to rush, but I need to stop by Garvey's Funeral Home. I forgot to take Paddy's eyeglasses. He'll look more natural for the open casket with them on, don't you think?" She patted me on the cheek, her fingers lingering for a moment, the wrinkles in her face softening as she smiled.

A million thoughts swirled through my head. Things I needed to know. Questions I didn't even know to ask. I only hoped I'd have time before Doreen left the state.

Hugh added to my bewilderment as soon as Doreen was gone. "Truth is, Georgia, you've got an albatross on your hands. Doreen told me she had some reservations herself. When Paddy made the will, you still had O'Dell, and heaven only knows what he was thinking. Perhaps that O'Dell would own up and do what he should've been doing all along and take care of his family. At the very least, Palmer's gesture was sincere, and he thought he was doing you both a favor by naming you in the will. In my opinion, a girl like you's got no business out there on the highway running a tourist court."

Immediately, I recoiled. *Girl like me?* I glared at him. "But the will seemed clear to me. While I do agree it's a tall order, I'm not so sure it's out of the question as you imply."

"I'm sure it's a thrill to be named a benefactor, especially in your current state of widowhood, but if I were you, I'd exercise the third-party option. Advertise for a manager, let him run the place. You'd have to oversee it, of course, but the place is run-down. I didn't want to mention it with Doreen here as it always stings to realize you've invested an entire life into something that's hardly more than a pile of rubble."

My hackles rose. "It's not that bad. I went out there looking for Doreen yesterday . . . before I learned about Paddy. Some paint and fixin' up will do wonders. I'm not afraid of the work."

"Not saying you are. But you should consider my advice. Don't take it personal—consider it a nice windfall you can turn into cash at the end of five years. The land oughta be worth a pretty penny or two." He pulled a cigar from his desk drawer, leaned back in his leather chair, and held a silver lighter to the cigar tip until an odorous cloud erupted.

The smell of it turned my stomach, Hugh's puffing a painful reminder of the days when he entertained my pleas of finding Mama and Daddy. The old hurts reared up inside of me. Our vagabond life back then, skipping from one place to another. And the childish dream that one day my parents would return to the Stardust and at least give me an explanation.

Ah, the Stardust. It came down to that, didn't it? Hugh might be right, but he also might be wrong. Something had taken hold of me. Determination to prove myself. Excitement over a new challenge. Freedom for Rosey, Avril, and me.

The heat rushed at me when I stepped onto the sidewalk, but my steps were light, and I had the sensation of floating like a carnival balloon that's just escaped the fist of a tiny child.

⟡

CHAPTER 7

Gossip about the Stardust would travel like lightning on the telephone party line, so instead of making a jaunt out there to try the keys Doreen had given me, I hurried back to Sally's to pick up Avril.

Sally was thrilled. "Yesterday you didn't know what you would do, and today the good Lord has made a way through the wilderness."

"It's not like I'm in Egypt, for heaven's sake." I explained what Hugh Salazar had suggested.

"You could let a manager run it, but you'd still have the responsibility. Besides, a change would be good for you. Think of your girls, sweetie. They'll love it with all that room to roam, and I betcha you'll have things spruced up in no time. You know, a coat of paint, some new window boxes filled with geraniums."

"One problem. I have no money."

"No, but the Magnolias have been panting for a new project since we finished up the flower beds over to the library. Honey, you see about fixing up the cottages, and I'll put the Magnolias to work on transforming the grounds into a showplace."

Bolstered by Sally's enthusiasm, I dropped by Aunt Cora's with the girls after supper and found her sitting on the porch with the sheriff.

Sonny hopped up and offered me his rocking chair. "Time to make a pass around town. Be seein' you, ladies." And I should have guessed by his hasty departure that he'd already delivered the news.

Aunt Cora asked the girls if they'd like to run around back and play on the tire swing. They streaked off, giggling. She sat there fanning herself, looking off in the distance. I'd always favored this time of day, soft shadows as the sun dipped behind the trees. Damp smells starting to rise from the bayou. Too early for fireflies, but the cicadas were already practicing for their nightly chorus. As much as the evening beckoned, I was too antsy for porch sitting with what I wanted to discuss with Aunt Cora.

"I guess you heard about Paddy Palmer."

"Sonny mentioned it."

"Did he mention anything else?" Sometimes you had to get Aunt Cora warmed up for tricky conversations. Let her take the wheel.

"Said it was cancer that got him."

"Yes." She wasn't making it easy for me, so I blundered on. "I have a dilemma of sorts. Apparently, Paddy wanted to keep the Stardust in the family, and he's willed it to me..."

Chin jutted up, head cocked a fraction to the side, she said, "So it's true...the rumors?"

"You've heard then?"

"There are no secrets in Mayhaw. Sonny ran into Doreen down at Garvey's when he went to check on leading the funeral escort." She smoothed a wrinkle from her linen skirt. "Of course, you turned it down."

"No, that wasn't an option. I was hoping you might go out to the Stardust with me, maybe tomorrow afternoon...just to see...

well, the possibilities. It's an opportunity for me to do something with my life, quit this waffling about—"

Her look cut me off, and in the shade of the porch, I couldn't tell if she was angry or perplexed. Only that her lips were drawn tight above her quivering chin. As if to keep the emotion from spilling out. It was a side of Aunt Cora I'd rarely seen. She was an expert at being coy and flirtatious or bossy and intimidating— always in charge. But never confused. Or anxious.

I touched her lightly on the arm. "I'm sorry I didn't come over right away to tell you. I had to get Rosey from school, fix supper. I see now, it would have been better to tell you before Sonny beat me to it... Well, Sonny's a character, isn't he? Always the first to know everything. I'm sorry. I owed you that much at least."

"At the very least." She stiffened and reached into her pocket for a hankie. Blotted the corner of her eye. "You've no idea what you've gotten yourself into." Her words hissed out. "Exposing your girls to merciful heaven only knows what. It's not a proper home for children. Strangers coming and going. It's a filthy place. Utterly filthy." And the way she spat out *filthy* I didn't think she was speaking of cleanliness.

"I'd still like you to go out there with me and have a look."

"The governor will dance at my wedding before I step foot in that place."

I saw the opportunity to turn the tables. "Oh? Are you and Sonny planning something you've not told me about?"

"Good heavens, no. We're only friends. He gets lonely and likes to drop a fishing line in the creek behind the house. Says it's an exclusive spot where the best channel cats congregate. I wouldn't know, but a couple times a week, he brings one up to the house for me to fix."

Whether Aunt Cora was glad to get off the subject of my news or was nervous when I asked her about Sonny, I didn't know. But at least I'd filled her in with my plans. And I hoped she'd changed her mind about coming to the Stardust. Maybe I wasn't so different from Aunt Cora after all. Living life on my own terms. Defying tradition. Going against the grain.

It should have bothered me more than it did.

※

Sally watched Avril again while I went to Paddy's service. A small clutch of people rallied around Doreen at the dinner afterward, commiserating, asking about her plans. When she announced that I would be taking over the Stardust, a dozen saints offered to help Doreen move her things and help me with anything I needed.

When I got a chance to slip out, I hugged Doreen and made arrangements to meet her the next day for a tour of the Stardust and get instructions on running it. After I put Avril down for her afternoon nap, I got the long-distance operator on the line and called the regional sales office in Tyler—the number I'd found in O'Dell's briefcase. Time to get all my ducks lined up.

I explained about O'Dell's accidental death and inquired about obtaining his latest commissions.

The secretary hesitated. "You're Mr. Peyton's wife?"

"Yes, ma'am."

"One moment, please." In the background, a screeching sound as if a chair was pushed back, then a sound of papers being shuffled through.

A man came on the line. "Tragic. So sorry to hear about O'Dell. One of our finest salesmen." He cleared his throat. "What can I do for you?"

I took a deep breath and said, "Mr.—I'm sorry, I didn't catch your name."

"Clyde. Clyde Baxter."

"Mr. Baxter, we buried my husband five days ago. Last Friday. I've just now been able to go through his things and begin to put my life back together."

I explained about O'Dell's drowning, not knowing how long he'd been in the bayou or even that—due to the traveling nature of his job—he was in fact, missing.

"I'm sorry for your loss, Mrs. Peyton. We've been concerned that we hadn't heard from O'Dell in a couple of weeks, but because our salesmen work independently, that's often the case. I'm afraid we'll have to look into this. We will need a death certificate from you. To expedite matters you can present it in person with your identification."

"Certainly. I'm in the process of getting the death certificate now. In the meantime, can you tell me what I can expect in the way of unpaid commissions or death benefits?"

"We don't carry life insurance for our employees, and I will have to prepare a statement regarding the commissions. I will tell you, we are hit hard by this. O'Dell was our top sales guy last quarter. Heckuva fella." I detected a choked-up tenderness in his gruff businessman's voice.

And for the briefest of moments I remembered the way O'Dell's eyes lit up when he practiced his five-point pitch. He *was* a good salesman. I'd bought his excuses plenty of times—the tall tale he'd told me about the waitress at Caddo Lake. The rumors he explained away about Sheila Price, a girl from the Sweet Shoppe. His taking his wandering eye on the road shouldn't have been such a surprise.

This wasn't the time to get my dander up, so I told Mr. Baxter I'd be in Tyler on the following Monday.

CHAPTER 8

Doreen had a feather duster in her hand, her arm swooshing in time to Hank Williams crooning about *jambalaya on the bayou* on the radio when I arrived at the Stardust. My heart tugged at the sight; she looked so natural behind the counter, the pinafore apron tied at the back of her neck and around her thick waist.

Her face lit up when I stepped across the threshold. "Come in, if you can stand the mess. So sorry I've let the dust accumulate. Poor Paddy took all my attention."

"You don't have to clean or make excuses. There'll be time for that..." Realization hit me in the gut. I would be the one ruffling the feather duster, and Doreen would be hundreds of miles away.

On the radio, Hank Williams finished with a flourish as Doreen did a little jig, her steps light. She made a final swoosh over the rack of keys. "You're right. Looks as if it'll have to wait. It's time to show you around."

"And give me a crash course in business management and the fine art of innkeeping."

"You'll be fine." She waved me back to a door in the corner of the office. On the way I noted the rocking chair where Doreen had rested, waiting for travelers. Maybe not rested, for she always

had a lapful of yarn, her knitting needles clacking, or I would find
her reading *Capper's Weekly* and clipping recipes. Sometimes past-
ing the recipes in a notebook.

This wasn't the time to dawdle, so I followed Doreen into the
living quarters behind the office. The smell of ointment and sickness hit me first. I swallowed hard and tried not to think about
Paddy. Or people dying.

A modest open area served as both kitchen and living room. Seat-
ing space on the right. A line of cupboards in a small L-shape on the
left. A round oak table straddled the two areas. Doreen assured me
the men from the church would clear everything out, and I could
see they had a tall order to fill—the accumulation of a lifetime.

"Over here is the bedroom Paddy and I shared. I'm thinking
you'll want the girls to stay in here. The light is nice and cheery
in the mornings. And if you don't mind, I'll leave this wardrobe
since there's not much closet to speak of."

I told her, "Of course," and tried to picture the girls' twin beds.
Yes, they would fit, along with their chest of drawers. But before I
had time to do more than a quick calculation in my head, Doreen
had shooed me along, showed me the bathroom—also small but
adequate—and then ushered me into the sunporch.

"We added this a few years back. We loved to sit out here of
a morning with the view of the cottages so we could tell if any
of the guests came our way to check out. We could still watch
out the other side for any deer coming up from the woods." She
pointed toward Zion. It didn't look so far from this vantage point.
Just separated by the length of a couple of football fields. A skittish
feeling came over me. It also wasn't that far from where O'Dell
washed up. I turned away from the window and surveyed the
room. This would be my room by default, but it was large and airy
feeling with windows on three sides. Weatherproof, it seemed.
Room for a stuffed chair on one side, my bedroom furniture on

the other. Even though I'd have a view of Zion, I couldn't let O'Dell's happenstance landing there color my thoughts. Shoot, every street, sidewalk, and business establishment in Mayhaw had reminders of O'Dell.

Doreen clucked her tongue and motioned me to the breeze-way that connected the "quarters" to the washhouse that the child, Merciful, had pointed out. The workroom was utilitar-ian and more than adequate, with spare linens stacked neatly on open shelves, an old wringer washer, and a newer automatic one. A pressing machine stood against the back wall, and I imagined Merciful and her momma working in this room as warmth and moisture swirled together in a hive of activity. Already I was hop-ing they would help me get ready for the grand reopening of the Stardust.

And almost as if she read my mind, Doreen turned around. "I used to take care of all the housekeeping myself, but for a few years now, I've resorted to hiring help. Best thing I ever did. You'd be doing them and yourself a favor to have Ludi come help."

"Ludi?"

"Ludi Harper. She lives over yonder." She pointed to the trees.

"How do I get in touch with her? Is there a road somewhere I haven't seen?"

"Nothing but a trail connects Zion to Mayhaw. The road they use is out a ways, off the road to the lumber mill. Easy to get lost out there, though, so if you want them to help, you can do what I do and hang a sheet out on the clothesline. Ludi will be here before you can snap your fingers and turn around three times."

"Thanks. I'll do that . . . when I'm further along with the plans."

"Take your time, sweetie. You've got five or six weeks until Memorial Day. That's when we always get the first big string of travelers."

She showed me the cottages, and there was no doubt it would

take every bit of that time to get them ready for paying guests. The bedspreads were frayed, broken springs in some of the beds. The units all needed paint, and more than a few had drippy faucets. Surely O'Dell's back pay would cover the initial repairs until I could sell our house. My heart raced at the ideas swirling in my head.

I was the new owner of the Stardust, a woman with her own business.

My own business.

A home with no reminders of O'Dell aside from the bayou. I would be doing something constructive and be able to remain in Mayhaw, and the glory of it carried me along from cottage to cottage. I even laughed when we got to number five—the one I'd stayed in with Mama and Daddy.

"I bet you have a lot of stories, Doreen, about all the folks who've stayed here over the years."

"Oh, my stars! You wouldn't believe." Then she gave a big wink. "That's something you'll have to discover yourself."

"Care to elaborate?"

"No, sweetie. All you need to know is Paddy would be happy you're going to keep the place going. 'Twould be a travesty to let all our memories go to dust." Her eyes drifted to another place, and for a moment I was envious of her devotion and long marriage.

"All I can say is I'll try. Ever since O'Dell drowned, I've been in limbo...trying to come to grips. It'll take me awhile to get organized."

"Sweetie, don't you know it? Paddy did me a favor by willing you the Stardust, and you'll do fine. Now, what say we head back to the office and I'll show you how I do the bookkeeping?"

The radio was still blasting when we got there, with Bobby Carl Applegate's nasal twang reporting on the farm market. Corn futures. Spring calves. Cotton prices.

Doreen switched off the knob and pulled the ledger from a cabinet beneath the counter. An hour later I had a decent idea of what I needed to know. Receipts. Bills to pay. Names and numbers of assorted vendors who provided supplies. Granted, the Stardust wasn't fancy. Just a few of those paper-wrapped soaps and whatnot.

"One question, though. You don't have any checks entered showing you paid Ludi Harper."

"That's right. I put her over here in miscellaneous in the ledger. Cash only. Folks over in Zion...some of 'em don't read or write. Ludi among them."

"Really? Right here in Musgrave County? I had no idea."

"Crying shame, but the good Lord didn't promise life would be fair. Only that he'd walk beside us. And Ludi knows the truth of that." She laughed and then looked around me. "Well, if that don't beat all? We just finished, and here's the crew come to pack my things."

We went out to greet the caravan of pickup trucks, and before I left, I hugged Doreen. "You know you've always got a spot here if you want to come back."

"Bless you. Even if Paddy insisted on putting that in the will, I'm off for the next leg of my journey. Reckon it'll be my last."

"Thank you...for everything. Don't be a stranger now, okay?"

I'm not sure if she heard me or not as she was directing a half-dozen men where to start packing and loading her things. And as I pulled from the driveway, I looked in the rearview mirror. Fruit basket upset. Doreen leaving. Rosey, Avril, and I coming.

My skin tingled with excitement. A new home. My own business. I looked in the rearview mirror at the neon sign.

Stardust.

Like an old sweet song, the magic flowed through me.

CHAPTER 9

Rosey and Avril acted as if I'd given them a lifetime supply of ice-cream cones when I took them out to the Stardust. They raced through the office and the quarters, their delight echoing in the empty rooms. When I hauled out the wash buckets, they hopscotched on the sidewalks and found stray tree limbs to use for ponies while they pretended they were Roy Rogers and Dale Evans.

Sally brimmed with the same excitement and supervised a cleaning and lawn-mowing crew on Saturday while I slapped robin's-egg-blue paint on all the walls in the quarters and a more appropriate cream-colored paint in the office. I planned to overhaul the cottages one at a time as soon as we were settled and I had a better picture of our financial status.

On Sunday morning, I could barely move and still had paint under my fingernails, but I got the girls up and took them to Sunday school, hoping to catch Aunt Cora. I found her in the foyer, where she eyed me with a frown. "Sonny tells me you're going through with it. Says you've already hired a crew to do the work."

"The Magnolia Garden Club has taken over the outdoor projects. I think Sally coaxed all the husbands into doing the mowing, telling them I'd throw a crawfish boil when we had the grand reopening. Beats me how I'm going to figure that out, but I'll worry about it when the time comes."

"That's the problem with you, Georgia—you charge right in without any backup plans."

"I need a backup plan to have a crawfish boil?"

"That's not what I meant and you know it. And it's not just your finances. I'm speaking of safety issues. A single woman with two children on the highway—"

Hazel Morton scurried up and thanked me for returning her potato salad bowl. "I'm sorry I missed you. Is it true? You're taking over the Stardust?"

I nodded, aware that Aunt Cora was perturbed by the interruption.

Hazel sidled up to me. "Mighty big job, don't you know? I was thinking, though, if you need help with some of the heavier work, my grandson, Joey, could sure use a summer job. He's right handy with a paintbrush."

"Thanks. I'll keep him in mind." I knew Joey. He hung out with a scrappy bunch of kids behind Brookshire's. Smoking cigarettes. Wolf-whistling at the girls. It wasn't Hazel's fault. Matter of fact, some of the goons who did the same thing when I was in high school turned out perfectly respectable. I just didn't have to expose my girls to them, and as Hazel walked away, Aunt Cora dipped her head in next to mine.

"See? That's the kind of trouble I see in your future. That Joey is a hoodlum. And you'll be so worn out from doing all the work yourself, you won't have time to keep an eye on the girls."

"Doreen gave me a recommendation for someone to help. It'll work out. You'll see."

She shuddered ever so slightly and sniffed. "I can only imagine."

And this time she seemed grateful when Hazel interrupted yet again and shoved a piece of paper in my hand.

"Joey's phone number."

Not hardly.

The truth was I had considered hiring someone to do some general repairs and paint the outside of the cottages, but I didn't want to get hasty and not have the money to pay them. Which I hoped would be forthcoming when I went to Tyler on Monday.

So, bright and early, I dropped Rosey off at school and headed to Tyler with Avril in tow. She sang "You Are My Sunshine" and "Zaccheus Was a Wee Little Man." What she lacked in musicality she made up for in volume, and we laughed and played I Spy until we pulled into the outskirts. We stopped at a filling station for directions and to use the restroom. Then on to a small business office behind the newspaper's quarters on Main Street.

The receptionist nodded toward the only other room in the office and offered Avril a peppermint.

"I don't supposed to take candy from strangers." She clung to my skirt and followed me through the open door, where we found Clyde Baxter, O'Dell's boss. He stood to greet us, a squirrelly guy, several inches shorter than me, with a nervous tic in his jaw.

"Aw, Mrs. Peyton, I presume."

I greeted him and handed over the death certificate, my driver's license, and our marriage certificate, which he hadn't mentioned but I'd thought of at the last minute.

Avril tugged on my sleeve, a twinkle in her eye. "Is he the real Zaccheus? I don't see no sycamore tree."

"It's *any* sycamore tree, sweetie, and no, this isn't Zaccheus. The real one lived a long time ago when Jesus was alive. Mommy has to talk to Mr. Baxter now, so I need you to be still."

Clyde Baxter cast a look at Avril like she was a boil on his backside and took a seat. I sat in the only other chair and pulled Avril onto my lap. As Mr. Baxter bent over the folder I assumed was O'Dell's file, the brown coil of hair atop his head unwound and hung down, covering one eye. He pushed it back into place and withdrew a piece of paper, which he slid across the desk.

A certificate.

Clyde's jaw twitched when he said, "O'Dell was the top salesman for the winter quarter. Normally, we'd honor him at a sales meeting and present him with a set of sterling cuff links, but the meeting was last week, and since O'Dell was indisposed..."

"Excuse me? He wasn't indisposed. You have to be alive to be indisposed." I felt sorry for the guy in an odd way, but how he'd risen to the manager level was beginning to concern me. "Do you have the cuff links?"

"I didn't think you would have any use for them."

"Me? No, I wouldn't, but it would be nice to present them to his mother. She *is* indisposed. Not well at all. Grieving. As you can imagine."

"Of course. I wasn't thinking." He reached in his drawer and pulled out a velvet pouch with a gold cord. "It's not much, but..." He handed it over. Avril slipped off my lap when I took them.

"I appreciate it. Now, about his commissions?"

"Yes, well...the news there is not very encouraging, I'm afraid."

A queasy feeling rose to my throat. "As in?"

"O'Dell's sales for this quarter are, shall we say, slim. We'll honor his current orders, but we'll have to send one of our other employees to pick up the merchandise from the warehouse and make the deliveries. The expense of that will come from O'Dell's commissions, I'm afraid." The jerking in his jaw was more pronounced, making the leaders in his neck protrude with each twitch.

Avril had crept closer to him and now stood at his elbow, squinting her eyes at him. "How do you make your face wiggle like that?"

"Avril!" I jumped from my chair and in two giant leaps was behind the desk. I snatched her up, my face flaming. "Oh, sweetie, it's not nice to ask personal questions of strangers."

She dipped her head, burrowing into my chest. I hefted her to my hip and looked at Mr. Baxter. "I'm sorry. Now, you were saying?"

He had his own sheepish look and said, "The final check is probably less than you were hoping for. He only had commissions coming for five weeks." He pulled an envelope from the folder and slid it across the desk.

Inside was a check for two hundred and twenty-three dollars. Good gravy. I swallowed the O'Dell-size lump in my throat. What did I expect?

I forced a smile and thanked him for his time.

He extended his hand. "I'm sorry for your loss."

Juggling Avril on my hip and holding the check in my hand, I didn't have a free hand to shake his. I nodded and turned to go. When I reached the door, he said, "You do have the cuff links."

I sailed out the door and put Avril in the front seat of the car, went around, and let myself in. As I jammed the key into the ignition, a twitch came in my own jaw. And rather than spit nails, which is what I wanted to do, I turned to Avril.

"How about we find ourselves an ice-cream parlor? 'Twould be a shame to come all this way for nothing."

CHAPTER 10

After supper I took the girls over to see Mary Frances and take her the cuff links. She got teary eyed and blamed it on the head cold she thought was coming on, but no doubt she was proud of O'Dell's accomplishment. Under different circumstances I might've been, too.

But stuffy sinuses or not, she still had a Pall Mall dangling from her fingers when she offered the girls an RC Cola. While they sipped from the ice-cold bottles, Mary Frances asked what our plans were for the summer. Polite, almost formal, she kept her lips drawn, her line of vision veering off to the pleated drapes behind me. Rosey asked if she and Avril could sit on the front porch, and I sent them on their way.

Then I plunged right in and asked Mary Frances if she'd heard about my inheriting the Stardust. No, she hadn't heard. I explained about Paddy's death and taking over right away.

"Getting out is so difficult, with reminders everywhere of O'Dell and my own Earl. Life is just passing me by. You and the girls didn't even stop by yesterday like you usually do on Sunday afternoon."

"I should've called, but after church—"

"I waited all afternoon." She wiped her nose with her hankie, her eyes bleary. Could have been the head cold. Or the gin.

"I'm sorry. I'm trying to get ready by Memorial Day, when the first summer guests usually arrive. The girls and I went to the Stardust and cleaned out one of the cottages so I can paint first thing tomorrow. I'm going to have paint in my pores forever with all the work to be done."

"Guess I know where that leaves me."

The whining was getting to me. Dank, smoky air hung like dingy organza around my mother-in-law. Ex-mother-in-law, but I wasn't sure if till death do us part applied only to O'Dell and me or his mother, too. And in my gut, I knew the answer.

I lifted my chin and looked square into her eyes. "I know where you think it leaves you, but you do have other options. You could get your driver's license and a nice car so you could get out more, or you might volunteer down at the library. O'Dell always told me he got his love of books from you."

She almost smiled. "That O'Dell. Yes, he was a book-lovin' boy." Then she drifted off into some other world, her rheumy eyes misting.

"Or there's your cousin over in Corsicana—"

She snapped back to the present. "Bertha? You call that an option? I'd rather wither away here than spend an hour listening to her go on about the latest cocktail party she went to and how many ties the mayor has hanging in his closet."

"I'm just saying you can't depend on me and the girls for all your social contacts. You're barely fifty years old. There are a lot of things you could do."

"That's fine for you to say—you've already moved on. Didn't spend five minutes grieving over O'Dell now, did you?"

I bit my tongue to keep from pointing out O'Dell's infidelity. Had I wanted to, I could've yanked the one last thread that kept

Mary Frances hanging on—the memory of a son whom she'd always seen as the embodiment of perfection. As it was, I stuck with keeping things on track. For her sake *and* mine.

"We all grieve in different ways, Mary Frances. But I have to move on. It's fortunate for me the Stardust fell in my lap when it did since O'Dell didn't leave much in the way of provision for the girls and me."

She tapped out another Pall Mall from the pack. The last one. She crumpled the wrapper and tossed it on the coffee table atop a pile of envelopes and papers. She flicked the lighter and lit up, then had a coughing fit. "Blasted head cold," she said.

We sat in silence while she puffed and I tried to think of an excuse to leave. I ambled over to the picture window and drew the drapes so I could check on the girls. They'd set their coke bottles on the porch and were playing with the girls from next door. The late afternoon light shimmered from Rosey's tangled mop of poppy-colored curls. A protective fire tumbled through me. I had O'Dell to thank for my girls, and although it might seem irrelevant, they also had a smidgeon of Mary Frances in them. Abandon her? Not hardly.

Turning back to the living room, I said, "You know you're welcome to come out to the Stardust and have a look around."

"For heaven's sake, it's practically next door to where O'Dell drowned. Or have you forgotten that the way you forgot to come over yesterday?"

I heaved a sigh. Back to square one.

"I said I was sorry. Why do you keep bringing it up?"

"Because."

It was like dragging something out of a stubborn child. "Because why?"

She stubbed out the cigarette and crossed her arms over her chest. "Because I had something exciting to tell you. I waited and waited and you didn't come." She leaned over and whisked the wadded-up Pall Mall pack on the floor, then picked up a large envelope.

"Here. See for yourself."

I undid the clasp and removed a document similar to the life insurance policy with Fiona Callahan's name on it. This, too, was an insurance policy. Five thousand dollars. And my name as the beneficiary.

Heat crept up my neck. "Oh, my."

"I finally remembered where I'd put it." Her voice, though husky, was small, penitent. "O'Dell didn't leave you penniless as you've implied. And I couldn't wait to tell you. I kept waiting and watching for you... but you never came."

I winced. My heart's cry since I was six years old, waiting, always waiting for the mommy and daddy who never came. I dropped onto the sofa beside Mary Frances and took her cold, bony hand in mine. "It's all right, sweetie. I'm here now."

Toward the end of the week, a thunderstorm came during the night, lightning flashes followed by booms of thunder. Avril crept into my bed first. "I'm scared, Mommy."

"It's okay, baby." I pulled her close as another jagged streak lit the room, thunder on its heels, so loud it shook the walls and brought Rosey flying into the room and under the covers.

Rosey covered her face when another flash and clap of thunder came. "I wish Daddy was here." Her voice was small, timid in the dark, as rain pelted the windows.

"I know you do." Even with the girls snug as bookends on either side of me, the bed felt cavernous without O'Dell. We'd always squeezed the girls between us on stormy nights.

Rosey whispered, "Rub my arms, Mommy."

I ran the back of my finger over her goosefleshed arm, up and down, then in lazy circles. Beneath my fingers, the taut muscles relaxed, her breathing settled, and she slipped into the arm-sprawled comfort of slumber.

Avril sat up. "Will Daddy be at our new house?" A blue-white shimmer lit her face, her dark eyes so much like O'Dell's it pierced my heart.

"No, sweetie. He's in heaven with Jesus now."

"Can Daddy stop the thunder?"

"I think that's God's job, but I bet Daddy's thinking it's time Avril went to sleep like her sister Rosey did. Here, let me rub your arms."

"Not my arms. My back." She flopped over, and I reached across and ran whisper-light caresses on Avril's back. Over the nape of her neck, slowly outlining first one shoulder blade, then the other, neither as big as a china saucer. The storm had calmed outside the window, drippy and no longer rattling the windows, but it left in its wake an empty spot. O'Dell had rubbed my back, too. Long strokes that eased away the weariness when I'd been up all night with Avril and her colic or the time Rosey had the big red measles and I didn't sleep for a week. There was no doubt, O'Dell had his charms. If only he hadn't felt compelled to share them with so many others. Maybe if I'd been a better wife...

No use crying over spilt milk. Merciful and her momma had it right. The next morning brought sunshine. The air wrapped a muggy film around me the minute I hurried the girls out to the car. Beads of moisture collected on my face, and I wished for a breeze to blow through the open windows of O'Dell's Ford as we drove toward the school. Instead, a swarm of gnats danced around my head. I waved them away, leaned over to give Rosey a kiss, and then watched as she skipped up the walk.

Avril and I stopped for a donut and coffee for me, a carton of chocolate milk for her, and headed out to the Stardust. The rain had brought out the smell of mothballs and Paddy's illness, which I'd hoped the new paint would take away. I went into our living quarters searching for the source of the odor. In the wardrobe Doreen had left behind, I found a box of partially dissolved mothballs tucked in the folds of an old quilt. I opened the windows to let the rooms air out, hoping the smell hadn't permanently penetrated the walls and pine floors. The quilt, a heavy wool patchwork, was tied with embroidery thread. It looked like it still had some use as a picnic blanket, so when I tossed the mothballs in the trash barrel, I toted the quilt along and threw it over the clothesline.

"C'mon, chipmunk," I said to Avril, then stopped. I'd never called her that. Never. That was O'Dell's name for her since her first baby teeth were two miniature Chiclets on top, tiny pearls that weren't joined by any other teeth until she was thirteen months old. How and why *chipmunk* popped out of my mouth came from some part of me I didn't know. Or trust.

Avril, though, seemed not to notice, and followed me along the sidewalk as I went to check on the first cottage I hoped to paint. Every few yards, she sidestepped to stomp her feet in a rain puddle. She was singing the ABC song at the top of her lungs, and I joined her in the last line. "Now I've said my ABC's. Tell me what you think of me."

I ruffled her head. "I think you're the best Mommy's helper in the world, and today we're going to paint. What color should we use—the blue or the green in this cottage?"

"Pink!" Avril wanted everything pink, and after giving her opinion took a giant leap to the left to jump in a puddle with both feet.

I should have scolded her, but I was working the keys on the O-ring trying to find the one labeled number one. When I found the key and entered, my heart plummeted. A chunk of plaster the size of a washtub had fallen into the middle of the room—onto the mattress. A patch of blue sky peeked through the lath that once held the plaster in place.

Avril stood in the doorway, her eyes as round as marbles. "Look at this mess, Mommy!"

"Oh, my. You are right, my sweets. Just look." I swallowed. Why hadn't I had the roof checked? All of the roofs? Had the storm blown shingles off? I spun around and, with my Avril shadow behind me, went from cottage to cottage to assess the damage. Nothing as bad as in number one, but six and seven both had bulges overhead with water-stained edges.

Immediate action was needed, but I didn't know what to do first—clean up the plaster in cottage one or call a roofer. Surely someone at the lumberyard could point me in the right direction, and with the promised money from O'Dell's *found* life insurance policy, I could get credit. The dollar signs mounted in my head. What if the insurance money wasn't enough? What if I couldn't afford to have the renovations done? Would I be breaking the terms of the will before I even moved into the Stardust's quarters? My stomach gnawed with the truth that my inheritance from Paddy might not have been such a windfall as I'd expected. I didn't blame Doreen for wanting to scoot on out as quick as possible.

I grabbed Avril's hand and marched toward the office to ponder the possibilities. Avril skipped beside me until we came to another puddle, then stretched to stamp her foot in it. Mud sprayed up on both of us.

"Avie. Stop it! You're making both of us a mess."

Her mouth drooped at the corners, her eyes bearing the same penitent look O'Dell had perfected when he didn't make it home for dinner because the fish were biting. I squeezed her hand. "It's all right, Avie. Mommy's just being cranky."

She stuck out her bottom lip as we made our way to the office. As we neared, I looked up. On the porch, a woman whose girth could fill a doorway stood with hands on hips, feet planted wide apart, an unreadable expression on her ink-black face. When she saw us, she drew her hand to her forehead to shield the sun, as if she wanted a good look. And when we got there, she eyed me first, then Avril.

I spoke first. "May I help you?"

"Yes'm. Miss Do-reen said you'd signal when you be needing

Ludi's help." Doreen was drawn out *Dough-reen* in a rich, full voice that vibrated the air between us.

My mind clicked through the morning's events. The mothballs. Throwing the quilt over the line. Then finding the hole in the roof. Worrying what I was going to do. *Ludi.* Yes. Yes! The colored woman who helped Doreen with the housekeeping.

"You saw the old quilt on the clothesline. The signal, you say. As a matter of fact, I could use some help. Do you know how to get ahold of Ludi? Is that why you've come?"

"Lawsy, missy, I am Ludi! In the flesh, ready to get to work."

"Oh, my. Then you know about Paddy?" I held out my hand. "I'm Georgia Peyton, the new owner of the Stardust. And this is Avril. Come in out of the sun so we can talk."

"Yes, ma'am, Miz Georgie. I'm pleased to meet you, though I been grieving a blue streak over Mr. Paddy's expiration. I been on my knees a prayin' someone like you be comin' along." She lumbered after me into the office, her hands worrying the apron she wore, an apron that carried the remnants of a half-dozen spatters of what looked like tomatoes, maybe a bit of gravy. Her hair, though, was pulled into a neat bun at the back of her head, and she smelled of wood smoke and earth and something faint but sweet. Her feet were stuffed into men's black leather shoes, the laces missing, which allowed her beefy flesh room to breathe at the tops. I winced, thinking the shoes must be killing her feet. She seemed not to notice so I didn't mention it.

"So you're Ludi. Ludi Harper, I believe." Her nod told me I got it. "I'm not sure what your arrangement was with the Palmers or even what your duties were. I would guess general cleaning and keeping the cottages stocked with fresh towels, soap, clean linens."

"Yes'm. And running the washer machine, putting the sheets through the ironing press, whatever the missus needed, that's what I do."

"Well, I'm temporarily closed, trying to get some remodeling done. Cleaning so the girls and I can move in." I pointed to Avril. "She's my baby, but I have another girl in school. Rosey."

Avril had been walking around Ludi since we'd come inside, and I hoped she didn't say something embarrassing like she had with Mr. Baxter about the twitching jaw. Instead, she put her hand in Ludi's and smiled. "I like you. You look like Rae Rae's Tansy. She's got a big lap like you do."

Ludi cupped Avril's chin in her ample hands, the thick fingers as gentle as her smile. "You know Tansy, do you? Why, she be my niece who work over to the Cotton house."

"Rae Rae say Tansy is the bestest samwich maker in Mayhaw." Avril's voice had taken on the same inflection as Ludi's, and I was at once relieved. I'd always thought children were good people barometers, and Avril had admiration shining in her eyes for Ludi already. "Can you come over when we get our furniture and let me sit in your lap?"

"We best be leaving that up to your momma."

Of course, I agreed. Not to her being a maid or cook for us personally. Heavens, the kitchen in our quarters was the size of a matchbox. But helping with the Stardust, certainly.

Ludi smiled a wide, toothy smile. "What we need to do to move things along, Miz Georgie?"

"I don't even know where to start. I wanted to paint and freshen things..." A sick feeling came in my gut when I remembered the plaster in cottage one, but Ludi had her eyes locked on mine, saying *hmmm, hmmm,* and nodding her head while not saying anything.

The next thing I knew, I was blubbering about the ceiling falling in, and not knowing who to call, and then Ludi's strong arm was around my shoulder, her hand patting the back of my head as she told me, "It's all right, sweetum. I knowed these cabins was a

fixin' to cave in one of these times. I kept a telling the man, and
he was fixin' to have some work done. Poor fella took the cancer,
and now you be in a fine pickle."

My face flamed at my lack of composure in front of a stranger,
but she summed it up—I was in a fine pickle.

"I'm sorry, Ludi." I straightened, ran my hands down the tail of
one of O'Dell's old shirts that I'd started wearing to paint in, and
said, "I don't know what came over me. The last few weeks have
been such a mess. First, my husband drowning, then Paddy, and
now trying to do all this work..."

"It can wear a body down fo' sure." She gave me another soft
pat and grew quiet. Took a half step away from me. "You say your
husband drowned? That be a while back?"

"Yes, someone found him over where you live. I'm sure it was
the talk of all of Zion."

"You be gotten that straight. 'Twas my boy Catfish what found
him washed up." Her head went side to side. "I sho'nuf didn't
know it was your man. Bless you, child."

My hand flew to my chest as I sucked in a bucketful of air.
Catfish. The child, Merciful, had mentioned he was her brother.
Ludi's boy found O'Dell? I couldn't think of anything to say. We
stood silent, facing each other, not quite knowing what to do
next. I had a million questions, yet my tongue couldn't form a
single one. The business of death is not a subject to broach like
picking out the color of paint for a rotted-out cottage.

That poor child. He must've been scared half to death himself.

Ludi opened her arms, and a mysterious force pulled me in. I
breathed her scent, woodsy and musky from the day's heat no
doubt, but also a hint of jasmine, and I wondered where on earth
Ludi got her hands on such a delicate fragrance. I buried my face
in her shoulder and let her ample arms hold me. If I could have,
I would have curled into her lap.

CHAPTER 12

A week and a half later, I had put my house on Crockett Street up for sale and filed the papers to get O'Dell's insurance money. The girls and I moved into the Stardust on the first of May—my twenty-fifth birthday. Aunt Cora brought a chocolate cake by the house that morning and saw Doreen's friends from the Methodist church loading my furniture into their pickup trucks.

She sniffed. "I'm still appalled that you're going through with this."

I took the cake. "Everything's going to be fine. You'll see. And you're welcome to come out anytime."

She shot me a look that said I'd better not push my luck, then in the next instant, she hugged my neck and wished me happy birthday.

The girls and I settled into the quarters, and blessedly, with Ludi's help, the work was coming along on the Stardust. Each morning got rolling when I heard the first faint strains of "Swing Low, Sweet Chariot." Ludi's deep, throaty voice came like honey across the open meadow that separated her world from mine.

Avril raced out to meet Ludi whenever she heard the singing

and met her with open arms. "Where's Merciful? Is she coming today? C'mon, I want to show you something." And Avril would pull Ludi's arm—or Merciful's, if she was tagging along—to show her the latest treasure. Sometimes a pretty rock she found in the flower bed. Sometimes a picture she colored. Then we would have to tell Avril we had work to do. Rosey had school until the last Friday in May and now rode the bus to and fro. Every morning she marched off swinging her satchel, waving good-bye, and smiling.

With the girls happy and Ludi coming to help, I knew I should be grateful. And more patient. But the Memorial Day deadline loomed and it looked like we'd never be ready. Ludi and I didn't have enough hours between us to paint and clean and do all the other projects. We had a sum total of three finished, and they still needed new bathroom fixtures.

The roof replacement was another issue gnawing at me. I'd been to the lumberyard and got someone to come out and cover the leaking roofs with tarps held in place with old tires until a roofer was available to do the shingles. "Three weeks, at least," Mr. Miller informed me.

"Can you recommend anyone else?"

"Not likely you'd find a roofer in Mayhaw that we don't already employ. You might try over in Jefferson or Longview, but they won't carry an out-of-town account, and you never know the kind of work you're getting from a stranger."

I'd called back a week later and he'd told me the rain we had over the weekend meant it was still three weeks before they could get to it. Drat. I let the receiver drop in the phone cradle and kicked the stack of boxes that held new faucets for the bathrooms. They were to be installed by one of the Methodist men who was a plumber, but he'd been called out of town—to see about his sister in Shreveport who'd come down with infantile paralysis.

Granted, I admired a man who made family matters a priority, but it didn't help my frustration.

When I called Sally complaining, she told me to relax and *breathe*. "Don't lose your focus, Georgia."

"How can I relax and not lose my focus at the same time? That makes no sense whatsoever."

"Try focusing on the ultimate outcome and relax. Take one day at a time. And I'm simply dying to show you the plans the Magnolias have drawn up. They're splendid. If you don't mind, I'll bring them by later and see what you think."

"You may find me on the roof hammering on the shingles myself."

She laughed and hung up.

Deep down, I knew it was that I didn't want to disappoint Doreen and miss the opening deadline. Plus I was going through O'Dell's anticipated insurance money faster than water swept through Hixon Bayou in the rainy season. Mattresses. Paint. Lumber for new window boxes.

I went to check on Ludi, who was patching a hole in the wall of number eight. She had plaster blobs in her hair and a smudge across her cheek, but she was humming "Amazing Grace" as she worked.

"Here, Ludi. I brought you some sweet tea." I set the glass down on the windowsill and watched her scoop up a trowel of plaster from the bucket we'd mixed that morning and then slap it on the wall. She smoothed it out in sure, even strokes like a painter at an easel. Sweat ran down the sides of her face, along the fleshy part of her neck, pooling in the soft spot at the base of her throat. She nodded at me and kept humming until the wall was as smooth as a sheet of glass. She set the trowel down and swiped her forearm across her brow. I handed her the tea.

"Thanks, Miz Georgie. I ain't never been treated like no queen before, and here you are, fetching me stuff and bringing me sweet tea." She chugged half a glass. "I'm mighty appreciative."

"No problem. I just came to see how you were doing."

She eyed her work. "Hmm. Never thought these clumsy fingers could do such a thing." She gave a hearty laugh, finished the tea, and handed me the empty glass. "You's a blessing to me, child. Don't you be forgettin' it."

"I'd say it's the other way around. I'll check on you later."

As I headed to the office, Avril met me on the sidewalk.

"Hey, Mommy, there's a man wants to see you." She pointed a pudgy finger toward the office.

"A man? Who is it?" I hoped to goodness gracious it was Mr. Miller from the lumberyard bringing me good news.

"Dunno. He said he's looking for the manager."

"Did he say what for?"

She pulled her shoulders up toward her ears, her chocolate eyes wide, innocent.

When we got to the office, a fair-headed man stood tall, hands holding a straw hat before him. His face was tanned and smooth except for a pale hat line on his forehead, and I guessed him to be close to thirty. Sitting beside him was a black-and-white dog, a long-haired spaniel or bird dog of some kind, its tail swooshing like a windshield wiper along the bottom step of the porch.

"Yes, sir, may I help you?"

"Certainly hope so. I didn't mean to scare your little girl." He extended his hand, clean with calluses worn smooth, his shake firm when I obliged.

Avril gripped my leg with both arms.

"I'm sorry if you're looking for a place to stay. We're closed until Memorial Day."

"That's what Cecil across the way told me. Said you're doing some remodeling and might could use a hand."

"Cecil a friend of yours?" I couldn't remember seeing this particular man before, and he drew his words out different from the way we did in East Texas. Softer, but a definite drawl.

"No, ma'am. I was passing through on my way to San Antonio when my car broke down. Lucky for me I was only down the road a piece and found the repair shop here at the edge of town."

"If you're passing through, why are you looking for work?" The dog lifted its chin, a long red tongue reaching out to lick the man's hand.

The stranger looked away for an instant, and I couldn't tell if he was shy or trying to come up with a believable story, but then he looked square at me and said, "Fact is, I'm a little low on cash. I don't have enough to pay to get the car repaired, and bein's mechanics is one skill they didn't teach me in the army, I got no business fixing it on my own."

"Wish I could help you, since you're a veteran and all, but cash is not something I'm swimming in right now, either. I'm sorry. Maybe you could try something in town."

"Yes, ma'am. Thought it was worth a shot."

He turned to go, put the straw hat atop his head, and signaled for the dog to follow. There was something intriguing in his demeanor, the way he stood tall but not cocky. Polite but not pretentious. And if the heat hadn't tampered with my judgment, I'd seen sincerity in his pale blue eyes.

He'd gone a few paces, his hand riding easily on the dog's head, his stride long but not defeated. This was the sort of situation Aunt Cora cautioned me about. Strangers who appeared out of nowhere, insinuating themselves on me. And the girls. It was generous of her to care, but this fellow seemed genuine. Humble.

I stepped off the porch. "Oh, say, mister. I have a question. If they didn't teach you mechanics in the army, then what did they teach you?"

He turned, removing the hat. "Things I probably shouldn't mention in front of your girl, ma'am. I spent the last year of my hitch in Korea. 'Fore the service, though, I took my plumber's license and did carpenter work."

"What do you know about roofing?"

A lopsided grin graced his face. "I reckon I've hammered on near a hundred of 'em in my life. Working for my pappy over in Macon."

"Macon?"

"Georgia, ma'am."

The way the syllables of my name rolled off his tongue like they'd been laced with molasses sent a hiccup through me, and I had to remind myself he was mentioning the state, not calling me by name.

"Why can't you call your *pappy,* as you say in Georgia to wire you the money to fix your car?"

"Nothing I'd like more, but he's passed. Him and my momma, too. Didn't leave nothin' to speak of. Just the tools I carry in the trunk of my car."

A man with skills and tools had my interest. "I'm sorry to hear about your folks."

"It's been awhile. They were God-fearing, and I know they're enjoying the streets of gold right now." He was working on the straw hat, shifting his weight from one long, skinny leg to the other, probably wishing Cecil had never sent him across the highway. Avril had squatted down to eye level with the dog,

"What's your puppy's name, mister? Does he bite?"

The man smiled a slow smile—the way I supposed they did in Georgia—and held out his hand to the dog. "Never bit a soul that I know of. His name's Sebastian."

The next thing I knew, Avril had her arms around the dog's neck, getting licked across the face, all the while cooing, "Sea-bash-an. Nice doggie."

"Avril, maybe you can pet the dog another time. Run on in and let me talk to the man here, okay?"

She flashed her dark eyes and stuck out her lower lip, then kissed the dog on the nose and stomped up the steps. If she was like this at three, I could only imagine her at thirteen. I turned my attention back to the stranger. The sun now bore down on us, the stickiness gathering into what promised to be a sweltering day. I brushed a damp curl away from my face. "There are a couple of problems I see with me giving you work."

"Yes?"

"First off, you haven't told me your name, and it's a fact I don't have much in the way of wages to offer. I can use the help, though, Mr.—"

"Beg your pardon, ma'am. Reese." He extended his hand again like we hadn't already shook hello. "Peter Reese. And I can't say as the amount you pay matters much. It's more'n what I had before. And I'd be obliged if you would consider a place to stay as part of my pay."

"The place isn't ready for guests yet, as you can see."

He assured me it wasn't important, and before any warning signs in my head had time to reach my tongue, I had offered him a place in number ten. The ceiling there was still intact *and* it was the farthest away from the office. I asked when he could start to work.

"The sooner the better on that roof. I'll just go get my things. I was wondering though...seems like I ought to know who I'm working for, ma'am."

I laughed, but even as I did, heat crept up my neck. "I figured Cecil told you my name. I'm Georgia. Like the state." I resisted the urge to offer *my* hand and added, "Georgia Peyton."

"Fancy that. Nice to meet you."

When Mr. Reese sauntered off toward Cecil's, he popped the

straw hat back on his head and held his hand on Sebastian's head. The dog trotted obediently beside him. An involuntary smile started deep in my chest, touched my lips, and I felt my eyes crinkle until I realized Aunt Cora would have a walleyed fit. My skin broke out in a sweat. We'd only lived here two weeks, and already I'd put myself and my girls into a vulnerable position.

On the bright side, Mr. Reese mentioned he was headed to San Antonio, so his stay would be short. I did hope the cottages sported new shingles before Cecil finished the car repairs. Still, I knew absolutely nothing about this man except that he talked slow and had nice eyes. I hollered for Avril and went into the office. As I debated with myself over getting the locks changed, Sally breezed in.

"You up for a night out?" She had on fresh lipstick and a pressed frock I knew didn't come from the Mercantile. More like Titche's in Dallas. But God love her, if I mentioned it, she would slough it off like it was nothing.

"Hello to you, too. What did you have in mind?"

"Tonight's the kickoff to the March of Dimes summer campaign. Didn't your aunt Cora tell you?" The light coming in the front door bounced from her hoop earrings.

"I heard the announcement at church. Aunt Cora went on and on with the girls, but snubbed me. She still thinks I'm putting the girls in peril by moving out here." *And will be pitching a fit to high heaven when she finds out about the roof guy.*

"She'll get over it. She's just steamed you didn't move into Mara Lee with her."

"Which she used as an excuse for not marrying Sonny."

"No worries about that anymore. Sonny had a date with Twila Flynn Saturday night."

I blinked and tried to swallow. Instead, I blurted out, "Are you sure? That'll be awkward. Twila's done Aunt Cora's hair forever."

"Mayhaw could use some drama, don't you think?" When she swooshed her arm, the bracelets she wore jingled, and in the next instant, the office door did the same when Mr. Reese stuck his head in.

"Pardon me for interrupting. Okay with you if I put these things in my room now?" His eyebrows, as pale as his hair, shot up in a questioning look. He had a guitar slung on his back, a canvas grip in his hand, and at his feet a tool case he'd set down to open the door.

Sally did a double take, her own eyebrows arching up.

"Sure. Mr. Reese, I'd like you to meet Sally Cotton. She and the rest of the Magnolias have made it their sacred duty to turn the landscaping of the Stardust into a showplace. Sally, this is Mr. Reese."

"Please call me Peter." He extended his hand, the nearly transparent hair on his forearm scarcely concealing his rippling muscles. And, I admit, I got a good look as I was trying to avoid Sally's eyes.

"Nice to meet you, Peter." She turned to me. "I didn't know you were taking guests, Georgia."

"Mr. Ree…Peter will be working on the cottages. Lucky for me he stopped in when he did since I can't get anyone from the lumberyard down here to fix those holes in the roofs. We have to get those done before we can repair the insides of the damaged cottages. It's a long story, and Ludi's doing all she can, working from sunup to sundown and then having to go home and take care of her own family." I knew I was blathering.

Sally held up her hand. "You can't take responsibility for the whole world, Georgia. And don't go making excuses for Ludi. Your colored girl wouldn't be here if she didn't need the money. And besides, her kind is used to working long hours and scraping by."

My jaw dropped, locked in a half-open position. I sucked in a big breath and said, "Sally, I'm going to pretend I didn't hear that. Ludi's been a godsend to me, and I won't have you speaking ill of her."

Her bracelets jangled as she waved her hand at me. "I didn't mean anything bad by it. You know I love our Tansy like my own sister. You need to relax, like I told you. And tonight's just the ticket." She turned to Peter, who still stood in the doorway. "You're welcome to come to the town square tonight, too. We're having a March of Dimes rally with free hot dogs, courtesy of Brookshire's, and Georgia's aunt has a surprise for the evening's entertainment."

"Thank you, miss. I'll keep it in mind."

I snagged the key to number ten from the rack and marched past Sally to hand it to him. "Mr. Reese, I apologize for my friend. Once you get to know her, you'll understand she speaks her mind without thinking, but under all the fancy clothes, she's got a heart of gold. There aren't any towels in your room, but I'll make sure you get some."

"Much obliged, Miz Peyton. Nice meeting you, Miz Cotton."

Sally tapped her foot, her latest ankle-strap pump like a metronome on the pine floor. "So, sweetie, do you think you and the girls can make it tonight? I hear the Pearl sisters are bringing their instruments. I know how you adore good fiddle playing. Besides, your aunt Cora would be in heaven if you and the girls came and supported the cause."

"I don't know. I'll think about it... I've still got things to do here." I went behind the counter and stapled the invoices for the faucets together.

"Hey, you're not mad at me, are you?"

"Not mad. Disappointed, I think." I took my time to find the right words. "You've changed, Sally. I hadn't thought much about it before, but you come in here dressed like you're going to a tea party at the state capitol and say things you didn't used to say or even think."

"I'm sorry if you don't approve of the way I dress."

"It's not that... You always wanted to be part of society and have nice things, and I'm glad you got what you wanted, but when you make snide remarks about Ludi, it makes me wonder. You've no idea how sweet she is and how hard she works... how much the girls love her."

"But she's a colored woman, Georgia. They have their own ways."

"And that's where I disagree. Aunt Cora used to say things like that, and I didn't agree with her, either."

"Then I guess we'll simply have to disagree. We shouldn't let it come between us. See you tonight then?" Her bracelets jangled as she started for the door.

"I said I'd think about it."

"Suit yourself, hon, but you look like you could use a night out."

After she'd flitted out the door, I realized Sally hadn't shown me the plans the Magnolias had drawn up. Her comment about Ludi still stung two hours later when Rosey got off the bus waving a mimeograph paper about the March of Dimes rally.

"Please, Mommy, can we go? It's for kids who can't walk 'cuz their legs are crippled."

"You know, I've been thinking we need a night out."

"Really? I can give the money from my piggy bank. I have lots of dimes."

"All right. But you don't have to give all your dimes. Only a few, okay? And I hear there's gonna be fiddle playing, so we'll have to see if we can find your cowboy boots and the outfit with the fringe on the sleeves, the one Aunt Cora gave you for your birthday."

"And my cowboy hat?" When I nodded, her eyes sparkled and off she went, spinning and smiling.

Sally was right. We all needed a break.

CHAPTER 13

Streamers wafted from the gazebo in Mayhaw's town square when the girls and I arrived. Already a sizable crowd had gathered and milled around the hot dog stand on wheels, some waiting in line for their free supper, others with their cheeks stuffed, talking to neighbors and friends. The smell was robust, the kind that makes your mouth water as you anticipate sinking your teeth into something as ordinary and yet decadent as a hot dog. I felt a pang of guilt that I'd left Peter a bologna sandwich and hadn't offered to bring him with us even after Sally had invited him. A job and a place to stay didn't include introducing him to the citizens of Mayhaw.

Hiring him had been a wise choice, I was still certain. He'd spent the afternoon inspecting all of the roofs and reported the construction was solid on the cottages—it was just a matter of taking off the old wood shingles and putting on new ones. He would make up a list and take it to the lumberyard the next day. As the girls and I piled into O'Dell's Ford, Peter was on top of cottage one with a tape measure.

A soft breeze riffled the flag at the center of the town square. The girls ran like banshees, practically turning cartwheels, and I was afraid the hot dogs we'd wolfed down might come right back up. Rosey squealed hellos to kids from her first grade class while Avril darted among the dozen or so tables sponsored by the various ladies' circles from Mayhaw's churches. Lemonade and coffee on one, baked goods on the others. *Free desserts. Donations accepted,* the signs said.

I looked for the table of the Bethany Street Church, the one we attended with Aunt Cora, and saw Hazel Morton waving us over. Shoot. She would ask if I'd called her grandson. I waved back and acted interested in the pecan pralines the ladies at the Missionary Baptist table set out.

"Yoo-hoo! Georgia!" Hazel's voice rose above the crowd. I nodded that I'd seen her but let the girls take their time picking out a cupcake apiece, then dropped a quarter in the gallon-size pickle jar like the ones Aunt Cora placed around town for donations. Only then did we go over to Hazel's table.

Hazel eyed the girls' cupcakes and sniffed. "We have cupcakes here, too, you know." She crossed her arms. "So tell me, are things going well out at the Stardust?"

"Quite nice, actually."

"My grandson said you never did call. I think he was expecting to hear from you."

"I've been terribly busy, and now...well, why don't you tell Joey to go ahead and put in his application around town."

Hazel let out a soft snort, and I was relieved when Aunt Cora bustled up to the table and held out her arms to the girls.

"Aren't you two the most delicious sight I've seen all day?" She had Rosey turn around. "Why, that cowgirl outfit I got you is cute as a bug. And Avril, oh, my stars, I think you're getting prettier every day. Got any kisses for your auntie?"

Both the girls giggled and kissed Aunt Cora, who'd bent down to their level. She really was a nice person. Really.

She turned to me. "Glad you could tear yourself away to come out. And you look lovely, too. That tangerine color is perfect with your complexion."

"Thanks. And sweet of you to say so."

She held her hand to her mouth and whispered, "Although people might talk about how quick you've come out of mourning."

"Do you think? I hadn't even thought about it. Since I was in mourning for two months before O'Dell washed up, I figured—"

"Shh. It's better to be the bereaved widow than the deserted wife. But you do look nice, just remember to tear up and put on your long face if anyone mentions you-know-who."

"Aunt Cora, I would never—"

Sonny Bolander strolled by arm in arm with Twila Flynn. I gave Aunt Cora a cautious look.

She flicked her hand and leaned toward me. "Best thing Twila ever did—taking Sonny off my hands. Goodness gracious, I was tired of his catfish stinking up my kitchen."

Someone inside the gazebo hollered for her. She winked at me. "I'll be fine, and so will you. Thanks for coming." Then she pinched Rosey's cheek and said, "I'll see you chickadees later."

People had started clustering in the chairs set up in front of the gazebo, so we drifted over as well. Sally waved us over to her spot in the fourth row.

She pointed toward the front of the bandstand. "Look at those posters, would you? Doesn't it break your heart?"

Oh. My. One showed two young girls, dark eyed and innocent, the smaller of the two helping the other with leg braces. The slogan *You Can Help, Too* marched across the top of the poster. The other had a sweet boy with crutches, a larger image of a soldier in a combat helmet behind him, and the words, *This Fight Is Yours*.

Sally whispered, "That could be Hud's cousin's little girl or one of our own."

"So sad. No wonder Aunt Cora is so dedicated to the cause." Inside, the images reached a spot I reserved for starving children in China and kittens abandoned by the roadside, but this had a too-close-to-home feel.

Rosey snuggled up next to me. "Look, Mommy. That boy in the picture has on a cowboy hat like me. Can I catch what he did and have to get crutches?" Her eyes were dark, fearful.

"We hope not, sugar. That's why we're here, for you to give your dimes to help fight polio."

"It makes me sad. I don't think I want to stay here."

"But you couldn't wait to come."

"I just wanted the hot dogs and to put my dimes in the jar."

Sally leaned over. "Look, there's the Pearl triplets on the stage now. I think Ozella's tuning her fiddle."

And indeed she was, soft, short scritches coming from the strings as she slid the bow across. On either side of her were her identical sisters, Opal on the harmonica and Olive—who was tone-deaf but bouncing with rhythm—on the tambourine. They were around Aunt Cora's age, and like Aunt Cora, none of them had ever married. I suspected it was because they couldn't bear to be separated, but their buckteeth and fashions that went out with the horse and buggy might have been responsible. Which was nothing like Aunt Cora, who still caused men's heads to turn when she walked into a room.

As a matter of fact, as the chairman of the local March of Dimes, Aunt Cora stepped up to a microphone in the middle of the stage in her lemon-yellow suit and sling-back pumps looking like she stepped off the cover of a *Southern Women* magazine. "Ladies and gentlemen, thank you all for coming."

Rosey settled back in her chair as Reverend Abernathy from the Presbyterian church gave the invocation and led us in singing the national anthem.

I always tear up at "the rockets' red glare" and dabbed my eyes as we sang. Next up was someone from the Texas Chapter of the March of Dimes saying the predicted outbreak of polio was feared to reach the tens of thousands, with Texas having hundreds of crippling cases already in the first four months of 1952. She put out a plea reminding us this was only the beginning of the season for the "summer disease."

A familiar scent wafted by—Aqua Velva—and my stomach turned over. Bobby Carl Applegate. His breath was warm on my neck as he whispered, "You look gorgeous tonight." I turned around, quirked my mouth in a fake smile, and nearly laughed. He had on a yellow-and-green-plaid shirt that gave a greenish cast to his skin. I turned back around quickly. Sally had her hand over her mouth, but I could tell from her eyes she was laughing.

The Pearls sat in the shadows at the back of the bandstand as Aunt Cora took center stage. "As you all know, we are a town famous for our talent show at the annual Mayhaw Festival, but when I was planning the program for tonight, I had an epiphany. Why wait two months to share your talent? Tonight we're going to have an impromptu dress rehearsal."

She went on to explain that for the next five minutes she would take names on slips of paper of those who wanted to participate. You could put in your own name or the name of someone you wanted to hear sing or dance or juggle. The catch was you also had to put an amount you would donate to the March of Dimes for the privilege. Names would be drawn for the order of contestants, with the Pearls serving as accompanists.

Rosey was about to squirm right out of her skin as she looked at me. "Please, Mommy, I want to sing. Put my name in the basket. Please. Pretty please."

"What do you want to sing, sweetie?"

"It's a secret." She pursed her lips, determination in her look.

"You sure?" She nodded. "Alrighty, I'll put your name in."

I wrote *two dollars* on the slip of paper with Rosey's name and decided if she chickened out, I could go with her onstage or else just pay the money, bein's it was a good cause and all. But when her name was the third one drawn, she sashayed to the stage, fringe swinging on her sleeves like she was the Shirley Temple of the South.

Aunt Cora beamed as she lowered the microphone. Rosey whispered to the Pearls what she wanted to sing, then walked to the mic and said, "This song is for my daddy, who has to watch it from heaven."

The air swirled around me as Ozella played a couple of beats, then nodded to Rosey. I knew what she was fixing to sing. O'Dell always sang "You Are My Sunshine" in his off-key way anytime we got in the car to dash off to a traveling carnival. Or out for a surprise ice-cream cone. Or when we went down to the bayou to gather Mayhaw berries that, being their nature, grew the best with their roots clinging to the edges of the banks, their branches heavy with fruit. The best way to get them was to shake the bushes, then go out in a rowboat and scoop them from the water with a butterfly net. A wave of panic clutched me as I realized we'd missed Mayhaw season this year, and now Rosey's voice floating with gossamer innocence across the town square brought it all back.

Tears burned like hot coals behind my eyelids, and if Aunt Cora had been watching she would have been proud that I was playing the grieving widow to perfection. And she couldn't possibly know that, contrary to what I said, my heart bled its own tears for O'Dell. For what we could have had. Cheat or not, he was the father of two beautiful girls.

Behind me, Bobby Carl breathed on my neck. "Hoo-whee! That girl sings almost as purty as you. What're you gonna sing when your turn comes?"

I shooed him back with my hand, waiting for her to finish. As the crowd broke out in applause, I turned around and glared at him. "Sorry, no singing from me tonight."

He wiggled his eyebrows. "Oh, yeah? Someone might've put your name in the hat. I know I'd pay a pretty penny to hear your honey voice."

"You better not have put my name in."

Rosey had made it back from the stage and threw her arms around my neck. I hugged her long and hard. "Your daddy would be so proud."

Only now, the simple act of a child felt tangled. Even if O'Dell were alive, he probably wouldn't have been here to see his daughter. The bitter taste lingered as Zenith Morris sang with great vibrato her rendition of "Blue Moon of Kentucky," and then Sue Ann McDonnell tap-danced across the stage to the Pearl sisters' accompaniment.

In the middle of Sue Ann's dance, a murmur started in the crowd. Sally looked around and scowled as others began fidgeting and whispering. By the time Sue Ann finished, it wasn't applause that greeted her, but the wail of the fire truck siren. Now everyone turned to watch Mayhaw's lone emergency vehicle pull out from its bay across the street and turn west. More chattering ensued, and Aunt Cora had trouble being heard over the crowd. No one listened to her, and a few of the men—those who served as volunteer firefighters—hastened away to perform their duties.

The smell of smoke teased the air, growing stronger with each minute. In my belly, a sourness churned. Mary Frances lived in the area where the smoke rose, and while I peered along with the crowd, Sheriff Bolander approached and looked at me, his eyes hooded beneath his Stetson. "Georgia. Bad news, I'm afraid. The place on fire is that of O'Dell's momma. You might want to come along with me now."

An icy feeling seized me, froze me to the chair. "Oh, no. Please, no."

Sally put her arm around me. "Lord, have mercy. What could possibly happen to you next? Go on now. I've got the girls. And I'm praying."

Somehow, I willed my legs not to buckle as I stood and scurried away, following Sonny. And each frantic step drew me closer to finding out what new disaster lay ahead.

CHAPTER 14

Night sounds from the bayou punctuated the stillness when I returned to the Stardust. With a glass of sweet tea to clear my parched, smoke-tinged throat, I sat on the steps outside my bedroom. An owl hooted off in the distance above the thrum of bullfrogs and cricket chirps that made me think of rusty banjo strings.

I took a long drink and gazed at the inky spot that was Zion. Flickers danced in the trees like fireflies. Lanterns? Ludi had told me they had no electricity, and that she cooked on a woodstove behind her home. What that was like I really couldn't imagine and only knew she never complained, reminded me even that the Lord had blessed her with a roof over her head and a good man. Neither of which my mother-in-law, Mary Frances, now had.

My mind raced through the events of the evening. Rushing along with Sonny to the fire, I'd seen the flames lick the sky, then watched as the roof of the clapboard house caved in, not knowing whether I was seeing the fiery grave of my mother-in-law or just a glimpse of hell. It wasn't known at first whether Mary Frances was inside or not, and as the firemen wielded canvas hoses like rope whips to harness the fire, a shout went out.

"We found her!"

My strength poured out the bottoms of my feet, my legs stringy and limp, but I willed them to hold me up until someone took my elbow and steered me down the street where they were loading Mary Frances into the ambulance.

They say disasters come in threes, and we'd already buried my husband, O'Dell, and Paddy Palmer. It was a divine act that Mary Frances had not ended up being number three, but the questions remained: Had she cheated death, or did another disaster loom?

From my spot on the back steps, I set down my glass of tea and pulled my knees up. As I hugged them to my chest, I thought about my mother-in-law. She'd escaped the fire and was found wandering in the alley half a block away wearing a puckered gingham bathrobe. No shoes. A nurse had replaced her smoke-tinged robe with a hospital gown, rolled up the robe, and said she'd dispose of it. That's when Mary Frances started screaming.

"Take the last blessed item I own on this earth, will you?" Her eyes pleaded with me. "Don't let them treat me like that, Georgia."

The nurse had winked at me, more in pity than anything, I think, but when Mary Frances wouldn't let up, I asked to see the robe. In the pockets I found a silver lighter my father-in-law, Earl, had given her years ago and a familiar velvet pouch. O'Dell's Salesman of the Quarter cuff links.

I took them to her, and she clutched them as if they were the Holy Grail. And to her, they were—the only thing she had left of the men in her life. She cried again as they washed her feet, which had cuts and scrapes from the rocks in the alley and which her drunkenness apparently had kept her from feeling. I longed to ask her about the fire, but she was so fragile, I couldn't bear to bring it up.

The simple truth was she drank liquor. Too much and too often. And no matter how many fancy bows or excuses you put on it, she had set her house on fire. Most likely a lit cigarette. Perhaps it caught fire while she was in the bathroom or getting another ice cube for her whiskey tumbler. That she was lonely, weak, and irresponsible was a realm over which I had no control, and deep in my heart, I believed God who made the heavens also watched over the less fortunate. Which included Mary Frances.

It was unknown how long she'd remained in the house and how much smoke damage there was to her lungs. Her disorientation—which came and went—and the blue tinge around her lips were of concern. Doc Kelley had suggested she stay in the hospital on oxygen for a day or two. He wanted to run a few tests and do a follow-up chest X-ray. And I knew he was giving me time to make arrangements for Mary Frances.

Her cousin in Corsicana came to mind. Mary Frances might pitch a fit, but Cousin Bertha had asked her to come. I would talk with her first thing in the morning.

The moon rode high in the sky, dull, obscured by a veil of smoke. A remnant of the fire, no doubt. Another possibility for Mary Frances niggled at me. The Stardust. She *could* come here. I shoved the thought away, but the nudge was insistent. I shook it off and felt a lick on my bare leg.

Sebastian. The dog who had come with the roofer. I ran my hand along the sleek fur of his head, which encouraged him, and before I knew it, he was alongside me, his head resting in my lap.

Why aren't you inside with Peter?

"Good question." The voice startled me, and through the shadows, Peter appeared. Sebastian loped obediently to his side.

"Question? I wasn't aware I'd spoken." A ripple through my body snapped the hairs on my arms to attention. "And heavens to Betsy, what are you doing up so late? You scared me half to death."

"I was asleep, but Sebastian whimpered to go out. I didn't

notice you'd come back. Sorry. I'll see it doesn't happen again."
He hooked a finger in the dog's collar and turned to go.

"It's no problem. It might even be good to have a guard dog
around. Guess he could lick a burglar into submission if nothing
else."

Peter gave a soft chuckle and looked over his shoulder. "That he
might. I keep him for company, not his killer instincts." He stepped
off into the night, leaving a rush of loneliness in his wake. I watched
him go, and then, as earlier in the day, I called out to him.

"Say, Mr. Reese, could I ask you a question?"

He turned, his face obscured by the moon's shadow. "Seems as
if you just did."

"Never mind then. I'll talk to you tomorrow."

He stood a few paces from me, head tilted. "Your question?"

"About the cottages... which one would you think we could
get ready the soonest? Something has come up, and we may have
a guest sooner than I'd anticipated."

"Not rightly sure, although the roof on number five is solid.
Depends on how much work is left to do on the inside. When is
your guest expected to arrive?"

"A couple of days, I guess. There was an accident in town—a
fire."

"I heard the sirens and smelled the smoke. Was it a friend of
yours?"

"My mother-in-law. She made it out, but her house is a total
loss. Poor thing has no place to go, so I thought I'd ask her to stay
out here until she decides what she wants to do."

"I wasn't aware you were married. What does your husband do?"

The temptation to tell Peter to run on over to the graveyard
and ask O'Dell himself played wickedly with my senses, but I bit
my tongue. "Nothing now. He's deceased."

"Pity. So sorry for your loss, ma'am."

"Thanks. That's neither here nor there. I just thought I'd fore-warn you about what we'd be doing tomorrow—getting a room ready."

"Appreciate it."

And this time when he turned to go, I let him. The moon had floated free from the smoky haze and brightened the sky, but the night smells lingered—a melting pot of what the day had stirred up. The smell of the bayou, heavy and wet from the recent rain, came up to mingle with all the other scents. Ashes. The hosed-down remains of Mary Frances's house. I caught a whiff of fried catfish and decided it came from Zion. They'd probably eaten hours ago, but that was the way with fish. The odor hung around long after the bones were tossed for the cats to fight over. It had been a long day, and it felt like two thousand hours had passed since I put Rosey on the school bus that morning.

Tomorrow would be another long day. For the present, I was glad the girls were staying with Sally. At least I'd have time for a cup of coffee in the morning. I might even invite Ludi to sit with me at the kitchen table and hatch out our plans for getting Mary Frances moved out to the Stardust.

Zion was wrapped in darkness now. No more flickering lights. I picked up my glass and opened the screen door. This was the life I dreamed of—making my own way in the world. As I slid between the sheets, an old adage Hugh Salazar was fond of crept into my thoughts. *Be careful what you wish for, Georgia. You just might get it.*

Back then it was finding my parents. Now, I wanted to make a new life for the girls and me. Why did it feel as if my world was getting ready to tip off-kilter? The thought tickled me. My life had tipped so many times the past few months that, as Aunt Cora would say, I no longer knew up from sic 'em.

CHAPTER 15

A thump on my bed roused me the next morning. Fuzzy headed, I opened my eyes to find Avril's face inches from mine, the smell of pancake syrup lacing her breath. Confused, I shook my head. "What are you doing here? Where's Rosey? And Sally?"

Sally sailed into the room, her eyes wide. "So glad you're here and not still with Mary Frances at the hospital. How are you, love? And your sweet momma-in-law?"

"I don't know. I'm not even awake." I sat on the edge of the bed, ran my fingers through my hair, and pulled Avril into my arms. "O'Dell's momma is going to be fine. She'll need a place to stay of course, but all in good time. They're keeping her in the hospital for a couple of days."

"That's a relief. Where will she go then?"

"Not sure, and it's too early to think about it."

Sally smiled, but her manner was all wrong. Stiff. Not telling me something. I smiled back. "Thanks for keeping the girls, and sorry I didn't get up earlier and come get them. Looks like I need to get cracking if Rosey's going to make the school bus."

I made it to my feet and grabbed my housecoat, but Sally hadn't moved. She chewed her bottom lip, blinking back tears. Maybe there had been an incident with the girls or...Hud. I shuddered. "Sally, are you all right?"

"No. Something's come up. Hud's cousin, the one whose little girl has polio, has now come down with it herself. Bad, from what they say. They've called the family to come down to Houston. His aunt is on the verge of a breakdown at the thought of losing her daughter and caring for Nina Beth, who still needs worlds of therapy. Hud's mom has asked us all to come. I've packed a bag to be gone for a week..." Her voice was strained, her ready composure ruffled.

"What about your kids? Do you need me to watch them?"

"No, Hud says the whole family should go. Although, to tell you the truth, I'm scared out of my wits over this whole infantile paralysis thing. I don't want my kids being exposed, but Hud assured me we'd keep them far away from the polio ward." Her voice hitched up an octave. "They've put his cousin in an iron lung. Can you imagine living in a tank, having it squeeze all the air from your body just so you can breathe? It's barbaric. And horrible." She braced her shoulders and flicked her hair from her cheek. "We're staying at the Palace Hotel. I'll call you later and let you know how things are."

Questions raced pell-mell through my head, but the feeling of impending catastrophe that visited my dreams now took up residence in the hollow of my chest. I held out my arms, then hugged my best, lifelong friend and muttered the stupid things people always say in times like this. "Don't worry. Everything will be all right. You and the kids...you have to go...it's the thing to do. You know I'll be praying."

Sally's chin quivered. "Thanks." Then she was gone.

Wide awake now and shaky myself, I looked at the girls. "So you've had breakfast, which I can tell from your syrupy breath.

Rosey, what do you want to wear to school?" I looked at the clock. Ten minutes until the bus.

"I'm sick, Mommy. Not going to school." Her voice told me she was faking, probably upset by the trauma of the morning, but my heart told me I needed my girls close. How bad could missing one day of first grade be?

"Here, let me feel your forehead. Where do you feel bad?" I reached for a clean rag and wet it under the kitchen faucet.

"My tummy. I think I ate too many pancakes."

Peeking under her shirt, I said, "Oh, my, yes. I'd say you had one too many. Here, put this rag on your forehead. Why don't you go put on some play clothes and rest while I get ready? We have a lot to do today as soon as Ludi gets here."

I went to the window and peeked at the field, hoping to see her lumbering along, but saw nothing. "I wonder what's keeping her. She's usually here by now."

Pounding came to the front door of the office. "Oh, good. I bet that's her now."

I slipped through the door that connected the quarters to the office and padded barefoot, an apology forming in my head for Ludi. But through the glass I saw it wasn't Ludi, but Peter. Straw hat and all. Shoulders slumping and heat creeping to my face, I opened the door.

"Morning, ma'am." He tipped his hat.

"Morning, yourself. Sorry about my appearance, it's been a rough morning."

"My apologies for interrupting." He cleared his throat. "I saw your friend's Caddy pull out so thought it okay to bother you. I have the list of supplies for the lumberyard. Do you want me to accompany you while you place the order? I'm..."

He must have noticed the dumbfounded look on my face. Me

in my bathrobe, my hair so messy a sparrow might mistake it for a fire bush. And all I could do was stare at him.

"So sorry, ma'am. I didn't realize—"

The school bus driver let out a long toot on his horn on the highway. Brushing past Peter in the doorway, I stepped out on the porch and waved the bus on. Sebastian sidled up to me, sniffed my robe, which hung open, and slurped my hand. I jerked away and pulled my robe tight around me. Peter at once snapped his fingers, and Sebastian went to his side.

"So sorry, ma'am. I...guess I didn't know what time... What say I come back later? There's other work I can do in the meantime."

"No, it's fine. Just one thing. Please stop calling me ma'am. Call me Georgia or hey you, but no more of this ma'am this and ma'am that."

"Yes, ma'am. No problem."

I glared at him.

"All right. Georgia. And like I told you yesterday, Peter's my given name."

"Fine. Now give me a few minutes to get organized and we'll go to the lumberyard. I'll introduce you to Miller, the manager down there, and see about getting you on my account so you can order things as you need them. No sense in my having to approve every nail and shingle or piece of wood you need."

And before he had time to answer I went in, threw on my clothes, brushed my teeth, and pulled my hair back into a ponytail. It would have to do for now.

"Come on, girls, we have errands to run. Rosey, bring the cold rag for your face if you think you need it. I'll leave a note for Ludi." I ran to the office to get a pen and paper and then remembered—Ludi couldn't read or write. A profanity was on the tip of my tongue. I threw the pen down, the rigors of the morning plowing into me with more force than a freight train.

Whatever possessed me to think I could pull off a stunt like running a tourist court? No money. No experience. Certainly no brains. And at the moment I was so tired, all I wanted to do was crawl back in bed and sleep for a month. The world would march on by with its disease-crippled victims and poor people who never learned the simple delight of scribbling a grocery list or writing their name at the top of a school paper. Even sad sacks like Mary Frances, who thought the answers to emptiness were found in the bottom of a liquor bottle. Maybe God wasn't looking out for the unfortunate after all.

I closed my eyes, a silent prayer on my lips, a surge of determination taking the wheel. There was nothing a few deep breaths, a decent cup of coffee, and the power of the Holy Ghost couldn't fix. And right now, I was in desperate need of all three.

I looked up. Avril and Rosey looked at me as if I were a Martian from outer space. Behind them, Peter Reese, whose blue eyes held the calm of a lake on a summer's day, spoke. "Pardon me for saying so, Georgia, but it looks to me like you could use a strong cup of coffee. If you're ready to go, I'm buying."

CHAPTER 16

Merciful Harper sat on the doorstep when we got back from the lumberyard.

"Morning, Merciful. Did you come with your momma?"

She hung her head, looked at me with the tops of her eyes. "No, ma'am. Maw can't make it. She sent me and my stinkbug brother."

"Catfish, right?"

"Yes, ma'am, but he don' want to show his face, so he's waiting 'round back. Maw says she's sorry, she feels terrible bad knowing you gots a lot to do." She stood up tall. "I'm a good worker, though."

"Is your mother ill?"

"No, ma'am. Mamey is." She clenched her jaw, no explanation forthcoming.

"I'm sorry to hear that. Is Mamey your grandmother?"

She nodded, tears forming in her inky eyes, and I could tell she was trying to keep her composure. I offered her my hand. "I think it's time I met this brother of yours. Around back, you say?"

Catfish stood a couple of inches taller than Merciful, was

barefoot like his sister, legs as thin as a tree branch from what I could see below his rolled-up britches.

"You must be Catfish. I'm Georgia. Happy to meet you."

I held out my hand, but he kept his shoved in his pockets, his eyes downcast and looking from one side to the next.

Merciful popped him on the arm. "Mind your manners, stink-bug. Miz Georgia wants to shake your hand."

Slowly, he pulled a hand from his pocket, extended it. Sort of. I shook it and told him I was glad to meet him.

"Your momma's told me you're the fisherman in the family."

"That's what I be fixin' to do today, but they wanted me and Merciful to hightail it outta there."

"And why's that?"

"You tell her, punkin' face."

I smiled to myself. Merciful, as cute as she was, had a face the same shape as a pumpkin. Extraround cheeks and a snaggle-toothed grin where she'd lost a couple of baby teeth. But it was a scowl on her face, not a jack-o'-lantern smile.

"Miz Georgia don' want to know 'bout our troubles." She stuck out her tongue at her brother, and then I did laugh. Rosey and Avril acted the same way sometimes.

I looked at each of them in turn. "You don't have to tell me."

Catfish looked at the ground and kicked at the dirt. "They's cutting off her leg today. Don't want us around."

A shiver raced through me. "Who? Your grandmother?"

Through pinched lips Merciful said, "Mamey's got the sugar sickness. Maw said it be best if Catfish and me get on down here and not be hanging around when they saw off the leg. It 'bout made me sick the last time."

My head felt woozy, too, at the thought. "The last time?"

"Mamey's other leg. She got the sugar bad."

I wasn't sure I wanted to know more, but I put my arm

around Merciful's shoulder and offered my other hand to Catfish. "I'm sorry about your grandmother, and your momma is right. I can use a world of help today. Catfish, there's someone I want you to meet. You'll be Mr. Reese's right-hand man while Merciful helps me."

Handing Catfish off to Peter was the coward's way out for me. In the few short minutes I was with Ludi's son, all I could think was that he was the one who found O'Dell. He was nothing more than a child. Ten or so, I guessed. And from what I knew of the condition of O'Dell's body when he washed up, it must've been a shock of biblical proportions. Chances were Catfish was trying to forget as desperately as I was, and I was sure Peter would welcome the help.

Merciful was delighted when I asked her to watch the girls for the afternoon. The three of them skipped off to pick wildflowers and look for butterflies. I made a quick call to the hospital to check on Mary Frances, relieved when the nurse told me she was resting like a lamb.

"Glad to hear it. Please tell her I'll be by in the morning to check on her, but if she needs anything, please call." I gave her the number, changed into one of O'Dell's old shirts and a pair of baggy pants, then went off to paint the cottage I'd picked out for Mary Frances. As I rolled on the paint, I let various conversations and arguments with Mary Frances about her love of gin and the way it was destroying her life keep me company.

By five o'clock I'd finished the room and went to check on the girls, who were now playing dolls with Merciful. Peter and Catfish were both on their knees atop cottage one, Peter hammering the shingles Catfish passed him. They'd taken to each other like flies to honey, it seemed, their motions smooth and synchronized.

Parched, and knowing Peter and Catfish must be, too, I went

in to make some sweet tea. I'd just put the kettle on to heat when Aunt Cora called.

"I'll get right to the point."

I flinched, regretting already that I hadn't called her to tell her about Mary Frances. "Please do. But first, let me apologize."

"It's a little late for that, isn't it? Half the town knows you've got some stranger sporting around town with you, buying you coffee, pretending to be some construction foreman or such. What in the world has gotten into you?"

"Wait. First of all, I'm not sure what you heard. I've hired a handyman to put new roofs on the cottages, not some pretty-boy escort. I tried to get local help, and they're all booked. If I waited, I wouldn't be able to get the Stardust open by Memorial Day. And you know what they say, time is money, so I considered it providential when Cecil at the repair shop sent Mr. Reese to help out. He'll only be here temporarily."

"You asked for references, of course."

"He seemed decent. Kind and not pushy. He acts like he knows his business."

"The whole situation you've let yourself in for is disheartening, Georgia. Why, oh why, won't you listen to reason? The Stardust is going to suck you dry financially and physically. You're putting the girls and yourself into harm's way, mark my words."

"We could always move in with you. Of course, we'd have to bring Mary Frances along."

"Don't say I didn't offer. But speaking of your momma-in-law, I took her a bouquet today, thinking I might see you there. She said you'd not been by at all. Poor thing's aged ten years overnight. It might be wise to use her insurance money and put her in the rest home. So tragic."

"I could never do that. And I did call to check on her. Stayed with her till half past midnight last night. Truth is, I'm going to talk to Dr. Kelley tomorrow about having her stay out here until she gets her strength back."

She gave a soft snort. "The fixes you get yourself into."

"Well, it's not like I had a choice in this. Don't worry, we're all going to be fine. Really. Tell me, how did the rally go last night?"

"Not as well as we hoped, but we plan to have a booth at the Mayhaw Festival. And we'll keep the donation jars out around town. The goal is to raise enough money to have an iron lung in every county in Texas. A half-dozen new cases were reported in Tyler in the last week alone. They're scrambling over there to turn one wing of the hospital into a respiratory ward."

"Did you hear about Hud Cotton's cousin? She's down in Houston in an iron lung."

"I'd heard a rumor but didn't know if it was true."

"Sally and Hud left earlier today to be with the family. His cousin's child is still recovering. I didn't know it was so contagious."

"It appears so the way it breaks out some places more than others. Praise be, Musgrave County hasn't been touched."

"Aunt Cora, I know we don't always agree on things, but I'm proud of what you're doing. And I'll make sure you get the money for Rosey singing at the rally."

"Don't worry. I already put in ten dollars with her name on it."

"Oh, my. You didn't have to."

"I know, but I'd give anything to ensure one of your girls doesn't end up on a poster."

"Me, too, Aunt Cora. Me, too."

By the time I made the tea and took it out, the hammering had stopped and Peter and Catfish were no longer on the roof nor anywhere that I could see. I asked the girls if they'd seen them.

Merciful answered. "They's probably out back washing up where the spigot be."

I wasn't aware of the spigot in the back, only the one at each end of the cottages where we hooked up the garden hoses. As I went looking, I heard Catfish talking, his high-pitched voice running as quick as anything.

"I thought a whale done spit a body out of the water up on the riverbank, just like Jonah in the Good Book. 'Cept it was big and fat, eyes bugging out like a bullfrog, lookin' like if'n you stuck in a pin, it would pop."

Nausea hit me like floodwaters, and I stepped in the shadows between two of the cottages. Catfish was talking about O'Dell, telling Peter of his conquest like he'd been on a Lewis and Clark expedition. Another wave of bile and disgust rose up, my head swimming. I was afraid to take another step or even breathe, mortified that Catfish would catch me eavesdropping.

"Was the worse thing I ever saw." His voice was choked with emotion, holding back sobs, not bragging as I'd thought.

I wanted to run, but my feet felt like they'd been driven into the ground with spikes. Peter spoke softly, words I couldn't make out. I felt clammy and hot and disgusted all at the same time. Of course I knew O'Dell's body was in a state of decomposing. Mr. Garvey at the funeral home had told me as much. Without the detail, of course. At the time I'd thought it only fitting since I felt murderous toward O'Dell for leaving us the way he did. I had no idea it had been so grotesque.

Collecting myself enough to move, I turned to go back to the office, but Peter called out behind me. "Say, Georgia, you looking for us?"

I turned and smiled. "Oh, here you are. I was bringing you and Catfish a spot of tea. If you're thirsty, that is."

"Plumb parched." He winked at Catfish. "How about you, care for a glass of Miss Georgia's sweet tea? I do believe it's the best I ever had."

Catfish sniffed, wiped a hand across his eyes, and in a thin voice said, "No, thank you. If it's all right, I'm goin' on home now."

I couldn't let him leave torn up like he was. I handed Peter the tea glasses and put my hand on the boy's shoulder. "Catfish, I know you feel bad. I heard you talking. The man you found was my husband. If you hadn't stumbled on him, we wouldn't have known what happened."

He fixed his eyes on the ground. "I didn't know it be yo' man."

"Sometimes bad things happen. You were very brave that day."

His chin lifted. "Maw say it be the right thing."

"Yes, it was. Now, would you like some tea?"

He shook his head and scurried away, calling for Merciful as he ran by the washhouse. The two of them flew like panthers across the field toward Zion.

Peter leaned against the cottage and took a long, slow drink. He ran the back of his hand over his mouth and handed me the glass. "I'm sorry. I had no idea."

"I feel bad for Catfish. I only hope he doesn't have nightmares the way I still do."

"I can only imagine. Again, I offer my condolences about your husband."

"Thanks. I hope I didn't scare your helper away."

"I have a feeling he'll be back. He's quite a kid."

"Come on up to the office in an hour. I'll have a supper plate for you." I turned to go but remembered the new roof. I hollered over my shoulder. "Good job up there, Mr. Reese."

Behind me, he muttered, "Peter's the name, Miz Peyton."

CHAPTER 17

Two days later I picked Mary Frances up from the hospital and took her to the Mercantile for new clothes and to Lovey's Rexall Drug for toiletries. When we emerged, she eyed Ralph's liquor store, but I took her elbow and gently guided her to the Ford.

She sat arms crossed, a scowl on her face, when I took the driver's seat. "I'm an adult, perfectly capable of making my own decisions." Her chin trembled.

I backed the car from the parking spot, hands tight on the wheel. "You know what Doc said. Alcohol is strictly forbidden with your medication."

"A touch of gin would give me a great deal more pleasure than swallowing those nerve pills he prescribed."

"I think you should try and tough it out. For Rosey and Avril, if nothing else."

"It's not what you think, Georgia."

"What?"

"The fire."

"What do you mean?"

She fidgeted in her seat like she had a hitch in her new underpants. "You assume I was intoxicated."

"I didn't say that." Of course, I thought it! But no matter how I turned it over in my head, I had plenty of my own guilt for pretending her drinking wasn't a problem. Mercy, I'd even helped her get the gin more than once.

"Why not call a spade a spade. It was my fault. But it wasn't like you think."

Her face softened, a look I hadn't seen since she'd first held Rosey in her arms. The worry lines melted, and her eyes took on a faraway look.

I said, "The only thing that matters is that you made it out. Now we'll concentrate on getting you better and decide what you want to do next."

Her jaw tensed. "Just let me say it while I have the nerve. The fire was my fault, but it was an accident."

"No one has said otherwise."

"I was wanting a drink real bad, but whether you realize it or not, I was trying to quit the bottle. I'd cut way back and ran out a couple days before. I was getting pretty shaky, but I kept thinking about what you said about I ought to get out, get a job."

"And you still can. I'm proud that you were trying to quit." I gripped the steering wheel, unsure of her new tactics. Maybe she had more smoke damage than Doc thought.

"I've had a lot of time to think, bein's no one comes around to see me anymore."

Ouch!

"I was thinking of taking a little trip, maybe going down to see Bertha." She let out a hacking cough into her fist. "Stupid fire's clogged my lungs."

"Go on. I'm listening."

"It doesn't matter now. My home is a pile of ashes, and right now, what I really need is a drink."

"Probably not a great idea."

"I know it's not, but I'm trying to tell you what happened. I was back in the bedroom looking for the map to see how far it was to Corsicana. I thought I might take the bus, and while I was looking, I found a picture album of O'Dell when he was a tyke. It was during the Depression, you know, and we didn't have two nickels to rub together, but there was O'Dell smiling and laughing, pulling a little wagon. I was on my own little trip back in time when I smelled the smoke. I admit, I must've left a cigarette burning in the ashtray—it's the only thing I can figure out. But the smoke was already so thick I couldn't see a thing. I ran out, and then I thought, well, why in tarnation didn't I get that picture album? I ran back in with my hand over my face, but I was too late. The next thing I know is I've got a mask over my face and people all around me."

My own throat clogged. How would I know she'd been trying? I hadn't exactly been there to give her any moral support. I put my arm out the window to indicate I was turning into the Stardust and looked at Mary Frances.

"Thank you for telling me. I'm sorry about your house." My jaw twitched. Whether Mary Frances believed it or not, I did have her best interests at heart.

When Doc had given me the lowdown on Mary Frances, he'd told me, "The B12 shot and the vitamins will help in the short term, but getting her interested in life again will make the biggest difference. She and I go way back. Did you know she was one of the brightest kids ever went to Robert E. Lee school? She could do algebra in the fifth grade and memorized the entire Sermon on the Mount from Matthew. Pity to see her like this." His face had a worn, sallow look, and he looked like he could've used a shot of B12 himself.

But his reminder of Mary Frances's former genius had given me an idea. She might be poor in spirit at the moment, but I was going to put her to work in the office. Not sure how that lined up with the beatitudes, but it was all I had at the moment.

Avril ran up to the car the minute we arrived. "MeMaw. Come look. I have a surprise."

Mary Frances stepped into the sunlight, patted Avril on the cheek. "That's nice, but what on earth is that infernal pounding noise?"

I hurried to her side. "We're getting the roofs replaced. It's darn near a miracle the way Peter and Catfish have put new shingles on half the cottages already. Another couple of days and they'll be done."

"I won't get a speck of rest with that hammering. Where's my room?"

"Right this way."

Sebastian, now Avril's shadow, followed behind, tail wagging. When we got to the cottage, Mary Frances stopped, put her hand to her chest. "O'Dell used to have a mutt almost like that. I'd forgotten until just this minute. You know, I'm not sure about staying here." She nodded in the direction of Zion. "Reminders everywhere of O'Dell. I know you've gone to a lot of trouble, but maybe I should get a room at the hotel downtown."

I shook my head. "You know what Doc said. I'm to take good care of you. Three square meals a day and plenty of rest and sunshine. The reminders are here for me, too, but I'm trying to dwell on the present and not the past."

"Easy for you to say. You have the girls. I have nothing."

"You have us, Mary Frances. Now come in and see your room."

The room was as homey as I could make it. A few pictures of the girls I'd taken from my quarters. One of O'Dell in his business suit, a sober expression on his face. I'd found a small bookcase at the thrift store and stocked it with magazines and one of the sets of *The Book of Knowledge* I'd retrieved from O'Dell's trunk.

Avril tugged on Mary Frances's arm. "Come on. I want you to see what I made."

I ushered us in while Avril went straight to the bed and picked up the picture she'd drawn of three stick figures. At first I thought it was her, Rosey, and me, but on a closer look I saw the larger figure had black springy hair. Merciful.

Mary Frances studied it. "Gracious, you drew a picture of a colored girl. Where did you ever get such an idea?"

"It's Merciful. She's my friend. Her mommy helped get your room fixed. Do you like the picture?"

"It's nice. Thank you, Avie." Her eyes scanned the room. "I don't see an ashtray. You surely don't expect me to give up smoking, too."

Shrugging, I said, "I was hoping you might limit the smoking to the outside since the weather's nice. I'll see about getting you a lawn chair to keep in the shade. The fresh air will be good for you."

"The only thing good for me right now is some peace and quiet."

I put my arm around her sloped shoulders and gave her a peck on the cheek. "Welcome home."

＊

Strangely enough, the Stardust felt more like home than I'd dared to hope. Steady progress on the cottages thanks to the hard work of Peter and Ludi, along with her children, made the vision of opening by Memorial Day more of a reality each day. Mary Frances joined us for meals, and except for the occasional complaint about the hammering, she seemed to be gaining ground.

And every evening, after reading to the girls and tucking them in to bed, I'd take a glass of sweet tea out to my back steps. The night sounds of cicadas and the murmurs of songbirds settling onto their roosts were like a sweet benediction to the day. Working from dawn to dusk had its satisfactions in the progress on the cottages, but it had brought a few surprises, too. Namely Peter Reese.

I hadn't expected to find myself watching him as he joked with Catfish, hoping he'd cast a wink in my direction. And when I had a decision to make, his opinion was the one I sought. It wasn't that I wanted the complication of a man in my life, and certainly not one who would be gone in another few weeks, but I trusted his judgment, and he was never pushy, demanding, or one to be disagreeable. Yet he maintained an air of mystery when it came to himself that, darn it all, I found compelling.

Night after night, I retreated to my steps on the back porch, and in my gut I knew it wasn't to drink in the scent and sounds of the bayou but to listen to the sweet strains of the guitar Peter played at his own front door. Haunting melodies like "Oh Shenandoah" or "Danny Boy." And I would imagine the long slender fingers callused from driving nails by day as they moved effortlessly over the guitar frets.

Often I would hum along and once stood and danced *one-two-three* as Peter played "The Tennessee Waltz." Sally would say I had it bad, but then Sally had a respectable man who came home at night. One who hadn't been born with the unfaithful gene.

By day, I blushed at my evening thoughts and pushed to get the work done. But as dusk settled over the Stardust, an ache in my chest returned, and one evening I found myself hurrying the girls along with their evening baths, making them do the chin touch after we said their prayers, and hoping all the while I wouldn't miss whatever tunes Peter chose to play for the night. Just as I headed out the door with my tea in hand, the phone rang. Expecting it was Aunt Cora with another reported case of polio in Musgrave County, I almost didn't answer it. A pall had hung in the air ever since a three-year-old boy from the lumber camp not six miles up the road had been diagnosed. Now everyone walked in fear it might be their child next. Newspapers shouted new stories every day about the outbreak, now called an epidemic. People were warned to stay inside during the heat of the day, not to go near water, never to drink from public water fountains, and to have their children do the "chin touch" at every meal and when they said their prayers at night.

It was a real threat, I knew, but I was determined not to let fear get the best of me. Personally, I believed the best way to bring disaster on yourself was by dwelling on it. And that night I was weary from dwelling on it, so I decided to ignore the phone. Then Rosey hollered from her bed, "Telephone, Momma!"

It wasn't Aunt Cora but a woman who asked to speak to Peter Reese, if he was available.

"If this is long distance, you may want to call back; it'll take a few minutes to get him."

"I'll wait." Sweet, high-pitched voice. Not the voice of a mother, but then I remembered Peter mentioning his mother had passed.

Peter had a fresh-shower smell, his hair still damp and curling at the tops of his ears when I fetched him and we hurried back to the office. I turned the phone around for him to talk from the lobby side, then slipped into the quarters to give him privacy.

He knocked softly on the door a few minutes later. "Thanks for coming to get me."

I joined him in the office. "Glad to. Hope it was good news."

He shook his head. "Actually, I need to leave sooner than I thought. I'll ask Cecil tomorrow about my car. If he hasn't got the parts, I may have to catch the bus to San Antonio."

My stomach pinched, the tiniest bit of alarm. "An emergency?"

He chewed on his lower lip and nodded. "I know this might put you in a bind and all, and I know the roofing job is a couple of days away from being done."

"If something's come up, then you need to go."

"I'm sorry." He looked at the phone. "I probably shouldn't have given your number for private business. This is something I have to do. Betty says it's my last chance. Now or never."

Betty. The girl on the phone. Things made more sense now. Guys who are in love don't look at other women. And to Peter, I wasn't a woman...just a boss. It was a relief in a way. Good to find out before I let myself get carried away.

CHAPTER 18

On Monday afternoon, Sally, just back from Houston, paid us a visit to check on the progress of the new landscaping. She looked stunning in a cream-colored sundress with cap sleeves and a gold lamé belt cinched at the waist.

"I see you got some shopping in while you were gone. Beautiful dress."

"I had to do something to pass the time. I simply couldn't hang around the respiratory ward with the kids. I wouldn't dream of putting them in danger. And I made sure Hud took a shower the minute he came back to the hotel. And kiss him? Forget it. I was terrified he'd picked up the germs from breathing the same air."

"How's his cousin?"

"Not good. Apparently there are different types of infantile paralysis, which I didn't know. Lolly has the worst kind, which attacked her throat and chest muscles. If not for the iron lung, she would've died within hours." She shuddered. "It's too gruesome to even think about. Nina Beth, her daughter, has the other type, which affects the muscles in the arms and legs. She's improving slowly, but with a paralyzed right arm and leg, she'll probably have permanent damage, maybe even a shrunken leg. Poor thing won't ever get to play basketball or be in a beauty pageant."

"I'm so sorry."

"I needed therapy of some type, so I took Hud's checkbook and left Houston in a better financial state than I found it. But I didn't come to talk about that. I want to see what the Magnolias did while I was gone. And I must say, you've never looked better."

"I'm a fright, Sally. Look at me." I held out my arms so she could get a good look at O'Dell's shirt and the rolled-up Levi's that had become my work attire.

"No, it's not your clothes. You have a glow about you. Is that a new shade of eye shadow you're wearing? And your hair, pulled up on top of your head. It's darling."

"Thanks, but no new makeup, and my hair is easier to manage with it up."

"Must be that cute fella you had working here when I left. Anything going on with him?"

"Peter? Good heavens, no. He's the handyman. Roofer, painter, plumber, whatever comes up. At least he was. He left a few days ago."

"So the cottages are all done?"

"Nearly. Mr. Miller from the lumberyard is sending someone out tomorrow to finish up. And on Wednesday, I have an electrician and welders coming to fix the neon sign out front. Can you believe it? This place is almost done!" Until that moment I didn't realize how much I'd missed Sally and having someone to talk to, to share my excitement with. I opened my arms, and like the best friends we were, we hugged until we both burst into a fit of the giggles.

Sally got control first. "I've missed you. Now, c'mon and show me what the Magnolias did."

We strolled arm in arm even though the heat and humidity took our breath away. Here and there we stopped to admire the junipers and Indian hawthorne the Magnolias planted alongside the gravel parking spaces, yellow rosebushes at the corners of the cottages. The window boxes, freshly painted, were ready to be filled with flowers.

Sally stood back and admired it all. "What do you think for the boxes? Geraniums? Petunias?"

"Something easy. Maybe a few bachelor buttons and some asparagus fern." As we circled back toward the office, we passed Mary Frances in her outdoor lounge chair, a cigarette in one hand and a magazine in the other. Beside her, Sebastian stretched out like a sentry.

"Sally? My goodness gracious, aren't you a vision on this hot day!"

"Thank you, Mrs. Peyton. You're looking well, too." Sebastian rose and came to lick Sally's hand. "I didn't know you had a dog."

Mary Frances smiled. "Georgia's handyman had to leave, so he left Sebastian with me. It reminds me of the mutt O'Dell had as a child."

Sally gave me a questioning look but patted Mary Frances on the knee. "I think it's splendid you've taken the dog. He'll be great company for you."

"Hmmph." She went back to reading her magazine, and we ambled off.

Later in the office, I plugged in the electric fan and propped open the front door to let the air circulate. Sally sipped a glass of sweet tea. "You've got more courage than I would, taking on Mary Frances. It's nothing short of amazing how much difference a couple of weeks has made."

"Thanks, I wasn't sure how it would turn out. So far, so good."

"What's up with the dog? You said Peter left, but if I'm not mistaken, a man doesn't up and leave his dog behind."

"I got the feeling he needed to get to San Antonio as soon as possible. It was a woman who called, and I'm nearly sure she was giving Peter an ultimatum."

"Girlfriend?"

"Who knows? He could have a wife and six kids for all I know. He never discusses his personal life. Cecil's having trouble getting the part for Peter's car, so I took him to the bus station. Not to change the subject or anything, but how does next Monday sound for having the crawfish boil? That would give the Magnolias time to finish here and let me get the million and one last-minute things done before I open on the twenty-ninth. It depends on if you and Hud can come that night."

"Hud will be down in Houston. He always spends the last week of the month there. But I'll be here, wouldn't miss it for all the oil in Texas. Have you thought about what you're wearing?"

"Gracious, no. I'll find something. Maybe the peasant outfit I wore in the talent show last summer."

Sally clucked her tongue and shook her head. "Sometimes I wonder about you. This is a big event in Mayhaw, and I assure you, the newspaper will be here taking pictures. Even if your handsome handyman's not around, you need to get dolled up once in a while. You never know who might see your picture in the paper."

"I do want people to take me seriously as a businesswoman, but as far as impressing suitors—forget it. I'm still a grieving widow."

"Get out of here. You don't need to pretend with me. We both know O'Dell cheated on you even before you were married..." She looked at me to see if she'd said too much.

I lifted my chin, giving her a steady, tight-lipped glare as she continued.

"Heaven knows, every time you turned around, there was some rumor. I hate to say it, sugar, but it's time you gave up that hunt for the O'Dell you've created in your mind."

"Sally!" My chest tightened. A sprinkle of gasoline and a match and I would be set to go off like a bottle rocket, but I'd rather swallow glass than lose control of the moment.

Hands up, palms out, I said, "Sally, we both know O'Dell had a rambling spirit. I'm trying to give him the benefit of the doubt since he has two little girls who love him. And he adored them. There is no point in bringing all this up. All it's doing is getting me riled up for no good reason."

"Something needs to get you riled. You're a beautiful woman, in the prime of your life."

"If that's true, and I have serious doubts, then why on earth did O'Dell choose this time to up and leave me for another woman?" The words flew out scalding and bitter. My face flamed when I looked beyond Sally at the figure that stepped across the threshold.

Mary Frances.

Her eyes flashed, and I didn't know whether it was confusion or anger or shock. Or the sudden realization her world had just been shattered.

Her jaw dropped to her chest. Fish-mouthed, she tried to speak, but no words formed.

Mustering a smile, I spoke with a feigned cheerfulness. "Hi, sweetie. What can I do for you?"

Wary, her eyes darted from me to Sally. "The phone. I came to use the phone." Her voice was rusty.

"Of course. Do you want me to get the operator on the line? Do you have the number?"

"No. I need to call the insurance man about the settlement on the fire."

"I thought he said a couple of weeks."

She spoke through tight lips. "A week or two, he said."

"I guess it wouldn't hurt to check then."

"Some other time. I'm not feeling well."

Sally offered her arm. "Here. I'll help you sit down."

Mary Frances flinched. "Stop. You both know I heard what you said." Her icy stare was aimed at me. "How could you?"

"How could I what?"

"Say something so terrible about O'Dell."

Decision time. Deny it and keep on with the charade. Or tell her the truth.

I should've lied.

Instead, I went to her and put my arm around her shoulder. "I didn't want to tell you. I knew it would be a shock, and I hoped he would tell you himself."

"Any problems in your marriage were no doubt from the tight leash you kept on O'Dell. It's no wonder my sweet boy took to being a traveling salesman to get away from you."

"Tight leash? Wherever did you get that impression? I was devastated. More than once, I might add."

Her body coiled under my grasp, and she pulled away. "You never spent a minute grieving for him. Flirting with that disgusting Applegate boy at the Sweet Shoppe. Trying to get me to tell you how much insurance O'Dell left you. What did you think? Were you planning to get you a big, fancy house like your friend here?" Her dark eyes darted to Sally, who, bless her heart, swooshed across the office and took Mary Frances's hands in hers.

"You know Georgia wanted nothing more than to be O'Dell's wife, forever and ever. You know Southern women are bred to forgive and look the other way. It's hard, sweetie, to overhear truths like that, but honestly, Georgia has been in agony for months. She's done everything to protect you and those darling girls of hers. Not to mention O'Dell's reputation."

"O'Dell would've told me if he was thinking about leaving you, Georgia. I never heard one peep from him." The venom in her voice came from deep resentment of being alone and the belief that a child always puts his mother first.

My own bitterness swelled. "I'm sure he would've told you eventually. I even hoped he would change his mind and come back. I know this upsets you, but I've been carrying this around far too long. Perhaps it's good you found out."

"For what reason? To break my already weary heart?" Her veiny hand rested on her chest.

"No. It clears the air, that's all."

"If, in fact, you're telling the truth."

"I have no reason to make up lies. Would you like the details? Her name? How much insurance money he left her?"

Her eyes grew round, her body shrinking away from Sally and toward the front door. She gave me a final glare and turned, her arms pumping as she stomped back to her cottage.

I steadied myself on the counter and took a deep breath. "That didn't go so well."

Sally now came to me with hugs, pats of reassurance. "She had to know sometime."

"No, she didn't. It was my own burden to bear. It had nothing to do with her and the love she had for her only child."

"O'Dell sure didn't seem to mind whose heart he broke."

"O'Dell is dead. He can't hurt me anymore. But here's the thing: he's the girls' daddy, and that counts for something. Inside, my loyalty to them and the hurt he inflicted on me are twisted together. They're the strangest bedfellows you can imagine." My attempt at a laugh was pathetic.

Sally looked at her watch. "Sweetie, if you think that way, O'Dell will have a hold on you forever. I know I'd be spitting mad, wanting some sort of revenge. Since you can't do anything to get back at him, you're just going to have to make your peace with it."

"It's not like I can run out to the cemetery and have a heart-to-heart talk with him."

"Of course not." She tapped her foot and looked at her watch again. "Look, I need to go. I'll call you later to see how Mary Frances is holding up. And you—I know you don't want to hear it—but things *will* get better. Your life isn't over. Not even close." She took a wad of bills from her handbag and shoved them at me. "A new dress. My treat. I want you to be stunning at the crawfish boil, you hear?"

She didn't wait for the answer and swooshed out the door.

I held the cash to my chest. Dear, sweet Sally. It would take more than new clothes to make me feel stunning. Too bad a new heart wasn't as easy to buy as a party dress.

CHAPTER 19

I knew I needed to go to Mary Frances, to apologize for O'Dell. Yet it wasn't me who had been unfaithful; I'd only inherited the aftermath. So instead I went to check on Catfish.

When I'd first mentioned the crawfish boil to Ludi, she'd said, "You be leaving that to Ludi, Miz Georgie. First off, you got no proper place to cook a mess of crawdads. They got to be cooked while they's still wiggling, and an outdoor fire be the way to go." She then volunteered Catfish to gather the stones and make an outdoor fireplace in the clearing behind the cottages. He and his friend Stick—a boy half a head taller than Catfish and aptly named—had been working steadily and now sat with their backs against a pair of sycamores. Sunlight filtered through half-grown leaves the color of green apples, dappled patches like confetti dancing around them.

Catfish jumped up when he saw me. "We's just taking a rest." He hurried over to a massive structure in the clearing. It stood waist high, a three-sided oven of sorts made of stones expertly stacked and mortared together. Flat stones fit together like a jig-saw puzzle to form an apron in front.

He cocked his head, eyes shining. "What do you think?"

"Goodness gracious, when your momma said you could build a barbecue, I had no idea it would be something so huge…and wow. This is something."

Catfish beamed, a wide, toothy smile. "We's waiting for the mud to dry, and Stick and I's talking about the best places to catch crawdads for your big doin's."

"It's going to take a lot of crawfish. I thought I'd have to go over to Longview to the fish market."

"Heck, no. We could catch 'em up fresh. Maw says we're the best crawdad fishermen on the bayou."

"Alrighty then. You know I don't argue with your momma. So tell me, how does this outdoor cooking work?"

The boys started chattering at the same time, sweat shining on their bare chests, the smell of hard labor clinging to their thin, youthful frames. Catfish pointed to the center of the oven. "There in the middle, we'll dig out the ground and put in a grate to hold the logs for burning."

"And this part was my idea." Stick pointed to a spot along the top. "See this gap? That's for a rod for hanging the pots on."

"You've thought of everything. Both of you deserve a treat. What say I scare up some brownies?" I winked at Catfish, whose hand went to his stomach.

"Yes, ma'am. That would be fine."

I left the boys and cut through between the cottages. The drapes of Mary Frances's cottage were drawn tight, the door shut, and no sign of Sebastian. I was tempted to knock but decided to surprise her with brownies and sweet tea, too, when I returned with a treat for Catfish and Stick.

My steps light, I hummed "The Tennessee Waltz" as I went to the office. A woman walking up the drive stopped me. She listed to one side, a purse dangling from one arm, a bottle clutched tight in the other. My gut twisted.

Mary Frances was rip-roaring drunk and coming my way, Sebastian following faithfully behind. She certainly hadn't wasted any time.

I didn't know whether to be mad at Mary Frances or heart-broken. Her sobriety had been short-lived, but it's a bitter pill to swallow to know you're the one responsible for the fall from grace of another human being. Mary Frances had begun to inch her way out of the black hole of grief. A ray of light had begun to shine in her eyes in the days since she'd come to us at the Stardust. A light I'd forgotten was there. She hadn't always been the cling-ing, desperate woman who'd lost her way and stumbled upon the bottle.

I went to her. "Mary Frances."

She shoved me aside, ducked her head, and staggered to her cottage, where she disappeared into a room as black as my heart.

Sebastian lay on the doormat outside her cottage when I took her supper. And even though I knocked and hollered, Mary Frances ignored me. I knew eventually I would have to go in whether she invited me or not and see how much damage she'd done to herself, but I gave her distance that night.

The next day she took the breakfast I offered by sticking her arm around the door, which she opened just wide enough for the plate to pass through. Doc said to make sure she had three square meals a day. I would hold up my end and see what transpired.

She stayed holed up four days. Time for the roofers Mr. Miller sent over to finish the shingles and for the electrician and a repairman to complete repairs on the Stardust sign, repaint it, and install new neon lights.

That evening when I knocked on Mary Frances's door to deliver her supper, she breezed out, hair combed and a smile on her face. "Thanks, Georgia. If it's not too much trouble, I'd like to join you and the girls tonight. And in case you were wondering, I'm going to be fine."

Thrilled but leery, I linked my arm in hers and escorted her back to the quarters. After supper, she sat with Rosey and Avril on the divan, the three of them looking at dog pictures in *The Book of Knowledge* encyclopedia.

Avril pointed a stubby finger at the middle of the page. "That one looks like Sebastian."

Rosey leaned in to the book. "No, this one. He has the same wavy tail."

Mary Frances laughed. "I think you're both right. Did I ever tell you about the dog your daddy had when he was a boy?"

I smiled to myself, hoping Mary Frances had indeed come to some sort of understanding with her inner demons. Time would tell, but for now, I was thankful. After drying the last of the dishes, I took a glass of iced tea and slipped out the back door. Rain clouds had moved in as they had the previous two evenings, bringing a mossy smell that tickled the back of my throat. Bullfrogs warmed their vocal cords, whether in anticipation of the rain or just a friendly hoedown in the bayou was anybody's guess, but it was a comforting sound. Mary Frances had made a turnaround on her own. I was proud of her and glad she had good memories of O'Dell to share with the girls. They needed that, and I vowed once again to keep O'Dell's shortcomings from them.

An uneasy feeling settled on me.

I set down my tea and leaned back on my elbows. As clouds shrouded the moon, passing black and angry over the luminous ball, I strained my ears, listening for—hoping for—the sound of a guitar melody to complete my contentment. I knew it was in vain.

Lightning skittered across the sky in the distance, the next flash closer, the storm approaching quickly. Another flash of lightning, followed by a crack of thunder, brought Sebastian scurrying to my side as he crouched, trying to hide under my legs. Rubbing his head, I told him it was all right, I knew what it was like to be abandoned.

"That's me, my friend. The one everyone leaves. My parents. My husband." *And now Peter.*

Raindrops splattered on the steps around me, a knot growing in my throat. I bent over and ruffled the fur on Sebastian's neck. "Come on, boy. Let's get you inside."

Sebastian turned and looked into the darkness, as if waiting for someone to appear. I shuddered. I'd spent a lifetime doing that, and yet looking back had never made a speck of difference. "Maybe things will turn out different for you, Sebastian. Peter wouldn't have left without good reason. And he knew we'd feed you and give you a good home."

He licked my hand, tail wagging, then followed me into the quarters where all was safe and dry.

CHAPTER 20

✦

The gravel parking space at the Stardust looked like a luxury car exhibition. Cadillacs, late-model Buicks, Sonny Bolander's patrol car, and Hugh Salazar's Chrysler Imperial. I'd invited Hugh to the crawfish boil on the spur of the moment. Partly to gloat over being able to carry off the job he thought I had no business doing, but also so he could see for himself I'd met the terms of Paddy Palmer's will and fully intended to continue. Lord willing.

The only person who didn't come that I'd invited was Aunt Cora. The girls and I stopped at her house after we'd been shopping for new dresses for the party, thanks to Sally's generosity.

"We'd love for you to come. Ludi and her children and Peter have worked so hard. It will even meet with your approval, I think."

"You haven't needed or asked for my approval since you were ten years old."

I shrugged. "I'm asking now. Please, won't you come?"

Her gaze was wary, and I hoped it was a sign of surrender. "I'd love to, but I'll be at a March of Dimes rally in Jefferson for the night. Since it's in my district I need to be there."

"So you'll come another time?"

"I didn't say that."

I wondered if Aunt Cora had a specific reason for disliking the tourist court or if the Tickle blood coursing through her veins kept the family feud alive. No one even remembered what Uncle Paddy had done to merit being an outcast. I wanted her to come and see Rosey and Avril in their new matching dresses. The lavender gingham was perfect for Rosey with her fair complexion and fiery hair and equally cute with Avril's dark hair and eyes. Even Mary Frances was bright-eyed and more engaging than I'd seen her in a long time. Sometimes, it's the small miracles, you know, and the night of the crawfish boil, I was overcome with all the miracles that had brought us this far.

Not a breath of air stirred, but the evening was warm, expectant, and my skin tingled beneath my new aquamarine sheath. Thanks to Sally, I'd found a dress I loved on the sale rack, pleased even more when I took a size smaller, and I liked the way the satin cummerbund made my waist look slimmer. I wouldn't say I had a swagger in my steps, but Sally was right—the new dress felt like a new beginning for me, too.

Silly of me, since the first person I ran into was Bobby Carl Applegate. "Hey, doll! It's amazing what you've done with this place."

"Hey, yourself." I thumped him on the arm. "I had a lot of help out here. Guess you're here to report for KHAW on the grand reopening of the Stardust."

"No. I'm not there anymore. I thought you heard. I'm an agent now. Gonna run with the high rollers." He had on a starched white shirt, a paisley cravat at the open neck. It was a transformation in both his usual bad taste in clothes and his demeanor. Only now, he seemed cockier than usual.

I offered my hand. "Congratulations. Guess we've both found our dreams. So which insurance company are you with?"

He stepped back, his upper lip raised into a sneer. "Not insurance. I'm a music agent. You gotta admit, I know what folks like, being on the radio the past six years. Figure I'll have a whole string of clients before you know it. Got one fella already lined up for the Mayhaw Festival in July."

"Sounds fascinating. Anyone I know?"

"Probably not. He's an old-timer who used to be in vaudeville wanting to make a comeback. Rudy Vallee–type guy."

"Sounds fun. Good luck to you."

He sidled up to me. "Got me a sweet roadster right over there. Gotta build my image, ya know?"

He pointed to a sports car I hadn't seen, a tiny two-seated convertible. "Want to have a look?"

"Not right now."

"Aw, come on." He put his arm around my shoulder and pulled me in the direction of his car.

"I need to check on the food."

"Just one look. When you see it, you'll be wanting to go for a spin." His hand clamped tight around me.

"Oh, for heaven's sake, stop it. And by the way, if you're not here with the radio, why did you come?"

He stepped in front of me, both hands on my shoulders now. "Because I wanted to see you. You're beautiful, and I can't stop thinking about you now that...well...I thought you might give me a whirl since you're available again."

"Bobby Carl, I know we've been friends forever, but I'm not what you would call available. Not the way you want. With a business to run and two girls to raise, I've no intention of seeing you or anyone." *And we'll not be going out.* No use in pointing out the obvious.

"So the rumors aren't true?"

My patience was running thin, but I took the bait. "What rumors?"

"I heard you got an employee of the male persuasion staying out here. A stranger who's a bit of a cad, if what I've heard is true. I need to know my competition."

A sigh passed my lips. "People believe what they want to." Even though Peter had gone and wasn't a cad at all, the rumors would fly until kingdom come, apparently. Bobby Carl, though, didn't need the details. "It's nice you care, but the man who's the subject of all the wild rumors is an experienced roofer, a man who's served our country, and from what I could tell, a gentleman." Longing for Peter inched along my spine. I let my eyes drift past Bobby Carl. I blinked. A long-legged gentleman was headed our way.

My mouth went dry, my legs turning to jelly. A tiny squawk came from my throat. I'd know that straw hat anywhere. *Peter.*

Bobby Carl turned to see what caused my reaction. "Someone you know?"

"Yes…the roofer I was telling you about." *He's back.* I put my hand to my chest so Bobby Carl couldn't see my heart pounding.

I raised my chin, the corners of my mouth tilting into a cautious smile, although I wanted to wince because Bobby Carl had pulled me into the crook of his arm, so close I felt his hot breath on my neck. I elbowed him and stepped forward.

"Hey, Peter. I didn't expect to see you."

"This must be the night of the crawfish boil. Hope I'm not too late."

"Right on time. Ludi and the kids are cooking up a storm back there. And I know for sure someone who's going to be happy to see you." On cue, Sebastian trotted up, feather tail waving, and I was certain a smile graced his drooling lips.

Peter released his canvas bag and dropped to one knee to let Sebastian lick his face, his arms. "Good dog."

He stood, his eyes misty, and when he removed his straw hat, swiped a hand across one of them.

Bobby Carl sighed. "Guess there's something here I'm missing. I thought you were living out here if you're the fella I heard about."

Peter nodded. "Don't know what you heard, but I'm Peter Reese." He offered his hand. "And you are?"

Bobby Carl offered a limp shake. "Bobby Carl Applegate, music agent. I see you're carrying a guitar there. If I'd a known you were tonight's entertainment, I could've given you some pointers on the proper dress for one of Georgia's social gatherings. These are the cream of Mayhaw's society."

I shot Bobby Carl a warning look. "Cut the agent act, all right? Peter's been away for a few days." To Peter, I said, "You'll have to get used to Bobby Carl. He's starting a business promoting musicians."

Peter's eyes held a hint of caution as he gave Bobby Carl the once-over. "If I decide to take my guitar on the road, at least I know who to call. Now, if y'all will pardon me, I'll see if Ludi needs my help."

Bobby Carl watched him go. "Can't see what you see in him. Looks like a drifter to me."

"He's a handyman...and good at what he does." The vessels in my neck throbbed. Peter was back, and I was stuck with Bobby Carl.

"It's the propriety of it; I only want the best for you, you know."

"Thanks. And I want the best for you, too. Which, at the

moment, might be the yummiest crawfish you ever sunk your teeth into."

"Not interested unless you'll be my dinner partner."

"Sorry. I'm the hostess and am sitting with my family."

I hurried away, but when I looked back, Bobby Carl sat behind the wheel of his sporty car, then peeled out on the gravel. I wove among the tables and greeted those who'd come. Trixie and Bud Matthews, Honey Sheldon and her husband, the mayor of Mayhaw. Hugh Salazar looked up and nodded. I thanked him for coming.

"Wouldn't have missed it for the world." He smiled and turned back to visiting with the mayor.

A group rallied around Sally, asking about Hud's cousin, and she repeated what she'd told me earlier in the week. She added, "The newspapers are literally dripping with stories, telling people not to go out in public. Hud called me this morning and said in Houston they're asking people to vacation at home in their own backyards."

Trixie gave me a sheepish look. "How awful for Georgia if the whole state decided not to leave their towns. Who would come and fill up these adorable cottages?"

I shrugged. "You know it's a scare tactic. It sells more papers."

Sally sighed. "I'm one of those scared plumb into next week. Honest to goodness, girls, if you'd seen that respiratory ward—"

"I didn't think you'd ever gone in to see Hud's cousin."

"We couldn't actually go in since she's still in isolation. We had to look through the window."

Sheriff Bolander approached with Twila Flynn dangling from his wrist like a sidearm. I had to admit she still had her *looks,* as Aunt Cora would say. And Sonny looked ten years younger, clapping his hand over hers.

In a tinny voice, Twila said, "They say polio's contagious."

Sonny nodded. "You can bet we're keeping an eye on the situation. Couple of counties already issued quarantines on public parks. Heard they even turned out school a week early down south where the thing's grown legs and run wild."

Hands on my hips, I glared at Sonny. "Gee, thanks, for bringing such cheerful news. I think I liked it better when all you fellas talked about was the weather and the fishing report on Caddo Lake." Not that I didn't recognize the gravity of it, but I wanted the evening to be carefree.

Sally, bless her, came to my defense. "You're right. This is a night to celebrate. Come on, now! Let's have some fun."

I slipped away as Sally chatted about going to see *Singin' in the Rain* while they were in Houston and that Debbie Reynolds was "cute as a bug's ear." I found Peter in back helping Ludi with the food and manhandling the heavy black kettles that hung from the rod of the stone oven. He had a dish towel tied around his narrow waist, the sleeves of his dress shirt rolled up. He must've freshened up, and to say he was handsome was an understatement, but no sense entertaining those thoughts. For all I knew he'd come to collect his things and return to San Antonio for the girl who'd called. Betty. It was a nice name, and Peter deserved someone nice. I hoped she was also pretty.

When I walked up, Peter winked. "Less than ten minutes, according to Ludi. She says this is the finest mess of mudbugs she's ever seen. Must've been two hundred pounds of them Catfish netted."

"It smells divine. Perfect amount of spice, I'd say. I hope you'll join us at the table. You deserve it after all the work you did on the cottages."

"No, any sap could've done what I did. The landscaping, now that's art. You go on and enjoy your night."

I thanked everyone for coming and asked them to be seated. Newspapers covered the long tables we'd borrowed from the church, ready for the feast. In no time, Peter heaved bucket after bucket of rosy-red crawfish mixed with fresh corn on the cob, tender onions, hunks of spicy sausage, and new potatoes Ludi had insisted on bringing from her garden. Halved lemons meant for flavor added a bit of color.

I passed out dish towels for bibs and invited everyone to dig in. Rosey held up a crawfish. "Look at me. MeMaw taught me how to eat mudbugs." She held the head in one hand, the tail in the other. With a squeeze and a twist, she exposed the tail meat, held it in her teeth, and sucked in her cheeks until the meat popped into her mouth.

Mary Frances chuckled. "That's my girl." Her laughter was the Dixie balm I needed.

Sally clapped for Rosey. "I swan, you're a true Southerner." Her own hands were covered in juice, but she and the other ladies of society didn't seem to mind. You simply had to dig in with both hands and eat when it came to crawfish. And crawfish was as much of a tradition in Mayhaw as genuflecting at the statue of General Robert E. Lee outside the elementary school.

An hour later, paper-thin crawfish skeletons, wilted lemons, and fuzzy corncobs with the kernels gnawed off were all that remained. The sun kissed the tops of the pines, its neon orange casting a glow on us all. Gold, lavender, and scarlet ribbons streamed across the sky, the dying sun's reflection playing its reverie.

The ribbon-cutting was to take place simultaneously with lighting the Stardust sign. Rosey had begged to flip the switch from inside the office and awaited my signal. The Magnolias lined up behind a ribbon held on either end by two of the husbands. I stood in their midst, Avril's tiny hand clutched in mine. Hugh Salazar, to my surprise, asked to say a few words.

"Georgia, you've taught this old coot I've still got a few things to learn. Paddy Palmer, rest his soul, would be proud." He looked around. "Now who the devil is going to cut this ribbon?"

Mayor Sheldon, Honey's husband, waved a pair of dress shears. Jess Porter, the reporter for the *Mayhaw Messenger,* lifted his camera in readiness.

I cleared my throat. "Thank you all for your help. I feel completely inadequate to express my gratitude to all who've helped—Sally and the Magnolias, and my stars, for all you fellas who did the heavy work and made all those window boxes. Y'all might not know it, but my first memory of coming to Mayhaw is staying right over there in cottage five. You might say I've come full circle." My voice shook, emotion clogging my throat. "Everybody ready?"

I leaned across the ribbon and waved to Rosey. Moments later, the neon sputtered to life, the points of the star reaching toward the heavens. Mayor Sheldon snipped the ribbon and flashbulbs blinded me as a roar went up.

My insides trembled, my knees shaky. A pair of hands rested lightly on my waist and a voice whispered in my ear, "Congratulations."

Tears I'd held back now sprang to the surface and tracked down my cheeks. I turned and looked into Peter's eyes. The world stopped spinning for a moment, my head awash in the neon haze. I had a few questions for Peter Reese, but not tonight. Tonight I wanted to celebrate.

I exhaled, aware again of the bubble of activity around me, and Avril tugged my hand. "Come, Mommy! See the lights!" We marched to the drive and leaned back, craning our necks. A more

beautiful sight I'd never seen. I scooped Avril into my arms and
twirled around as she giggled. I set her down, found Rosey, and
the three of us joined hands, forming a circle. I threw back my
head and danced under the neon light of the Texas sky, stardust in
my eyes.

CHAPTER 21

L udi sat on a metal stool in the washhouse, her eyes bright. "Yes'm. That was some doin's last night. It done my soul good to see all your fine friends sucking the heads of them crawdads, having a high time. Miz Do-reen would be mighty proud of what you done here."

"I couldn't have done it without your help. I came here running from my own shadow, hoping and praying I didn't make a mess of things."

"The Lord knows what we be needin' 'fore we even ask. The way you come along and pay me now ever' Saturday. The way you watch after Miz Mary Frances. I believe the Lord Jesus musta whispered into Paddy's heart 'bout givin' you the Stardust."

"You have more faith than I do, Ludi. Not that I don't believe things work out for the good, for I suppose they do eventually. You know I've sailed a few thank-yous up in gratitude for you and your kiddos. Guess they're resting up over in Zion today?"

"Mercysakes, what give you that idea? They're out there trying to weasel yo' man Peter into gon' fishin'. Last I be hearin' he said they gots to clean up ever' speck a litter on the grounds and then some 'fore he's gon' fish." She winced and leaned over to rub the side of her foot.

"I'm glad they're helping Peter, who, by the way, is *not* my man—"

"You don't be knowin' that. Maybe the Lord's got plans he ain't informed you about yet."

"You're a fright, Ludi. Now let's get these cottages ready."

✦

My intention was to open at noon the day before Memorial Day for those who might strike out on vacation a day ahead of the holiday. That morning I took Mary Frances to the cemetery to place flowers on O'Dell's and Earl's graves. I'd chosen an arrangement for Paddy's grave as well and was surprised to see a dozen or more flower bundles blanketing the soft mound where his body rested.

Mary Frances held up better than I expected, and I tried to remain aloof and not think too much about it. It wasn't hard as I had to keep an eye on Rosey and Avril, who had to be cautioned to not walk over the tops of the graves and to stay on the paths. Rosey stood for a long time staring at O'Dell's grave. To me she said, "Do you think Daddy misses us?"

"Of course he does. You were his sunshine."

She smiled and blew a kiss toward the grave. Overhead, the sun had given way to a bank of clouds, the air heavy, sticky with the scent of roses and daisies and honeysuckle. Sticky like my marriage to O'Dell, but as Mary Frances ran her fingers across the letters of Earl's headstone, my eyes teared up. At least one of us had happy memories.

When we arrived back at the Stardust, Peter leaned against his Studebaker, Sebastian at his feet. His straw hat shielded his face, and I wondered if he was waiting to say good-bye. At least if he did, he'd be more courteous than the others in my life who had left me.

A twinge came in my chest. Good-byes in person didn't taste any better than notes left in sugar bowls.

The girls jumped from the car and ran to Sebastian. Peter pulled himself up and took off his hat. "Feels like a rain comin' on."

I fanned my face with my hand. "I'll say. Anything happen while we were gone?"

"Matter of fact, Cecil got my car done."

"I see that...so I guess you'll be leaving? Not sure how I can ever thank you for all you've done."

"No thanks necessary. The way I recall, I came here begging you to take me on, so if anyone's got dibs on being grateful, it would be me...if I were leaving."

"You just said you were."

"No, ma'am. You said I was. I said my car was fixed. Two completely different things."

My underarms got sticky, my face hot from looking like an idiot. "Sorry. I assumed you'd come back for your car."

He held his hat over his heart. "I am glad to get the old girl back. Seems, though, the repair costs were more than we first thought—"

"Ah, so you need money."

"It's not what you think."

"Oh, so you're the mind reader now?" My voice was more flippant than I intended, and Peter looked away quickly. I had the feeling he was calculating the pros and cons of whether to continue the conversation or just shake hands and drive on down the road.

Instead, he took my elbow and glanced at the girls playing

with Sebastian. "Could we take a walk? I have something to show you."

"I hope it's not another problem with the cottages. Ludi and I checked them thoroughly."

"Not the cottages. Something else."

"All right." We fell in stride, silence heavy like the air around us. "I've been meaning to ask about your trip. How was it?"

His face clouded as he shrugged. "Hard. I'm sure you could relate. Burying those you love is never easy."

The stormy blue of his eyes stole the air from my lungs. "The woman who called? She died?"

"Betty? No, her husband. Complications from his injuries in Korea. We were in the same platoon." He spoke in a flat tone, his eyes aimed at his shoes.

"I'm sorry."

"We all carry the ghosts of our pasts, I guess. You. Catfish. Me."

Silence deafened me, waiting for him to continue, hoping he wouldn't.

His Adam's apple bobbled in his throat. His eyes were still moist when he looked at me. "Come on, let me show you what I've been thinking."

He led me to the clearing out back. Leftover lumber dotted the area in various grids. He pointed under the trees. "What do you think of putting a few picnic tables over here? There's nice shade, and I could get Catfish to help me cut trees for the lumber we'd need."

"You're assuming, of course, we'll have guests who will want to take advantage of a picnic spot."

"We already have the barbecue. In the summer, people would prefer to eat outdoors rather than take whatever they've cooked back to their cottages." He raised his eyebrows in a questioning look.

"I had thought of adding a swing set or something for children to play on."

"I've laid that out over here. We'll want it far enough away from the cooking area to be safe. Cecil has all sorts of pipe and junk behind his shop I could salvage. We'd have to get new chains and seats for the swings. Maybe later add a teeter-totter and some sidewalks."

"Don't get carried away. We haven't even had our first customer yet."

"You will."

"I guess that means you're going to stick around awhile."

"I've no place else to go." His voice was upbeat, but the way his shoulders drooped and his eyes remained dull made me think he would carry the scars of his friend for a long time.

I was an expert on scars.

᛭

Late in the afternoon a man with a crew cut and ears that reminded me of doorknobs approached the counter. "It says you have a vacancy. Any chance you can put up a family of five?"

I smiled, giving him the information about the cottages and the rate per night. I'd rented four cottages since noon. I grabbed the key from its hook. "Let me show you before you decide."

As we walked across the parking lot, his wife and three small boys with the same round ears as their father and bounding with energy joined us. "This room has a hide-a-bed that should work with the size of your boys here. And there's a hot plate and separate sink in the kitchen corner. You're welcome to use the community icebox on the stoop behind the laundry."

His wife, a petite blonde with a headscarf tied under her chin, said, "I love it. We'll take it."

She and the boys stayed behind while the gentleman went back with me to make the arrangements. After he paid for one night, I gave him a welcome packet with a map of places to eat in Mayhaw and information about fishing on the bayou. "Ruby's Café is nice for a family. Just half a block down."

"What about fish we catch in the creek?"

"We have the icebox, but I'd rather you keep them in an ice chest until you can cook them. We have cooking facilities behind the Stardust. If you need an ice chest, Cecil across the road has a couple different sizes, and the ice plant is two blocks down, take a left, and go till it dead-ends. You can't miss it."

He thanked me and left. Personal service was one of the things I hoped would make guests comfortable and want to return for another stay. Peter's plan for the picnic tables and swings for the kiddos added to my excitement, and I allowed myself to day-dream. Happy children racing through the grass, playing tag or Red Rover, and squealing with laughter on the swings. *No Vacancy* would flash across the slim rectangle at the bottom of the Stardust sign, and people would drive away disappointed to see we were full. *If only we could've stayed at that cute place with the cottages that looked like postcards from Switzerland.*

It was a silly fantasy, but one that was materializing before my eyes. Five of the eight available cottages already rented. And as I strutted around, feeling all smarty-pants, Aunt Cora's voice from the past popped into my head, "Pride cometh before a fall. So get yourself down off that pedestal and make yourself useful."

One thing about Aunt Cora, she wouldn't abide boasting or sassing in any form, especially if it was your own accomplish-ments that swelled your head. The air in the office was stuffy, even with the fan going. Or maybe it was me feeling the rush of excitement and realizing my folly in being boastful. I pulled out the rubber band holding my topknot and shook my head, letting my hair fall to my shoulders. Although my neck was damp with humidity, it was freeing and made me feel a bit giddy.

I looked in on the girls in the quarters. "Want to come outside for a while?"

Rosey had a pencil propped on her ear. "After awhile. I'm the schoolteacher, and Avril's my pupil. She has to finish her coloring before she can have recess."

"Alrighty, then. I'll be on the steps out front having a glass of tea."

If anything, it was more stifling outdoors, like the world was holding its breath, waiting to exhale. Overhead, the sky had taken on a pale, watery color. We'd have rain before morning as sure as my name was Georgia Lee Peyton. I hoped it didn't ruin the holiday for those tucked in my cottages. I slipped off my sandals and wiggled my toes on the warm wooden boards beneath them. When I looked up, Mary Frances was headed my way, a stern look on her face.

She didn't waste any time with greetings. "Guess you're so busy you forgot about fixin' supper."

"Hello to you, too. And no, I didn't forget supper. I thought we'd have grilled cheese tonight since I don't know who might be coming next for a room."

"Hmmph." She pulled her cigarette purse from her pocket, fished out a Pall Mall, and lit it.

I patted the step beside me. "Have a seat."

We sat without talking, her puffing, me watching the newest guests unload their car and disappear into their cottage.

Mary Frances spoke first. "How long do you think O'Dell was in the bayou after he drowned?"

The question came out of nowhere. I wasn't even certain I'd

heard her right, but her eyes were steeled on me, waiting for an answer. "I don't know. Why do you ask?"

"I remembered something while we were at the cemetery...a phone call."

"From O'Dell?" My stomach clenched, and I wasn't sure I wanted to know.

"I think it was about a week before they found him. I wasn't thinking too clearly then."

She hadn't thought clearly since Earl died, but I didn't remind her of this. "You remembered it now, though."

"Earlier. I've been beating my brains out trying to think it all out. He had something to tell me and wanted to do it in person."

"Any idea what?" *Fiona Callahan. Was that it?*

"No, but he acted nervous. Do you think someone could've killed him? Either on purpose or by accident?"

"No. Sheriff didn't find anything unusual. O'Dell didn't have any enemies that I know of."

She sent a few puffs of smoke out into the already stale air, then turned abruptly to me. "Who was the woman O'Dell was seeing? You said he had an insurance policy in her name."

"He did. I still have it in my bedroom. Do you suppose that's what he wanted to tell you? Maybe let you hold on to it?"

"I'd think he would give it to her, so that doesn't make sense. Nothing does. Maybe he had second thoughts and was thinking of coming back to you."

"Then he would've called me, don't you think?"

"Would you have taken him back?"

"Children should have a daddy. For them I suppose I would have. It's not something I dwell on in light of what happened. I've wondered, though, what I should do with the policy."

"Burn it. That's what I would do."

"I don't know."

Wheels crunched on the drive as a station wagon pulled to a stop. A head popped out the window on the driver's side. "Ya got any vacancies?"

"Yes, sir. Come on in and I'll set you right up."

Mary Frances threw down her cigarette butt and ground it out with her shoe. "Looks like it'll be awhile on those grilled cheese sandwiches."

"It does. Unless you want to get things started. I'd like that... to have you be more a part of the family activity. Maybe even help out some in the office."

"Not tonight." She shuffled off as the man introduced himself and rented a cottage for the entire weekend.

Only two vacancies.

$$\ast$$

My dreams came in fits and spurts that night. No matter what position I tried, I couldn't sleep. And then when I did, everything was twisted and bizarre. I blamed Mary Frances, but the rain pounding the windows might've been partially responsible. Oddly enough, the girls didn't come running into my bed as they usually did even though fierce streaks of lightning lit up the windows. Thunderclaps shook the walls, and with each one, a vision of O'Dell being swept through the bayou, the water engorging his body, leaching it of all its color, ricocheted through me.

I got up and put the kettle on to make myself a cup of tea. Worrying the sheets into tangles certainly hadn't helped. And whatever O'Dell intended to tell his mother now rested in the bosom of the bayou—bobbing along the dark waters among the cypress.

I'd nearly finished my tea when the buzzer sounded in the office. *Who on earth would be out on a night like this?* I started to ignore it, then thought better of it. What if it was Mary Frances?

Or someone in need of a dry spot to get in out of the rain? Aunt Cora's warnings of all the awful things that could happen zipped through my mind, but I grabbed my robe and went to open the door.

A man of sixty or so ducked in the door, his hair plastered to his head, clothes sopping wet. "Sorry to be so late." He took a good look at me, then stammered, "Y-you... you're not Doreen. Or Paddy. Mighty sorry, ma'am. Didn't mean to bust right on in."

"It's fine. I'm Georgia Peyton."

"Are you open? The light was on. I got a late start, didn't figure on the rain being so blasted hard. Only thing that kept me from running my car into the bar ditch was seeing the neon sign."

"I'm glad it was a beacon for you. Are you a friend of the Palmers?"

"Of sorts. I reserve a room for every weekend during the summer starting with Memorial weekend. Didn't Doreen tell you?"

"No." I told him about Paddy's passing and Doreen moving to Oklahoma. That I was the new owner.

"So sorry to hear about Paddy. Fine fellow. Any chance you have a room?"

"Two left. Take your pick. Number one or nine."

"Nine suits me. I can show myself in."

He fished a wad of bills from his wallet and passed them over to me. "We'll settle the bill later. I'm ready to get these wet things off and get some shut-eye. The fish'll be biting like piranhas at first light with the bayou stirred up like this." He took the key, scribbled his name in the guest log, and showed himself out. He'd written Malcolm Overstreet, a name I didn't recognize. Oh, well. He'd paid me a hefty amount. I gave him time to get to his car before I turned out the porch light.

One cottage left. It wasn't a matter of pride. I was merely doing what I was meant to do—provide a spot for weary bodies and happy vacationers. I stood at the window and peered through the rain at the neon sign. The red and blue and yellow letters swam together, a wavy welcome even in the storm. I rested my chin on the sill and let the glory of it wash over me.

CHAPTER 22

Rain kept us all in the next morning, but by midday the sun won out over the clouds. When Ludi didn't show up, I busied myself with taking fresh towels to the cottages. I hoped it was just the rain that caused her absence and not another setback with her ailing mother.

After supper, though, she appeared at the back door, twisting her coal-black hands in her apron, working it like a lump of bread dough. The evening sun had that angle that made everything hard to see, like you needed to squint to see if your eyes were deceiving you. Mine weren't.

Behind Ludi stood a rake-thin woman about my age with hair of spun gold. She held the hand of a towheaded girl of four or five and also quite thin. They both looked as if they'd had the life spooked out of them.

Ludi rolled her eyeballs up so all I could see were half-moons hanging down in the whites of her eyes. "Georgie, I knows it ain't the best time, but I got myself a problem."

It appeared Ludi had two problems since there was a white woman and a white child standing behind her. And after a second look, I saw that the woman only appeared thin because of her height. She was, in my estimation, at least seven months pregnant, and the way she rubbed her back and winced, I suspected she might be in labor.

"Ludi, what's going on? Are these ladies your friends? Do you need a doctor?"

"No, ma'am. I's hopin' you could put them up in one of your units. I know you's getting pretty full up, but..." She gave a long look at her companions. "It's like this. They was in an accident in the rain. Their car skidded into the crik near as I can tell off Mason Road. The momma, here, she weren't making no more sense than a hoot owl in Hades when they wandered up in Zion last night."

The woman stepped forward. "I'm feeling worlds better now. My headache's nearly gone, and I think the walk is what made my back start acting up. I'd be so grateful to have a place to rest so I can figure out tomorrow how to get my car."

"I do have one vacancy. Number one—right here close to the office. Are you sure you don't need a doctor? I'm not equipped for delivering babies."

She smiled, the glow of pregnancy adding interest to her delicate features. "Rest is all I need. My little girl's as tired as I am, so we just want a good night's sleep."

Ludi's head bobbed back and forth following the conversation, and when I agreed to show the woman the room, she was nodding with practically her whole body. She took the child—Bonnie, her mother called her—by the hand and hollered over her shoulder. "I'll show them the room while you do the book work. Do you want me to fetch my keys in the washhouse or be waiting for you to bring the key?"

"I'll be right along, Ludi, with the key."

I checked on the girls, grabbed the key and the registration book from the lobby, and headed to cottage one. Fireflies, the first I'd seen at the Stardust, flitted from one Indian hawthorne to the next along the walk, filling me with a buzzy glow. All my cottages were full—just like my dream, and I couldn't wait to throw the *No Vacancy* switch on the Stardust sign. In the neon blur, the cottages stood, and at the far end, Peter's silhouette as he sat with his guitar on the steps. Soft strains of "Swing Low, Sweet Chariot" came through the shadows, and by the time I got to the cottage where Ludi waited, she'd joined in with humming, the sound from her throat thick as blackstrap molasses.

The woman thanked Ludi for helping her, assured both of us she didn't need a doctor. She then gave me cash for one night's lodging and signed the guest book. Ludi checked to make sure there were towels, and we left the mom and her daughter to get some rest.

On the way to the washhouse, Ludi was still twisting her apron in her hands. "Shore do 'preciate your helping, Miz Georgie. Tell you somethin'... a white woman and her child ain't got no business in Zion. Worried me plumb silly somethin' gon' happen to her and the authorities be making trouble for Zion."

"Why would they do that? You were being a Good Samaritan."

"White folk got different ways to make trouble for colored peoples. Not ones like you and Mr. Peter, but some of them from your crawdad party the other night, they might get a stitch in their britches if'n somethin' happened over to Zion."

"Are you worried something might happen to the woman? Or her child? Is there something you're not telling me?"

"No, ma'am, I just ain't never seen no one holdin' their head and rockin' back and forth and moanin' forty ways to nothin' like she was. Me and my sister talked it out, and we was fixin' to make a litter to carry the poor thing up here so you could fetch a doctor. Then the Lord Almighty answered our prayers, and she took a turn for the better. Here we be. You want me to sleep here in the washhouse and keep an eye on her?"

"Gracious, no. You go home. I'll check on her later. You've already done more than most people would have. She'll be fine, I'm sure."

She shuffled off toward Zion. A glance toward the newcomers' cottage assured me they'd already gone to bed. Uneasy, but satisfied all was well, I went in the back door.

"Hey, girls. Get your jammies on while I put these things in the office, and I'll come read you a story."

Rosey followed me into the office instead, telling me Avril was learning her ABC's and tomorrow they were going to play school again. "And maybe we can get that new girl to play, too."

"What new girl?" I threw the *No Vacancy* switch and changed the sign in the front window.

"The one who just came. She looked lonely. And scared. I think she needs a friend. And maybe to learn her colors or her shapes. I'll be the best teacher."

"Oh, I'm sure you will, but you can only play with the guests if their parents agree. They'll probably be leaving tomorrow, but if not, you can see if she wants to play."

"What are their names?"

"I'm not sure. I think the girl is Bonnie. But I didn't catch the mom's name." I put the money in the locked drawer and opened the guest register. "Here, let's see. Her name is...oh. Oh."

My head swirled, and I tried to clear my throat, but I couldn't utter another sound. Words wouldn't form in my mouth. When I tried to swallow, my throat was frozen.

And no matter what, I could not tell my daughter the woman staying in cottage one was Fiona Callahan—the woman who stole her daddy.

CHAPTER 23

M ommy? What's wrong?" Her small, determined hand clamped my wrist.

I gulped down a bitter taste and willed myself to respond to my daughter. "Well, nothing a scoop of ice cream won't fix. Let's see if we've still got some Neapolitan in the icebox freezer."

"You didn't tell me the lady's name."

"Her name's Fiona. Now, about that ice cream. Which one do you want?"

"Strawberry. And chocolate."

"You got it." I slammed the guest register closed and let a final shudder work its way out of my shoulders. What was Fiona Callahan doing in Mayhaw? I hoped she didn't start asking questions and that her showing up was entirely happenstance.

After our ice cream and reading *The Bobbsey Twins at the Seashore* to the girls, I tucked them in and took a stroll around the front of the cottages, to clear my head more than anything. The scent of pine and damp earth mixed with the occasional whiff of petunia wrapped its arms around me as I walked along the gravel path. Nearing Peter's cottage, I slowed, hoping he might still be playing the guitar. Instead, an owl hooted high in the sycamores behind the Stardust, leaving the *who, who* dangling like the questions I had about Fiona.

Why had she come? What did she know of me? Or the girls? Did she even know O'Dell had died?

Other thoughts galloped in, unbidden. Whose baby grew in her swollen belly? Was it even the same Fiona Callahan? For certain, if it was O'Dell's mistress, she was nothing like I expected. Not a ravishing beauty with painted lips. In fact, she had a waif-like quality, an innocent beauty, and even I was drawn to her porcelain perfection, flaxen hair, slim fingers that trembled as she stroked her abdomen and laced fingers with her child.

Poor O'Dell didn't have a ghost of a chance resisting her. Or maybe it was the other way around and he'd pursued her. The fire in my belly that had started the minute I read Fiona's name in the guest register now roared, licking its lips. I thought I'd put O'Dell's transgression out of my mind. Obviously not.

I kicked at the gravel, only vaguely aware that a yellow light had appeared in my side vision. Peter stuck his head out his door. "Georgia, is that you? Everything all right?"

Sebastian darted toward me, giving me a welcome lick on the hand.

"Perfect. Getting some fresh air."

Three long strides and Peter was by my side. "Busy day?"

"Yep." I squinted my eyes, sure I'd seen a light flicker in the cottage Fiona and her daughter occupied.

"Something wrong? You seem upset."

"Thinking, that's all. Actually, I'm glad you came out. Did I ever tell you I sit on the steps every night listening to you strumming your guitar?" Peter stood close enough that I could smell the shower soap on his skin. I forced myself not to look at Fiona's cottage and focused on Peter instead, who grinned cockeyed.

"You do? Why haven't you said something?"

"I'm not sure. Maybe because the songs you play seem personal, like they're meant for someone else." In the time since he'd been back, I'd noticed changes in him. Reluctance to talk about his buddy who died. A furrow between his brows that hadn't been there before. A wounded look, and yet at times he seemed fine. The way he stood behind me, his breath on my neck when we'd had the lighting of the Stardust sign. Our plans for a picnic area.

"Music *is* personal. You can take the same song and ask four people to play it, and they'll each have their own sound. Play a different lick at the end or change the rhythm."

"Where'd you learn to play?"

"I can't recall. My pappy played banjo and fiddle, and I can ham around on those, but I got my first guitar when I was ten or twelve. I hear you sing a pretty little song yourself."

"Where'd you hear that?"

"Rosey told me you sing every year in the local talent show. That sometimes you win a ribbon."

"I'm not all that good."

"Someday I'd like to be the judge of that myself."

"The talent show's not until the Mayhaw Festival in July."

"I can't wait."

A disturbance at the far end of the cottages stole our attention. A human cry. Sebastian waved his tail, weaving nervously between our legs. The door to Fiona's cottage burst open, and the child, Bonnie, ran out. "Help! My momma fell over. Somebody please help!"

From inside the room came an agonizing scream. Cottage doors popped open, and guests from the Stardust streamed out. Peter and I raced to the room, and with each pounding step, I felt my legs carrying me to the brink of disaster, hurtling me into something that was going to change the course of our lives forever.

And while I'm no prophet, my intuitions that night were dead-on.

CHAPTER 24

Fiona lay curled in a ball on the floor, her head tilted back and out of sync with the rest of her body. Moans echoed from the walls of the cottage. Bonnie, round-eyed and lips trembling, stood tugging on her mother's arm.

Peter scooped Bonnie into his arms, his voice gentle. "Come on, sugar. Let me sit you over here." He deposited her in a chair, then leaned over Fiona. "Tell me where you're hurt."

Oblivious to his question and those who'd gathered, the guttural sounds continued, neither more nor less as Peter touched her arm, her back, her legs. When he tried to move her head, though, a high-pitched scream pierced the air. "Georgia, call the ambulance. I'm afraid to move her, and she's burning up with fever. Was she ill when you checked her in?"

I told him what Ludi had said, about Fiona's accident in the rain and that she had a headache. "Do you think she could be in labor? Is the baby in danger?"

"I have no way of knowing, but it doesn't seem to be the baby. Do you know her name?"

I told him, her name like a cancer on my tongue. Then I raced to the office and called the operator, requested the ambulance.

In the doorway to the quarters, Rosey stood, rubbing her eyes. "I had a scary dream. People were screaming."

"I don't think it was a dream, sugar. One of our guests has fallen. That's what you heard. I've called the ambulance. Now I want you to be brave and stay here in the office and watch Avril. You can look out the window, but *do not,* under any circumstances, come outside. It's dark, and there are a lot of people out there. I'll see if MeMaw can come over and stay with you. Do you understand me?"

"Yes, Mommy. Why are you shaking?"

"Because the lady is very sick and needs to go to the hospital. I'm worried, but I have to go now."

A half-dozen people milled around outside, including Mary Frances. I ran to her, gave her a brief rundown of what happened, and asked her to sit with the girls and listen for the phone.

Fiona remained on the floor when I went into the cottage, Peter and Mr. Overstreet kneeling beside her, two or three others hovering nearby. Her face was waxy pale except for flaming circles on her cheeks, which I attributed to the fever.

I wet a washcloth and knelt beside her. "Fiona, it's going to be all right. Help is on the way, and we'll take care of your little girl. Is there someone I can call?"

No response, only jerky, trembly movements with the groaning. The man with the doorknob ears stood a few feet away, arms crossed. "Betcha anything she's got the polio."

His wife argued that it looked like an epileptic fit.

Someone else scoffed. "It wouldn't surprise me none if she got drunk and fell down."

I glared at the man who'd spoken. "Excuse me, but I'm sure that's not the case. She wasn't feeling well earlier in the day."

Mr. Overstreet was the only one who remained calm. He felt

her pulse, took a small flashlight from his pocket, and shone it in her eyes.

Doorknob Ears said, "You mean to tell me you let sick people check in here with all the talk on the radio about the outbreak of polio? If I'd known, we'd have been happy to find another place to stay."

Peter looked up. "That's enough from all of you. If you're not going to be of some help here, please stand outside. Georgia didn't do anything intentional, and for you to be supposing this and that when we don't know what's wrong is a waste of time."

The air in the room felt lighter when the gawkers left, but the insinuations remained an unspoken whisper in the room. *Polio. Infantile paralysis.*

The cloth in my hand had already turned warm from the few moments I held it on Fiona's forehead. Peter offered to rewet it while I continued to kneel. "Fiona, please listen to me. You have a fever. We need to let your family know you're sick, that you need them. I can call them for you if you tell me their names or where they live."

Nothing.

And in the next instant, the wail of the ambulance and its swirling colors were upon us. Sheriff Sonny Bolander entered the cottage first, which threw me off momentarily, until I realized I couldn't remember if I'd told the operator it was a medical emergency and not a wreck or some such. Behind Sonny were Les and Victor, the same two who'd hauled Mary Frances to the hospital the night of the fire. They tried to elicit the same information from Fiona as we had, with the same measure of success. Her moans had turned to whimpers, and from the spot where Peter, who now held Bonnie in his arms, and I huddled against the wall, it appeared to me Fiona might be losing consciousness.

Oh, dear God, reach down and rescue us from this terrible situation.

My silent prayers, though, seemed as frail as Fiona Callahan strapped to the stretcher, and as they wheeled her away, I wondered if that was the last I'd see of her. Death seemed but a heartbeat away, and its snare twisted inside me, a double-pronged hook like the knot I already had for O'Dell. A part of me wished her gone from my life forever. Another part wept for this poor woman and Bonnie, who watched as her mother was lifted into the ambulance, perhaps never to return.

Sheriff Bolander broke the muddle of my thoughts. "Georgia, you will need to go to the hospital to provide information since you were the last person to talk with her before she became ill."

"I'm sure I have nothing to add. I would prefer for you take her information—" I scanned the room, hoping to find a handbag, and was relieved when I spotted a shoulder bag with mud caked on it sitting on the nightstand. I grabbed it. "Here, take this. She and the child didn't have any luggage as they abandoned their car when it got stuck in the mud. She was hoping to get a good night's sleep, see about the car, and then be on her way. Surely any information you need is in there."

He eyed me. "Something is fishy about this whole deal. Your aunt Cora was right. You ain't got no business running a blasted inn out here on the highway. For all you know, this woman is a fugitive runnin' from the law, and you're caught in the crosshairs. Where's her car?"

Peter stepped forward. "Pardon the interruption, but Georgia only did what any decent human being would've done under the circumstances. I'm sure you'd have done the same in a similar situation. I'd be happy to go with you to the hospital to be of whatever service I can. This woman's current illness should be the priority here."

Bonnie's long legs wrapped around Peter's waist, her arms around his neck. She hadn't spoken since her first cry for help. I held out my arms to her. "Would you like to come with me? I can get you a cookie and a glass of milk while these men and the doctors take care of your mommy."

She eyed the sheriff and Peter, then let me take her. "I want my momma."

"I know you do, sugar, but she needs to be in the hospital tonight."

Sheriff Bolander frowned. "Maybe she should come with me. If the momma can't talk, this child might be the only source of information we got."

"I hardly think the hospital is the place for a child. If she says anything to me, I'll let you know."

"I'll have to notify the authorities if something happens to the momma and we got an orphan on our hands."

"What a horrible thing to say. Go on. You and Peter, go to the hospital. And please call when you find out how Mrs. Callahan is." I marched past them, carrying Bonnie. "Let's go, sugar, and get you a snack."

Mr. Overstreet offered to see Mary Frances home after I gave her a brief rundown. I didn't want to alarm Bonnie by saying too much; the poor child was already terrified. And it was certainly not the time to tell Mary Frances that the woman who'd become ill was her dead son's mistress.

*

A gentle knock came at the door during the night.

Peter poked his head in when I said, "Come in." Bonnie slept curled in my lap, her thin fingers entwined in a lock of my hair.

Her soft, even breaths held a scent of sweet milk, her tangled hair as pale as a dandelion puff, her dress wrinkled and spattered with mud.

Peter lifted her gently from my arms and followed me into the quarters, where I turned back the covers on my bed. He eased her into bed, felt her forehead with the back of his hand. A simple action, yet tender. Worried, perhaps, that she might be carrying the same thing as Fiona. I bit my lip, not mentioning it as the two of us returned to the office.

I willed myself to remain calm, hoping the hammering of my heart wouldn't be apparent to Peter. "How was Fiona? Any idea what's wrong?"

"It's bad news, I'm afraid."

I gripped the counter. "How bad? She's still alive, isn't she?"

"Alive, but gravely ill. Polio. Doc Kelley did the spinal test to make sure. She's delirious, barely able to breathe. They're sending her to Tyler, which is the nearest hospital with an iron lung."

"Oh, my." The room swirled like my stomach. "I think I need to sit down." I backed up and sank into the rocker where I'd held Fiona's unsuspecting, innocent child.

"Sheriff asked if you would mind keeping the girl until he finds her kinfolk."

"Of course. So he found information in her handbag?"

Peter pulled over a straight-backed chair, the only other seat in the office, swung it around, and straddled it with his arms resting on the back. "Not much. There was an Arkansas driver's license, but it expired a couple of years back, and it only had a box number. I forget what town. He said he'd start checking in the morning."

"Arkansas? Are you sure?" Could there be two Fiona Callahans? O'Dell might've been secretive about his meanderings, but I was nearly certain he hadn't ventured all the way to Arkansas.

"That's what was on the license. Perhaps she was traveling

when she slid off the muddy road. I'll see if Ludi can tell me more tomorrow."

"We need to find her family. The poor child's scared to death."

"The sheriff found a couple other items in the purse." He shifted his weight and took a deep breath. "A set of dog tags and a couple of photos."

"Dog tags, as in military?"

"U.S. Army. The sheriff will run a check on them. One of the photos was of a man in fatigues—also army, not a good-quality photo. Looked an awful lot like some of the ones I sent my folks when I was in Korea. I'm guessing it could be her husband. Course it could be a brother since there was a more recent photo with a man holding Bonnie, and it looked like Fiona was pregnant."

The room spun faster. The photo would tell the story, but even with the thread of hope that this was not O'Dell's Fiona, I knew in my gut it was. I closed my eyes and swallowed.

"Georgia, are you all right? You've turned a little green around the gills."

"I'm tired, but to answer your question, no, I'm not all right. Not even close. I'm scared."

"Everyone is. The doctor said it's the first case here in town. I thought he was anxious to get her placed somewhere else. And it's not good news for the Stardust."

"What do you mean?"

"Any public places where polio victims have been come under scrutiny. I'm not trying to alarm you, but your sheriff said he would be conducting a full investigation."

"You don't think he would close the Stardust?" My anger toward O'Dell and fear for Fiona now turned into a cloud of doom.

"I've no way of knowing. But he will alert the Department of Health."

"What a mess."

"There's no use worrying tonight. Why don't you get some sleep?"

My limbs felt as heavy as concrete blocks, and carrying around the knowledge that I was connected to Fiona in a bizarre turn of events only added to the weight. The urge to blurt it all out to Peter surfaced, like somehow it would ease the burden.

Trust him. Keeping the truth about O'Dell and Fiona would serve no useful purpose. Even Mary Frances needed to know. Perhaps if I had Peter to lean on, telling her would be easier.

Peter rose from the chair and offered a hand to help me up. "Tomorrow will be better."

Taking his hand, I rose. "I'm not so sure. There's something I haven't told you, and I'm not sure I should even do so..."

"About what?"

"Fiona Callahan."

"Did she tell you something?"

"No. I'm not sure it has any bearing, but I'm nearly certain she came to Musgrave County on purpose."

"How could you know that? Did you know her?"

I nodded. "Of her. My life has been a tangled mess for quite some time. You came onto the scene when I thought things might be headed the other way, that somehow I would get the threads straightened out."

"You lost me there. What could this possibly have to do with this stranger who checked in to the Stardust?"

Bracing myself, I looked into Peter's questioning eyes. "Fiona Callahan had an affair with my husband. He'd already left me and the girls when Catfish found his body in the swamps near Zion. I think she came to find O'Dell."

His eyes widened. "Sweet mother of pearl. You've been carrying this around not telling anyone?"

"My aunt Cora and Sally knew why O'Dell left me. The whole town's known for ages O'Dell was a womanizer. I kept hoping..."

"I am so sorry. I thought your reluctance to talk about your husband was due to grief."

"Grief comes in many colors. What O'Dell did to me is over and done with. But now..."

"You can't change the past."

I laughed. "You sound like Aunt Cora. I'm sorry to bother you with all of this; I thought it would be easier if I told someone."

Peter stepped toward me, hands on my shoulders. "Until this moment, I didn't know why God brought me to the Stardust. Now I know. I'm as dense as a fence post, evidently."

"Now I don't follow what you mean."

"I'm nothing but a drifter. I figgered you knew that when you hired me. That I'd be here and gone before you could whistle Dixie. What I didn't plan on was getting attached to this place. And you."

My eyes burned with tears or weariness, I wasn't sure which, but either way, I couldn't grasp what he was saying. He felt sorry for me after what I'd confided in him. Pure and simple. After a good night's sleep he would realize he'd made a mistake, might even decide that staying here was unhealthy. I bent my head so I couldn't see his face, but he tilted my chin with his fingers.

"Georgia, sometimes you have to lay out a claim, drive a stake, and put your life on the line no matter what. I have a feeling you've done that here at the Stardust. Took a risk and worked for something you cared about."

"A lot of good it did me."

"I doubt you'll let one setback stop you." His eyes clouded, as if he wasn't sure what to say next.

Goose bumps skittered down my arms, but I kept my gaze on him. "Just because you're from Georgia doesn't mean you have to slow dance around what you're trying to say."

His hands cradled my face and neck, his breath warm and close. "I want to get to know you better, help you out with this crisis. You've been hurt, but I realized something in San Antonio. Life is short. Too short to spend it drifting around the country. I'd like to drive my stake in Mayhaw. Get a job, put down some roots, and see what happens."

He kissed the tip of my nose, then drew me into his arms and held me.

When he kissed the top of my head, the hot tears I'd held at bay slid down my cheeks. My arms slid around his waist, and I told myself to be careful, that getting attached was dangerous, and love might be lethal.

Don't get too close.

People leave.

My heart, though, didn't get the message.

CHAPTER 25

W hile wrapped in Peter's arms, I remembered O'Dell's journal with his sales list. I hadn't wanted to know at the time who the other woman was, but now I needed to learn more so I could get Bonnie reunited with her family. It was also a good excuse to get away from Peter before I got caught up in something I would later regret.

Peter waited while I went into the quarters to retrieve O'Dell's briefcase. We found Fiona's name with *Kilgore* written beside it, but no street address. It wasn't much, but Peter offered to relay the information.

The earlier moment of tenderness fled, and I was glad of it. Concentrating on Bonnie took priority, and with luck, she would soon be on her way. Hopefully, people would forget that the Stardust had birthed Mayhaw's first case of polio. I prayed it was the only one.

Morning came way too soon, and I felt disoriented when Rosey shook me awake from where I'd slept on the divan. "Morning, Momma. Time to get up." Three jam-covered smiles hovered over me.

"Morning to you, too. I see you've met Bonnie. And made breakfast, too."

"I toasted the bread, but Bonnie spread on the butter and jelly. Is Bonnie staying here now?"

A fleeting memory pinched my stomach. Something in one of the brochures Aunt Cora had given me on infantile paralysis. *The infection can spread through any hand-to-mouth contact. Thorough hand washing is imperative.*

Jelly smudges on the girls' fingers and chins. I'd seen how my girls spread jelly on toast before, licking their fingers and the spoon. A vision of millions of polio germs being licked and spread and swallowed made me want to throw up. I leapt from the divan and herded the girls to the kitchen sink.

"Let's get your hands and faces washed." With water as hot as I dared, I lathered soap on each girl's hands in turn and held them under the faucet, willing whatever germs might have lingered down the drain. Separate washcloths for their faces. Then I marched them into the living room and told them to sit.

"Girls, I know we've talked about this before, but I'm going to tell you something *very* important. You cannot drink after each other. You may not use the same forks or spoons. You know you have to wash your hands when you go to the bathroom, but now it's more important than ever."

Rosey bounced on the divan, a sassy look on her face. "I know all this. We did the germ rules every day at school."

"Good. I'm glad you know them. You can help Avril and Bonnie remember. It's very important."

"You said that. Can we go outside and play?"

"We need to help Bonnie with a bath and see if she can wear one of the dresses you've outgrown. We want her to look nice when her family comes to get her."

Bonnie, who sat with her hands between her legs, looked at me, her lower lip trembling. "When's my momma coming back?"

I knelt before her. "Bonnie, your momma is sick and has to stay in the hospital for a while. I know you're sad and scared, but someone will come for you soon."

Her chin jutted up, a steely look in her eyes. "She's not coming back."

"I'm sure she will, but it might take awhile."

Rosey put her arm around Bonnie. "My daddy left, and when he came back, they put him in a hole in the ground."

"Rosey, that's not what Bonnie needs to hear."

Bonnie chewed on a fingernail. "My daddy got put in a box and sticked in a hole, too."

Avril, who had been quiet, tugged on my arm. "I want to go outside and play with Sebastian. Please."

I nodded. "That's a splendid idea. Rosey, go out with your sister and remember to stay in the back."

After putting Bonnie in the tub, I threw on my own clothes, then ventured to the bathroom to get more information from her. "I'm sorry about your daddy. I bet your momma is thinking about him and you, too, right this minute. Was that what you were doing when your car went in the mud? Coming back from your daddy's funeral?" It might be the Arkansas connection. Perhaps they'd once lived there and moved to Texas.

"That was a long time ago. When I was three. I'm four and a half now."

"I bet your grandma and grandpa were sad, too."

She shrugged and clapped the bubbles between her hands. "Aunt Teddy was there. She smelled like Christmas."

"Was your uncle there, too?"

Bonnie scowled. "I was sad. He gave me candy."

An aunt who smelled like Christmas and an uncle who was sensitive to a child would surely want to provide a home for Bonnie. "Where do your aunt and uncle live?"

She made an O with her mouth. "O Sarks."

"Arkansas, then?"

"Don't know. Can I have a pink dress? Momma says pink is my best color."

"You and Avril are going to get along fine. Pink is her best color, too. And I think I know the perfect dress for you. Come on, let me shampoo your hair and get you dolled up."

"What's your name, lady?"

"I guess I've not told you that, have I? I'm Georgia Peyton, but you can call me Georgia."

"Georgie, can we go see my momma?"

"Maybe before too long. We'll see."

After combing the tangles from her hair and putting on the pink gingham dress Rosey had worn two Easters ago, I sent her out to play. As fine as Bonnie's hair was, it would be dry after ten minutes in the sunshine.

When I unlocked the office door, I didn't see Peter's Studebaker in its usual spot and trusted he'd gone to see the sheriff about locating Bonnie's relatives. But I did see two gentlemen marching toward me. If their expressions were any indication, they were not happy patrons.

The man with big ears stomped into the office first and shoved the key in my hand. "My family and I are leaving. I just went to the donut shop for coffee and the woman you let stay here is the talk of all downtown. She's got the polio. I knew it all along. So help me—"

The other gentleman, pock-faced and quite pleasant when he checked in, slapped his hand on the counter. "I want a refund. My wife is on the verge of a nervous breakdown after last night. She's suffering with a migraine right now, and our vacation is ruined." His nostrils flared, and I half expected smoke to pour from them.

I pasted on a smile. "Refunds are made only if you're unable to complete your stay. You were paid up through last night, so I think we're even."

"Even, you say? I'll get even if my wife or one of our kids comes down with polio." He looked at the other man. "I heard the same thing you did, only over at the tire shop when I went to get a quart of oil for my car."

They both glared at me, waiting.

"I'm sorry about your wife. You might take her to have her headache checked. You can find Doc Kelley's office—"

"We're not spending another minute in this town."

"Headache is one of the symptoms of infantile paralysis. Does your wife have a stiff neck or trouble touching her chin to her chest?"

"Excuse me. I thought you were an innkeeper, not a doctor."

"I'm sorry. Just trying to help. I wish both of you well. I'm distressed myself about what happened last night. I truly didn't know. I can take your keys, and please, if you're passing through again, I hope you'll consider staying at the Stardust."

The man with the bad complexion fished the key from his pocket and handed it over. "In your dreams, lady. You'll be lucky if you don't get sued or shut down."

I watched them go, sad because they spoke the truth, but also feeling I should shake it off. There would be more customers. And hopefully no other unpleasant incidents.

A few minutes later, Ludi trudged in, her eyes round. "I seen the child I brung over outside, but no one answers the door at the cottage. I thought it best to check with you before I barge in and see how she be."

"Ludi, I'm sorry. She was sicker than we thought. I had to call the ambulance."

Ludi fanned herself with her hand. "Lordamercy. I'm sorry I got you in this mess. What she got?"

"Doc Kelley says it's polio. They've sent her on to Tyler. I'm waiting for Peter to get back now to see if he's found out anything more."

"Mercy, mercy. My man say he'll look for her car. Can't be far away since she walked on up to Zion. It's a mystery, that one. And the poor child. What's to be done with her? And us? You ever think it might be one of our own gets the crippler next?"

Ludi gave wings to the fear riding low in my gut, but I refused to think about it. I explained that I was keeping Bonnie and told Ludi to leave Fiona's room as it was until I heard from the sheriff. "We want to do whatever we need to meet their regulations and see if they can tell anything from the room. I have my doubts…" Cooperation might make the difference between getting a quarantine slapped on us or not.

"What you be needing me for?"

"Several of our tenants have already left. Scared off, I think. There'll be their rooms to clean." I gave her the numbers.

"I sho'nuf never expected this."

"It's all right, Ludi. We'll make it through. We'll keep busy and things'll work out."

What worked out, though, was that the *Mayhaw Messenger* ran the story of Fiona Callahan on the front page of the Sunday edition, which arrived at five o'clock on Saturday afternoon. Word spread like a brush fire. All of the guests fled except for Mr. Overstreet, who dropped by on Sunday afternoon to see about his account.

"I've seen a lot in the thirty years I been coming to the Stardust. Not letting this scare me away."

"I appreciate it. If there's anything you need, please let me know."

"I like what you've done with the place. I was speaking with the young man from Georgia. He mentioned having a new barbecue pit out back. Maybe you and the rest of the regulars here could join me in a fish fry?"

"Don't you want to take home the fish you're catching?"

"Nobody to take 'em home to. My wife passed a couple years ago. Sure do enjoy fishing, though. Doreen used to fry up what I caught while Paddy and I told each other lies. Sure miss seeing them."

"Me, too. And I'd love to have a cookout. How about tomorrow evening? Will you still be here?"

"I've been thinking of extending my stay another couple of weeks, maybe longer. Like I said, there's no one to go home to."

It was settled. He and Peter would manage the outdoor cooking, and I would make a couple of side dishes and bring the ice cream. At least it gave me something to think of besides all the empty rooms and Fiona's tragedy.

I called Aunt Cora that afternoon, too, and after listening to her tell me I'd brought this on myself, I got in a word edgewise.

"Aunt Cora, I know what you're saying has some truth in it. I accept that, so please, let it rest so I can tell you why I'm calling."

"I'm listening."

"The woman with polio is the same woman O'Dell left me for. I don't know how this bizarre incident happened, but it's not important. What's important is that she already had a child when she met O'Dell. I believe her husband died, possibly as a soldier. The sheriff is trying to locate that information. What I want is to find the child's family so she can be reunited with them. I was hoping the March of Dimes might help."

"I suppose I could put my personal feelings aside to do that. Of course, I'm going to be busy helping to calm the fears of the people of Mayhaw. I can feel the hysteria gaining momentum, and I'm worried sick about Rosey and Avril."

"Thank you. I'm concerned about the girls, too, but they've already been exposed by being around Bonnie. We can only hope and pray Bonnie's not a carrier or a victim herself. She's a sweet girl, one who I'm sure a relative would welcome."

"So tell me what information you already have."

I gave her the scant details and thanked her. We both promised to call if there were any changes. There was nothing to do then but wait.

With all the waiting I'd done over the years, nothing compared to the fear that crawled under my skin, more oppressive than the heat that shadowed our town and crept into my dreams.

This time I wasn't waiting for someone to return, though, but praying that polio wouldn't.

CHAPTER 26

On Monday, I needed groceries for the fish fry, so I called Sally to see if we could come by on our way to Brookshire's.

"I'd love to see you, Georgia, but I'll have to pass this time. I'm on my way to the beauty shop."

"Okay. I just had a free moment and thought we'd get the kids together while we chatted."

"I don't think that's a good idea. I'm keeping my kids inside. Hud thinks it's best now that...well, you know everyone's worried, and you...you especially know that with what all's happened."

"It's okay, Sally, you don't have to explain. We'll get together some other time." *Like next winter.*

"I'm really sorry. The Magnolias think it might be best if we don't come out and do the usual maintenance that we do on our projects. Weeding, watering, et cetera."

"No problem. I think I can handle it. You've done a lot, and I appreciate it."

They didn't owe me, and yet it felt like a snub. I shook it off and hollered at the girls to get in the car.

The aisles of Brookshire's played out in a similar fashion. People who knew me waved, then turned their grocery buggies around like they'd forgotten something in the cheese section. I told the girls to stay close and not touch anything as I zipped along, trying to get out as soon as possible.

Hazel Morton hollered from one end of the baking aisle. "Georgia, thought you'd like to know my grandson, Joey, got a job mowing lawns."

"Glad to hear it."

She cupped her hand around her mouth like a megaphone. "Sure am glad it didn't work out with you hiring him since you got the polio out there at the Stardust."

I winced and sped up so we could speak in normal tones, but she put her buggy in overdrive and whisked around the corner.

Shake it off. I knew it wasn't personal, that fear now pulled the strings of all our lives. I put an extra carton of Neapolitan ice cream in the cart and went to the checkout. Rosey saw a boy from her class—Stewie French. She ran over to him, but when Mrs. French saw her coming, she practically yanked Stewie's arm out of the socket getting away.

Rosey turned to me, tears brimming in her eyes. "Momma, why'd she do that?"

"I think she must be in a hurry. And it's time we got out of here, too. We don't want our ice cream to melt."

The Stardust felt like a haven when we returned. I gulped in a big breath and sent the girls to find Ludi while I carried in the groceries. When Ludi came to the back door, I invited her and her children to stay for the fish fry.

"Miz Georgie, you think that be a good idea? You know how people talk."

"You know, Ludi, I don't care what people think. Y'all are like family. The girls adore Merciful, and Peter gets a kick out of

Catfish and his stories. Besides, I bought your favorite Neapolitan ice cream."

"You shore do know my weakness. If'n it's all right with you, I'll go on over to Zion when I be done here and check on my momma, but we'll be back. Yes'm. For ice cream, Ludi will come back."

Peter helped Mr. Overstreet with the fire while Catfish whittled on a cypress knee—a rounded piece of wood from the bayou. I'd grown up seeing the protrusions clumped at the edges of the water in proximity to the towering, moss-cloaked mother trees. When I was a child lying in bed with the windows open, I would imagine the sounds coming from the bayou were the knees telling each other stories. The smooth, twisted roots did indeed look like miniature bald-headed people, and Catfish had a real knack for carving them into lifelike creatures.

He'd carved a couple of smaller ones, eight or ten inches long and slim enough to hold in his palm, and presented them to the girls: a frowning catfish for Avril and a warty frog with webbed toes for Bonnie. His long fingers held the small knife expertly as he shaved tiny curls away, working on a "special" one for Rosey.

Mary Frances was in a good mood, puffing her Pall Malls, feet up on the chaise lounge we'd brought from her cottage. Her face glowed, and I was glad I'd not told her that Fiona had been O'Dell's lover. The evening was too perfect to throw a damper on it.

When the men declared we'd be eating soon, Ludi and I got the cold dishes from the kitchen. We spread quilts and blankets on the ground and ate out of tin pie plates, having a real picnic. Malcolm Overstreet, wearing bib overalls and Old Spice, took his plate piled high with food and sat on the grass beside Mary Frances.

"So tell me, Mrs. Peyton…is that what you want me to call you?" The slanting afternoon sun glinted off his hair, giving it a russet look. In spite of the gray fringes, he was still a handsome man.

"Oh, please, Malcolm, call me Mary Frances." A bit of color flushed her cheeks, and inside I smiled as Mr. Overstreet asked her what brought her to the Stardust. I didn't want to eavesdrop so I gathered the girls and seated them on a quilt and brought them plates.

Peter set the cooking utensils aside and stoked the fire. "We'll have marshmallows later if you remembered to buy some."

"I sure did. Come on now, get some supper."

"As you wish." He sat cross-legged, Catfish on one side assuming the exact same posture as Peter and Sebastian on the other, head between his paws, tail swooshing.

Ludi groaned and let her body down. "Y'all are going to have to get a rope and pull me if'n I cain't get up."

Her children snickered, but I turned to Catfish. "I saw you whittling a while ago. How do you pick which cypress knees to carve?"

"It's easy. I only pick the ones what done broke off under the water. My daddy told me it's a sin to break one off."

"Really? Why's that?"

"The knees that's attached be connectin' one cypress tree to the next and the next. That's how the trees get their air and feed. Cuttin' one off is the same as a person cuttin' off his arm where he cain't be feedin' hisself."

"I've always seen the knees, but I figured they were part of the root system."

"My daddy say cypress knees is like people. We's all connected someway or another. 'Cuz you be here right now don't mean you ain't connected to someone down the bayou."

Ludi nodded the whole time her son talked. She winked at me. "Catfish ain't got much book learnin', but he's a smart one, that be a fact."

"And an artist, too, from what I've seen."

Catfish wiggled his bottom, sitting up taller. "My daddy taught me how to use a knife, but he don't know nothin' about how to make somethin' purty."

"You do have a gift."

He ran his fingers over the cypress knee in his hand, making an adjustment or two, and presented it to Rosey.

Her eyes grew round. "What is it?"

Catfish lowered his head, his voice barely a whisper. "It's a mermaid."

She held it in her palm, her fingers tracing its delicate lines. It wasn't a fish or another critter from the bayou, but a perfect likeness of Rosey's face. Swirls were carved in imitation of her hair, and near the bottom, the natural twist in the wood made a perfect mermaid's tail.

A grin broke out on her face. "How'd you make it look like me?"

"That's what comes from down here." He pointed to his chest.

She passed it around for everyone to see. Mary Frances shook her head. "No doubt about it, Catfish is a genius."

Fireflies began their evening dance in the pale indigo that had fallen. I leaned back and stretched. "Anyone ready for ice cream?"

Peter popped up. "I'll help you."

After fetching the bowls and Neapolitan from the quarters, I dished it up from a small serving table and surveyed our gathering. Like the quilts where we sat, we were a patchwork bunch. Different in a dozen ways and yet connected. Like cypress knees.

Peter went to fetch his guitar, and as he strummed, he looked at Ludi. "Sing along, okay?"

He played a short lead-in to "Swing Low, Sweet Chariot." Ludi hummed the first line, warming up, then in a rich, mellow voice sang the next line, then a verse. She motioned for us to join in the chorus. Merciful had a childlike version of her mother's warm, clear voice when we sang "I've Been Working on the Railroad" and then "You Are My Sunshine," which Rosey requested. While we sang, Bonnie crawled into my lap and twirled a strand of my hair around her finger. The sweetness of the melodies didn't stop the ache that crept into my heart for Bonnie. Although she didn't put into words the loneliness and fear I'm sure she felt, sadness lived in her eyes. I remembered that feeling and pulled her tight against my chest, aware that Peter was now singing alone.

Goose bumps prickled my arms and legs. His voice, deep and clear, sang an old sweet song. *Georgia. Georgia on my mind.* A lump filled my throat, and I let my tear-filled eyes wander to Catfish, who'd flipped over on his back and rubbed a cypress knee like it was a worry stone. My heart swelled as Peter's voice faded with the last strains.

Our eyes met, and silence, like a breath held, hung in the air. Stars twinkled overhead, a sliver of moon peeking through the leaves of the sycamores. The dying embers of the fire turned from orange to red like a living molten lava. A stick of wood burned thoroughly to ash broke in half, sending up a spray of red-hot sparks.

Shivers tracked the length of my spine.

CHAPTER 27

While I was catching up on my book work, Sheriff Bolander appeared at the office door, one hand twisting the knob, the other hitching up his britches.

"Georgia, you got a minute?"

"Certainly. Come in." A warning buzz started in my stomach and fanned quickly to my arms and legs. I put the books in the drawer and locked it, then turned my attention to Sonny.

Sweat beaded up on his forehead under the brim of his Stetson. *Fiona. Something's happened.* I crossed my bare arms to rub the tingles from them. "What's on your mind?"

"If I had a nickel for everything that's crossed my mind the last three days, I'd be headed to Florida to retire in luxury. We've got us a situation."

"What's that?"

"Aside from all the people you've riled in this town, there've been other developments."

"Well, tell me straight then."

"If I only knew where to start."

For a moment I felt sorry for him, that what he was fixing to tell me hurt him, too. I took a deep breath. "Is it Fiona? Is she going to be okay?"

"Last I heard she was in an iron lung, unable to breathe on her own. They put one of those holes in her throat. Tracheotomy, I think they call it. Said she couldn't swallow and was drowning in her own spit. Worse case they've seen in Tyler. So no one knows if she'll be okay or not. My guess is not. Which leads to another thing. The kid."

"Bonnie. Her name is Bonnie."

"Yeah, we might've made a connection to her relations. Them dog tags in Fiona's purse belonged to her husband, Rusty Callahan. He died three weeks after he arrived in Korea. I reckon when they sent him home, she was given the tags. The burial was in Green Oak, Arkansas. I'm waiting on a call to find out if any-one from there might take the girl in."

"Bonnie said she had an aunt Teddy. What if they can't take her? Are there other options?"

"Temporary custody in one of the church orphanages is the best bet, but I doubt they'd be too keen on taking her with the polio thing—too much risk of starting an epidemic."

He leaned against the doorjamb and swiped his free arm across his forehead. "There's one other thing…"

"I'm listening."

"We found photographs in Mrs. Callahan's purse. A soldier in one of them. And another one…"

I knew what was coming. The picture with O'Dell that con-firmed his association with Fiona. Although it still stung, there was nothing I could do so I told the sheriff Peter had told me about the snapshot. "Was the man in the photo O'Dell?"

"I'm sorry to say, but yes, it was. I didn't let on to your Peter Reese. Thought it best to check out the evidence before I broke the news to you."

"There's no need to spare my feelings. I'm coming to terms with the fact he was a lousy husband."

"So you knew about this Fiona, and you still let her stay here?"

"I didn't know her name when she checked in. She was ill, and I didn't look at the guest register until later. I recognized her name from the life insurance policy O'Dell had in his briefcase. I'm surprised you didn't find it when you investigated O'Dell's death, but it doesn't matter now. I think she probably knew he lived here and came to find out why he hadn't been to visit her."

"Sounds logical. You say she was from Kilgore, but we've not been able to locate where. They've been hit harder with polio than we have. She was probably infected when she showed up here."

"So...about Bonnie, I see no harm in her staying here for a while. Maybe you'll hear something soon."

"If you don't mind, I'd appreciate it."

"I don't mind."

"Thanks. One other thing." The sweat now ran in rivulets from his brow. Either this was some terrible news or Sonny Bolander himself was coming down with something. I let him sweat it out.

He cleared his throat. "Here's the deal. I've had a lot of calls. People are on edge. You might get some phone calls of your own, maybe even nasty letters."

My stomach felt as if I'd been punched. Heat rose to my cheeks, sweat beads forming on my own forehead. "Because of one case of polio?"

"People go nuts over things like this. Just wanted to warn you. I wouldn't expect too much business if I were you."

"Surely, in a week or two, the panic will die down and people will start to trickle in."

"The deal is, I might still have to shut you down. I have a whole town to answer to, not just a handful of misfits like you have staying here."

"Misfits? Who are you calling misfits?"

"Just saying. And I wouldn't recommend taking the Callahan girl off the premises for the time being. That's what's got most people riled."

"What do they think? She's a monster?"

"I'm sorry. But not half as sorry as you'll be if we get an outbreak here in Mayhaw, and I have to shut you down."

He tipped his hat and ambled out the door.

I clenched my fists and wanted to spit. Instead, I sank into the rocking chair, pulled my knees up to my chest, and let its back-and-forth rhythm lull me. All this work and money down the drain. Even from the grave, O'Dell and his philandering had reached out to hurt me.

While I rocked, I realized Sonny Bolander hadn't said anything about an investigation from the health department. No one had been in the cottage since they'd taken Fiona away. Was the cottage a breeding ground for disease? Ludi had the day off since we were low on guests, but I felt the urge to do something. Peter might have a suggestion, but he'd gone fishing with Mr. Overstreet, and Mary Frances slept most days until noon, so I had the day to figure it out for myself.

I checked on the girls and found Rosey delighted to have two "students" to teach. As I watched their innocent fun, the sick feeling I'd had all weekend worked its way into my throat. We were all at risk. More so with the infected cottage right under our noses. Cleaning it would at least give me the satisfaction that I'd tried. I told the girls I had work to do and got their promise to stay inside until I came back.

My arms tingled with dread as I took the key to Fiona's cottage and marched over there. Inside, the room smelled dank. *Was this the smell of polio?*

The *crippler* could be lurking right now, clinging to the walls, multiplying unseen until it wrapped its arm around one of us.

Holding my breath, I stripped the bed first and piled the covers by the door. I stepped outside and gasped, inhaling buckets of clean air. Then I went back in, tossed a throw rug and towels on top of the linens, and looked around. Washing just the linens wouldn't be enough. I eyed the pleated lamp shade. The folds were the perfect place for germs to hide. I yanked the lamp from the socket and added it to the pile. I groaned when I looked at the mattress. Fiona had lain on it, I was sure. I would worry about it later.

My muscles quivered as I threw more things on the pile. I looked over my shoulder, thinking I'd seen a shadow. *Calm down.* Outside for another fresh breath. My lack of oxygen was making me see and imagine things. But I wasn't imagining the sour spot in my stomach. The revulsion. And anger.

Polio would not get the best of me. Just because I'd let O'Dell make a fool of me with Fiona didn't mean I would give up now.

A pillow I hadn't seen in the corner mocked me. I grabbed it and threw it atop the other contaminated items.

What now? Disinfectant for sure, but I could pour a washtub full of Clorox on every surface Fiona had touched and it wouldn't be enough.

I stomped to the washhouse, my blood pumping in my ears. Would boiling kill it? Standing on the concrete floor, I eyed the shelves, hoping the answer would jump off and land at my feet. That's when I saw a box of matches. The ones we used to light the hot water pilot. I grabbed them and went to the barbecue pit. The ashes from the fish fry lay lifeless, dull below the grate.

Two or three logs and some kindling would be enough to get a fire going. In minutes, a healthy flame flared. Yes! I sprinted back to the cottage and scooped up an armload of linens. My heart pounded, but I didn't dare breathe in the germs.

Throwing everything on at once would snuff out the fire, so I dropped the pile and hurled one item at a time, waiting until it caught fire before I added the next. Ugly yellow flames devoured sheets, pillows, towels. The stench of burning goose feathers from the pillows filled the air, stinging my nostrils, smarting my eyes. Each item I threw in gave me more satisfaction. Black clouds of smoke boiled out the top of the fire pit's stonework. I held one arm over my face and used the other to slam a lamp onto the fire. It hissed and cackled as perverse pleasure rippled through me. I charged back to Fiona's cottage and ripped the curtains from the windows.

I pitched them into the fire and crossed my arms. Flames licked the fabric, which sent up a shroud of black smoke. When every last shred had been thrown in, I sat down and watched it burn. Belching noises came with the snaps. I hugged my knees to my chest and buried my face in them.

You can't hurt me anymore, O'Dell Peyton.

I coughed from the smoke and stench until tears sprang from my eyes. Bile came in my mouth. I leaned over as vomit poured out. Another fit of coughing came, and I struggled to breathe. Heat raged through my body, my skin scorched.

Shouting came from behind me. Strong hands reached under my arms and pulled me back.

"Georgia! Can you hear me?"

Peter's voice. Other voices. I closed my eyes and drifted off.

CHAPTER 28

Long coils of auburn hair fell to the floor as Ludi snipped and clipped around my head, getting rid of the singed curls. It was the final act of cleaning me up after she'd put herself in charge. She'd seen the smoke, as had Peter and Malcolm Overstreet, and had come to see what was burning. While I wasn't burned and didn't even know my hair was singed, I'd been almost delirious, coughing, filthy, a mess inside and out. She hustled me over to the washhouse, stripped off my clothes, and wrapped me in a sheet to take me to the shower in the quarters. A good scrubbing had worked wonders.

My face flamed, not with heat from the fire, but embarrassment. *What had come over me? Had I finally cracked under the pressure?* I'd been so consumed with proving myself that I feared I'd gone overboard with cleansing the cottage and our lives. I wasn't entirely sorry. I had rid the cottage of the germs, but in my zeal I'd not protected myself from the smoke. My throat still felt dry and scratchy.

Ludi stood with hands on her hips. "That's the best I can do. You want to see for yo'self what I done?"

I went to the small oval mirror over my dresser, shocked at the difference in my appearance. "I've never had short hair." I turned to the side to get a better look at the bob I now sported. "You know, this might be just what I needed. A new look. You did fine."

"It ain't your hair what worries me. You best be watching that cough."

"I'll be fine. How about one last thing? Get me the green sundress from my closet. Just because we have no customers doesn't mean I can't look nice. And while you're at it, pull all of those men's shirts off the hangers and take that grocery sack with O'Dell's shoes. I won't be needing them anymore, and maybe someone in Zion can use them."

"You sure?"

"Absolutely." I took the dress she handed me, slipped it on, and let her zip me.

"Mr. Peter been hanging out in the front. Says he wants a word with you."

"Thanks, Ludi. For everything."

She started out, lugging O'Dell's things, then stopped. "Miz Georgie, I ain't one to interfere, but I been thinkin'. Ever since I first laid eyes on you, you've had the determination. You fixed up the cottages. You always tryin' to make people happy. You took us to your bosom. I 'preciate that so don't take what I be fixin' to say the wrong way."

"Whatever are you talking about?"

"Well, I think there comes a time you got to quit strivin' and let the Lord take over. You been a pushin' and strivin' like a crazy woman. You cain't stop the polio no more than you can stop the sun shinin' in the sky."

"Is that what you think I was doing by burning all that stuff?"

She nodded. "You ever think God mighta had a higher purpose for bringing that woman and her little girl to your place?"

"Destroying my business doesn't seem like a higher purpose. And I'm not sure if you know this, but Fiona Callahan was my dead husband's mistress. It wouldn't surprise me if the baby she's carrying is his. Not that the poor babe has a chance with Fiona so sick, but her coming here was nothing but a reminder of the bitterness of my failed marriage."

"I din't know she was your man's mistress, but it goes to show what I was tryin' to tell you. We's all connected one way or another. And it's the good Lord who do the connectin'. You be thinking on that."

"I will. I promise." I held up two pairs of earrings. "Which ones do you think look better with this dress?"

She pointed to the gold dangling ones set with green rhinestones. "Thanks, Ludi. Good choice."

I clipped the earrings on and went to find Peter.

He and Rosey were bent over a checkerboard in the office and both greeted me when I entered.

"Momma! What happened to your hair?"

"Ludi cut it. What do you think?"

"I like it. Look, Peter's teaching me checkers. I beat him the last game."

Peter smiled, surveying my hair, and I was certain it was approval I saw in his eyes. "She's a quick learner."

"That, or you're a great teacher. Where are Avril and Bonnie?"

Rosey made a move and said, "MeMaw came and got them. Mr. Overstreet took them all to town so MeMaw could go to the drugstore."

A brief moment of panic went through me. The sheriff had told me not to take Bonnie around town. I only hoped no one saw her and put together that she was the child from the Stardust. I thought of Ludi's warning to quit striving. I couldn't change it, so I might as well not worry. I watched Peter and Rosey play, then offered to fix lunch.

In his weeks at the Stardust, Peter hadn't eaten in our quarters with us. I'd always made him a plate or given him a sandwich. I invited him and Rosey into the kitchen to finish their game as I put together tuna salad. A short time later, while we ate, I told them Sheriff Bolander thought business might be slow for a while.

Peter took a drink of iced tea. "Was he the one who suggested you burn the things from the cottage?"

A slight flush crept up my neck. "No, that was all my hare-brained idea. My way of lashing out at polio. I must admit I got carried away."

"Guess you didn't plan on getting a new hairdo out of the deal." He cocked his head and looked at me. "You ask me, it looks nice."

"Thanks. And if business slacks off, I'll have to figure out another way to make do. I don't even want to think of what will happen if he shuts us down."

"I've had time to think, too. I think I'll head over to the lumber mill this afternoon and see if I can't get on there. I'd still have time to do odd jobs around here in the evenings. Rosey here thinks a swing set would be mighty fine."

"I won't have money to invest in that."

"It's all right. I think I can manage."

Maybe Ludi was right. My striving had taken its toll. The idea that God was in control gave me a warm feeling.

The feeling lasted less than a minute. Before I had time to clear the table, Sheriff Bolander was on the phone yelling at me for allowing Mary Frances to take Bonnie downtown.

"Honest, Sheriff, they left while I was doing something else... before I had a chance to discuss it with Mary Frances. I'll be sure it doesn't happen again."

"Darn straight you will, or I'm shutting you down. Maybe even put you on quarantine. I've already had three phone calls."

"Anything new to report on Bonnie's aunt?"

"It's only been four hours since I talked to you."

"Just wondering."

"Perhaps you need to spend less time wondering and pay more attention to what goes on out there."

"Thanks for calling."

CHAPTER 29

Peter started working at the lumber mill the following Monday, "getting out of our hair," he said. But it was excitement that shone on his face when he picked up the lunch I promised to have ready.

Ludi spent two full days scrubbing Fiona's cottage with Clorox. One morning, having run out of things to do, she reorganized the washhouse. After lunch, I sat with her on the back steps sipping sweet tea and fanning away the heat. When she'd cooled off, she mentioned Fiona's car.

"My man said he be lookin' up and down the bayou for it, tracin' every place it might have run off the road. Nothin'. He says it wouldn't be the first vehicle swallowed by the bayou. Place or two is mighty deep."

"I was hoping it might give us some clues. Registration papers or some of their belongings. Tell Mr. Harper I appreciate his looking."

She nodded and we got to work, falling into our own rhythms. When I wasn't busy with the girls, I devoured the infantile paralysis section in *The Book of Knowledge*. I knew every symptom by heart, observing the girls for the slightest bit of headache or fever and secretly did the chin touch myself. No one was immune. And no one could predict who the next victim would be.

In the gentle haze of evening, we all played games of horse-shoes and ate whatever Malcolm caught in the bayou that morn-ing. Like a well-oiled machine we went through our duties and our days waiting. And waiting.

For what, none of us knew.

✦

Sweat shone on Catfish's ebony back as he pushed the reel mower across the grass. Peter had sharpened the blades, and Catfish had begged to be in charge of pushing it. It was only ten in the morning, but already the sun bore down, wilting us and everything in its wake.

As Rosey watered the flowers the Magnolias planted, Ludi and I trailed behind her, pulling dandelions and henbit from the moistened earth. Every time he passed by Rosey, Catfish stopped and took a slurp from the garden hose.

Just as we finished, Mary Frances emerged from her cottage, dressed in a new pale green shirtwaist and strappy sandals.

I straightened and wiped the sweat from my brow. "You're just in time for lunch." I turned to the others. "Get washed up, and I'll get out the egg salad and lemonade."

Mary Frances snapped her handbag open and pulled out a lace hankie. "None for me, thanks. Malcolm is meeting me here for lunch."

"My gracious, you two are getting to be regulars down at Ruby's Café."

"Can't beat a good chicken-fried steak. Except today's Wednes-day. We might try the meat loaf special."

"Better than egg salad, for sure."

"Oh, there's Malcolm now."

I waved as the two of them left. The banishment from town apparently applied to me and Bonnie only, as I hadn't been getting any more warning calls from the sheriff.

While Ludi and the kids returned the tools to the shed, I went in to start lunch and check on the girls. Merciful met me, hands on her hips, the spitting image of Ludi in miniature.

"Those girls won't stop their fussin'. They both wanna be the momma, and I'm plumb wore out hearin' them."

Avril poked her head around Merciful, a blanket shoved under her shirt to look like she was expecting. Bonnie had introduced the game when they were playing with their dolls. Now she came up behind Avril and snatched the blanket from under her shirt.

"It's my mommy who's gonna have a baby, and when she comes back, she'll bring the baby."

Avril squinted her eyes at me. "Is she right, Momma?"

"Sort of, sweetheart. Bonnie, your momma left because she was sick. Remember? She can't come back until she gets well." I had no idea how I would tell her the baby might not even have a chance. Dealing with an absent mother was worry enough.

A vacant look came in Bonnie's eyes. "But she's coming back?"

My stomach knotted. The truth might rupture her world beyond repair. I pulled her into my arms, remembering my own childish hope that my parents would return for me. My adult self told me Aunt Cora had been sparing my feelings that my parents didn't want me, but the child in me needed to know. I could have wrestled with the truth and moved on.

I kissed her cheek. "I pray every night that she will."

＋

The next week three more people in Mayhaw contracted polio. Some people blamed the heat. Some blamed it on dairy products—Brookshire's had hundreds of bottles of milk go sour on their shelves for lack of sales. And some people blamed the Stardust. Understandable, but when none of the victims had a connection to me or places we'd been in town, they looked to other sources. Life dragged on, but fear was as thick as the muddy waters of the bayou.

It was a relief to be insulated as we were, confined almost. But Bonnie worried me. My attempts to draw her into conversation about her relatives only made her cry for her mother. I thought if she saw Fiona, it might help. It was the least I could do.

Doc was up to his ears with work, but for Bonnie's sake I called him one afternoon. He seemed surprised to hear from me. "I didn't figure the child was still with you. It's been nearly three weeks."

"Sheriff Bolander and the March of Dimes are working to find her kinfolk. But in the meantime, I think it might help Bonnie if I took her to the hospital to see her mother. Do you know if that's allowed?"

He said he would check.

The next day, I got two phone calls, the first from Aunt Cora.

"Hon, I thought I'd let you know we've located an aunt and uncle in Arkansas. Theodora and Elmer Benning. The woman sounded confused, but when I finally made myself clear, she apologized. Said she couldn't come as her husband's been in the hospital with hernia surgery."

"Did she sound nice? Like she would be comforting and loving?"

"I couldn't tell. She said she'd think about it. I gave her the information and asked her to come at her earliest convenience. I do hope she comes before the Mayhaw Festival. I've already penciled you and Rosey in for the talent show."

"I didn't suppose the festival was still on, with the public being so afraid of getting polio."

"It's more important than ever. I met with Mayor Sheldon this morning. People are afraid, but more than that, they want to know what they can do to help. Even your pal Bobby Carl has a celebrity talent lined up for a special concert to benefit the March of Dimes."

I snorted. "My pal?"

"He's always had a crush on you."

"So are you wanting to fix me up with him now that he's working with celebrities?" I shuddered.

Aunt Cora sniffed, unamused, and I told her to let me know if she heard any more from Mrs. Benning.

I'd no more than hung up when a physician from the Tyler hospital called me. "Dr. Kelley said you called about Mrs. Callahan."

"Yes. Her daughter's been staying with me, and the poor child is afraid her mother won't be coming back."

"Understandable. Mrs. Callahan is still in guarded condition in the iron lung. She has both bulbar and spinal polio, which is not unheard of, but often these patients don't survive. I believe she has out of sheer will to live and for the child she carried."

"Carried? She lost the baby?"

"On the contrary. We took the baby by cesarean to ease the strain on her back. Healthy six-pound boy."

I did a quick calculation in my head. Yes, it was possible. Fiona could have been further along than I thought. I felt a little dizzy. Would I be able to tell if it was O'Dell's child?

"Is he okay? Does he have…I guess I don't know much about these things. Is he in danger?"

"We don't observe any signs of polio in him, if that's what you mean. He's quite the pet in the nursery."

"I'm sure. So what will happen with him?"

"That's a matter of concern. We'd hoped that a relative might come forward, but there haven't been any visitors."

An uneasy rumble came in my gut. The baby was Bonnie's brother. "What options are there?"

"Foster care is a possibility. Or a children's home. He's not a candidate for adoption since his mother can't give her consent in her condition. Best course would be for a relative to take temporary custody. You say you have Mrs. Callahan's older child? Are you related?"

"I'm not. I'm just keeping her until someone comes for her. We've been able to locate an aunt and uncle in Arkansas, but no arrangements have been made."

"We hadn't heard this." The line fell silent, and I thought perhaps we'd been disconnected, but then the doctor cleared his throat. "We'll try to do what's best for the infant."

A million images flashed through my head. Bonnie and her brother together. The two of them separated. Me with a newborn propped on my hip while I greeted clients at the Stardust.

What's best for the infant.

"I suppose I could care for him until the relatives came."

"It's a lot to ask. I wouldn't—"

"I'd have to consult with a few people here. I don't know."

"It is something to consider. We'll be releasing the baby from the hospital next week."

"Next week? So soon."

"We're a hospital, not an orphanage." Although the words were cruel, the doctor's tone was kind, caring.

"I'll let you know. What I actually called about was to see if I could bring Bonnie to see her mother."

"How old is the child?"

"Four."

"She's a little young. Seeing a loved one in an iron lung can be quite startling, but it often helps the patient to see family members. What day were you planning to come?"

"As soon as possible."

"Excellent. How about next Monday? By then we'll know if you've decided to take the infant as well. We could have the paperwork ready and let you take him that day."

My head spun with the details, the what-ifs. My arms grew numb, and when I hung up, I felt as though I'd run a thousand miles. What would I say to Mary Frances? The child was most likely O'Dell's. Should I even tell her? I hated to tip her world off balance again.

She was only one consideration. There were my girls. The Stardust. Aunt Cora would be beside herself. And me? Could I handle a baby?

Maybe this was what we'd all been waiting for. I picked up the phone and called Hugh Salazar. He could draw up the appropriate documents and steer me through these dark waters.

CHAPTER 30

Hugh Salazar looked over O'Dell's life insurance policy with Fiona's name as beneficiary. I'd already explained to him and Aunt Cora, who I'd invited for moral support and because of her involvement in the March of Dimes, what I was considering—taking the baby until the family came or suitable arrangements could be made.

Blessedly, neither one of them lit into me or told me I'd gone off my rocker. Mr. Salazar looked over his glasses. "There's no reason not to submit this. It's bought and paid for, and the money may be needed to ensure she gets good medical treatment."

Aunt Cora sat at the edge of her seat, ankles crossed. "The NFIP covers the cost of many polio patients. No one is turned away who's in need."

When Mr. Salazar and I both gave her a questioning look, she explained. "It's the National Foundation for Infantile Paralysis. Fiona will get the best treatment available; that's what the foundation ensures."

I kept my hands in my lap, determined to be sensible at all times. "Is it possible to set up a trust fund for the children? Something to be used by them in the future?"

Aunt Cora nodded. "It might be an incentive for the relatives to come and get them if it meant taking the children would be a hardship."

Mr. Salazar folded the document. "I'll look into it. Georgia, it's generous of you to want to take the infant. You don't fancy latching on to the money yourself?"

His tone had reverted to the one I was all too familiar with—patronizing, as if my motives weren't pure. I kept my voice even. "Not at all."

"I know your business hasn't been what you expected—"

"I'm getting by. I have the life insurance O'Dell left, and I'm still expecting the house on Crockett to sell. But that's not the point. I wouldn't have come to you if I didn't trust your advice. I need that . . . and your blessing, if you must know. I consider keeping the children a temporary situation at best."

He wished me well and told Aunt Cora she got better looking every day. *Old coot.* Some things never changed.

⚹

On the trip to Tyler, I tried to prepare Bonnie for seeing her mother. She ignored me and bounced in her seat, chattering like we were going to the circus.

"Mommy said we're going to call the baby Willie. I have a brother, right?"

"Yes, and Willie's a good name."

"That's what Uncle Mitch says."

"You have an uncle named Mitch?"

"Yes. And Aunt Eyes."

"Aunt Eyes? Are you sure?"

Bonnie blossomed, more animated than I'd ever seen her. But who in the world was Aunt Eyes?

"Aunt Eyes says I'm funny."

"Was this when you went to the Ozarks and saw your aunt Teddy?"

"Nope. It was yesterday."

"We were at home at the Stardust all day yesterday."

"The yesterday before Momma got sick."

My hands gripped the steering wheel. We put out pleas all over the map for relatives when, right here, Bonnie was simply brimming with information. Not that it made sense, but it gave me hope that, with encouragement, we could fit the puzzle pieces together.

"Where did Aunt Eyes live?"

"In town. Not like Aunt Teddy. She lives with the chickens and pigs."

"On a farm?"

"Old MacDonald." She put her feet on the dash, then leaned over and rubbed the shiny patent leather of her new shoes. "Do you think Momma will like my shoes?"

"Of course." The moment to find out more was gone, and as the Tyler hospital loomed before me, I realized I'd not told Bonnie half of the things I intended.

As we stood at the reception desk, Bonnie clutched the diaper bag we'd packed with things for the baby—a sky-blue outfit with a sailor collar, diapers, a receiving blanket. In the car I had a cushioned basket for the ride home.

Back at the Stardust, the portable crib normally available to customers stood ready. Ludi had made it her personal mission to organize the layette Mary Frances and I purchased at the Mercantile.

I explained to the lady at reception who we were and that I had an appointment with the legal department. Hugh Salazar had prepared a document stating I would become the temporary guardian and outlined the conditions for the discharge of the baby to my care. Even though he had his unsavory moments, Cora's attorney and now mine, I supposed, had been thorough in making the arrangements with the hospital.

Bonnie danced around and tugged on my skirt. "Please, can we go see my mommy first?"

"We have to do this first so they can get your brother ready to go."

"I want to see my mommy."

The receptionist ushered us into the administrator's office, where a woman with wire glasses looked over the papers, signed them, and had me do likewise. Her assistant witnessed the signatures and notarized them. We were free to pick up the baby. The assistant offered to escort us to the nursery on the second floor, but I asked her to meet us there in thirty minutes, because Bonnie wanted to see her mother first.

Although I had braced myself for being uncomfortable when we went to see Fiona, my palms sweated and the collar of my dress made my neck itch. I pushed the elevator button and, when the doors opened, told the attendant we wanted to go to the respiratory ward on the third floor.

When the elevator jerked to a stop, my heart jumped to my throat. I reminded myself this was for Bonnie, and I would not let my distaste for Fiona and O'Dell's affair affect me. The uniformed attendant opened the door and wished us a pleasant visit. When we stepped out, we were met by a cacophony of clatters and hissing sounds, thumps and screams. The smell was distinct. Rubbing alcohol and body waste. The scent of ammonia burned my nostrils, and I wanted to run back in the elevator and return the way we'd come. But it was too late.

The elevator doors groaned shut behind me, having spit us out into an open area with a U-shaped desk, a work area behind that, and two long rows of doors on either side. These, I assumed, led to the patient rooms. Or ward, as the receptionist had said. If the nurses' workstation smelled this horrible, I could only imagine what it would be like in Fiona's room.

A young nurse with brassy blond hair pulled under a batwing nursing cap greeted us. I told her who I was and that we were there to see Fiona Callahan. "This is her daughter, Bonnie."

"Oh, I'm so thrilled you've come. She's been so lonely and depressed. That's the worst for the people here. The isolation from the world, not being able to see their families. Some can't even turn their heads, and none can sit up." She smiled at Bonnie. "Are you ready?"

A momentary panic seized me. "Do you think she should? She's rather young…"

"It's up to you. The patients on this ward are stable … and safe."

That sounded good, but I just hoped it wasn't too traumatic for Bonnie.

We followed the nurse onto the ward. A half-dozen iron lungs filled the room. Hisses and swooshing noises came from the tank-shaped machines affixed to metal stands, and I had the feeling I was in a boiler room of some kind, a factory. Only here the products were human. One of the machines was white, another one dull green, and several mustard yellow. They all had portholes on the side and viewing windows above those. The patients' heads protruded from one end, giving them the appearance of being separated from the bodies. Bonnie gripped my hand as the nurse led us to one of the mustard ones near the back of the room.

"Mrs. Callahan, you have visitors." The nurse didn't direct her voice at the head protruding from the machine, but at a mirror attached to the top edge of the unit. She motioned for us to stand, as she did, at the end.

It felt awkward, but at the same time gave me the opportunity to distance myself from the cold, fierce metal encasing Fiona's body. My own underarms ran with perspiration, my breaths jagged as though they were trying to keep rhythm with all the respirators in the room.

"Hello, Fiona. I've brought Bonnie to see you. Can you see her?" The calm in my voice surprised me, and I was glad I hadn't come out sounding like a Martian, surrounded as we were by the alien sounds.

Pale eyebrows furrowed above Fiona's dull amber eyes.

I moved Bonnie into better alignment. Fiona's eyes widened, becoming moist at once. The muscles of her face twitched, lips moving, and I thought she might be trying to pucker them for a kiss. A rubber collar cradled her neck, but a metal device in the center of her throat looked uncomfortable and menacing. I knew it was necessary, though, to keep her airway open. To keep her from drowning in her own spit, as the sheriff had said.

Bonnie's eyes darted from the mirror to the iron lung, back to her mother. She'd not spoken since we entered the ward, yet she didn't appear afraid, only curious. Now, she looked at the nurse. "Can I touch her?"

"Certainly. Better yet, let me get you a stool to stand on. We have other children about your size who come to visit."

The step stool brought Bonnie to a more approachable position. She leaned in and kissed Fiona's cheek. "I say my prayers every night, and Avril and me play dolls. Rosey is bossy and tries to make me learn my numbers, but sometimes she's nice."

Her small, thin fingers smoothed Fiona's hair. "Don't cry, Mommy. You have to be brave so you can get well."

Honestly, Bonnie acted like it was the most natural thing in the world to be talking to her mother in an iron lung. While she chatted, I let my eyes wander to the other patients.

Their total helplessness chafed my insides. The rhythm of the machines, while offbeat and disturbing, provided life-giving support. My own circumstances and inconvenience seemed small in comparison. One of the iron lungs had three portholes per side instead of four as Fiona's did. I chewed my lower lip. A young girl with long dark hair occupied it. A child like my Rosey. Avril. Bonnie. My breath left me.

Thank God for Aunt Cora and the others who dedicated themselves to helping. My admiration for Aunt Cora grew three sizes in that moment.

Bonnie leaned over Fiona again, a twist of her mother's hair curled in her fingers. "I love you, Mommy." She hopped off the stool and looked at me. "I'm ready to go now."

I stepped where Fiona could see me in the mirror. "We're all praying you get better soon. Bonnie's been an angel, but she misses you. We've tried to locate your family—"

Fiona's eyes widened, then blinked rapidly like she was trying to tell me something. "You have someone in Arkansas? Is that right?"

More blinks, but I couldn't tell if it was *yes* or *no*.

"Blink once for yes, two for no. You have family in Arkansas?" One blink.

"Do you have other family?"

A puzzled look. No blinks, but she formed an O with her mouth. I took a chance. "O'Dell?"

One blink.

"You were coming to find O'Dell?"

One blink.

"There was an accident. O'Dell was . . . hurt." The painful look on her face and her fragile condition stopped me from telling her the truth. "You have to work on getting well, okay?" She closed her eyes. Whether to shut me out or because she was too tired to keep them open, I didn't know.

Bonnie took my hand, her grasp firm as we left the ward, leaving behind the swooshes and clatters, the smell of sickness.

Too late I realized I'd not told Fiona who I was or how I knew about O'Dell. Nor had I asked permission to send Bonnie to Arkansas. I wasn't even sure I could bear to see her go.

CHAPTER 31

The nurse, a looming woman with steel-gray hair and eyes that matched, took the things we'd brought to dress the baby. When she'd finished, she handed him to me as the administrative assistant looked on.

Déjà vu flashed before me, a lump growing in my throat. The infant looked exactly as I remembered Avril. Same silky black hair. Same quivering chin with the dimple in the middle. Fighting back tears, I held the baby so Bonnie could see. She stood on tiptoe, her pale gold eyes locked on her brother, and reached to touch the blanket that swaddled him.

"Can we call him Willie?"

"If that's the name your mom picked out, then that's what we'll call him."

Bonnie asked to sit in the backseat by Willie's basket on the way home. Within minutes, she and Willie fell asleep, making the drive eerily quiet.

Mary Frances met us at the door when we returned to the Stardust. "Thank goodness, you're home. Got the baby, I see."

"Hello to you, too. I'm sorry to be so late. Did you and the girls have a good time?" I held the baby close, nervous about whether she'd see the resemblance and make the connection before I had a chance to talk with her. Regret that I'd not told her Fiona was O'Dell's *other* woman made my skin itch.

"The girls were fine. It's been a hive of activity the whole day. I've been up and down answering the door or the telephone every five minutes."

"Oh? Anything important?"

"First an older gentleman I've never seen before trying to rent a room. I told him he'd have to come back later."

"I showed you the check-in routine."

"I was making cinnamon toast in the broiler and didn't want it to burn or catch the house on fire." She let that dangle as if to remind me that stranger things had happened.

"Never mind, then. I'll see him when he comes back."

"He said he'd drop in later with his agent."

"I bet it's one of the acts Bobby Carl Applegate's trying to get going. He's probably hoping I'll give him a discount. Who else called?"

"Doc Kelley called. And your aunt Cora. Both wanted the same thing—to see when you'd be home and to tell you there's been another case of polio." Her indifference to the baby puzzled me, but Mary Frances had always been self-centered to some degree and obviously had no reason to have an interest in a child who was going to be gone in a few days.

Her voice hitched up an octave. "Can we go outside? I need a smoke."

"You're welcome to step outside, but I need to get the baby settled. He's on a three-hour feeding schedule, and it's already twenty minutes past the time he should've had a bottle. Want to see him?"

"Later. I need a smoke."

Bonnie had already skipped back in the quarters to see Avril and Rosey, and the three of them came squealing through the connecting door, all clamoring at once to see baby Willie. Thirty minutes later he'd been fed, burped, changed, and had every inch of his silken body inspected. Having an infant to care for wasn't going to be the problem. Much harder would be keeping three little mommas from spoiling him rotten.

When I returned to the office, Mary Frances was on the porch smoking. I joined her and thanked her again for staying with the girls.

"It was fine. I didn't mind."

"I'm sorry to hear about the new case of polio. I guess Aunt Cora didn't have any more to report on finding Bonnie's aunt and uncle. I hope the polio connection doesn't put them off."

"It's a terrible disease."

"Seeing Fiona in an iron lung about broke my heart."

Mary Frances shuddered. "I can't even imagine why you went."

"I needed to go for Bonnie."

"It gives me the creeps. Seeing those posters plastered in the windows downtown is enough to gag me."

"It is a reality, though. A danger we're all vulnerable to."

"So how was Bonnie's mother?"

"She's improving slowly. She's no longer in isolation, and the cesarean relieved some of her back pain."

"Did you need me for anything else?" She moved from one foot to the other and kept looking over her shoulder at her cottage.

"Why don't you sit down?"

"Not right now."

"I've been meaning to have a talk with you…to tell you how thankful I am that you're here with us. I had my doubts, but you've been a trouper."

"That's what people say when they're getting ready to deliver bad news. So what is it? You're asking me to leave?"

"Oh, gracious, no. Not at all. But what I have to tell you might upset you. I've just now gotten up the courage."

She ground out the cigarette with her new open-toed pumps. Red polish like rose petals dotted her toes. Prettying herself up, as people in the South were fond of saying.

I inhaled a bucketful of air. "You remember I told you O'Dell had a life insurance policy with the name of another woman?"

"Yes. I told you to burn it."

"I'm glad I didn't. Fiona Callahan was the woman."

She stepped away from me, turning away to cough into her fist. "Bonnie's mother? The one with polio? Are you sure?"

I nodded, perspiration bubbles breaking out on my forehead. "That's what I think he wanted to tell you."

"I think I will sit down."

I dropped onto the steps by her and took her hand. "There's no way of knowing for sure, but there's a strong possibility baby Willie is your grandson."

The words hung in the air, droplets of truth. I felt as if I'd given birth myself. The sensation, though, was freeing.

Mary Frances didn't move or speak, just stared at her toes. When she looked up, her eyes shone with tears. "O'Dell always wanted a boy."

Indeed. O'Dell had seemed a trifle disappointed each time I'd delivered a girl. After Avril came, he'd disappeared for three days. Fishing the bayou, he said, but I always felt I'd not been able to give O'Dell what he needed. A bitter taste came in my mouth.

"When you feel more rested, why don't you come back and see baby Willie?"

"Maybe. The thing is, Georgia, I see now what your motives were in dropping this little bomb. You think I should assume responsibility for the baby."

"Good heavens. That's not it at all. I'm sorry if you misunderstood. I took this on because I couldn't bear for him to be sent to a children's home and grow up separated from Bonnie."

"It appears you do the right thing only when it's convenient. You didn't even bother to tell me I have a grandson before you dumped him in my lap."

"I didn't..." I knew it was no use. "Why don't you go lie down? You've had a long day."

+

Peter stopped in after work to ask how our trip had gone. Rosey insisted it was Peter's turn to hold Willie. He gingerly took him and cupped him in his hands like he was a raw egg in danger of breaking. Willie let out a squall.

Smothering a smile, I told him to relax. "Hold him closer to your body. Babies have a startle reflex when they aren't cradled."

"Like this?" He worked Willie into the crook of his arm. The crying stopped, but in all the ruckus, I hadn't heard the office door jangle.

Bobby Carl stuck his head in the connecting door. "Yoo-hoo! Oh, you are here." He scowled at Peter. "Handyman, huh? Sorry, bud, I didn't realize you were living in here now."

Linking my arm with Bobby Carl's, I led him out to the office. "What can I do for you?"

He ignored me. "Who's the kid?"

"Long story. We're babysitting."

"I brought you a customer." He nodded to a tall, thin man with an easy smile. He looked to be around the same age as Malcolm Overstreet, but with a full head of fair hair fading to white at the temples.

"Georgia, this Van Sweeney, the client I told you about."

"Welcome to the Stardust. I'm Georgia Peyton." I offered my

hand, and Mr. Sweeney didn't shake it but lifted it elegantly and kissed the back of it.

"My pleasure, Georgia. This place is just as charming as it was the first time I came." His eyes crinkled at the corners when he smiled, and his accent was Southern but not local.

Bobby Carl put his hands on the counter. "I tried to get Van to check in to the hotel downtown, where I'm sure the accommodations are better."

When I scowled at him, he shrugged. "Don't want folks to get the wrong impression, bein's Mr. Sweeney's a celebrity and all. He's come early to work with the March of Dimes committee for a couple of weeks before the benefit."

"It's all right. We'll try to make him comfortable." I turned to the guest. "Bobby Carl told me you used to do vaudeville."

"Never did make the big time, but I had a whale of a time singing, doing the old soft-shoe in small towns across America. Mayhaw was one of the more memorable stops."

His slim, manicured fingers made me think he wasn't a fisherman, but I handed him a brochure anyway. "Here are some of the places to eat and information about fishing the bayou in case you're interested. I don't know when you were last here, so there may be some changes. And you might want to check out the town square on the Fourth of July. They have a Mayhaw jelly tasting and bicycle parade."

Bobby Carl danced from one foot to the other. "Kid stuff. The *big* celebration is the Mayhaw Festival."

I nodded and looked at each of them. "Now, which one of you am I to collect the money from?"

Mr. Sweeney pulled out his wallet. "This is on me since I fancied staying here. How much for ten days? And my band's coming the end of next week. Could I reserve three more rooms while we're at it?"

A rush went through me when I realized this would be a nice windfall in light of the piddly number of customers I'd had the past few weeks. I did a quick calculation in my head and told him he could pay for the band when they arrived. After he paid me, I grabbed the key to number eight and asked if I could show him the room.

"I think I can find it." A serious expression came on his face. "Pardon, but you look mighty familiar. You ever worked in Nashville?"

"No. Been right here most of my life. Let me know if you need anything. Our housekeeper will keep you stocked with fresh towels and make up the room each morning."

"Most appreciative." He gave a half wave and held the door for Bobby Carl. As they left, all I could think was why would such a nice man let Bobby Carl talk him into being his agent.

CHAPTER 32

L udi and Merciful lapped up Willie like a kitten with a saucer
of milk. I didn't have to do much more than get up for his
night feeding. The second night we were home, Bonnie joined
me on the divan and stroked Willie's dimpled fist while I held the
bottle.

"I bet your aunt Eyes and uncle Mitch would like to meet your
brother. Maybe we should call them. Do you know where they
live?"

Bonnie shrugged. "Aunt Eyes got mad."

"At you? Or your momma?"

"Momma. Told her to go on and get out." She yawned and
leaned next to me. In an instant she was asleep, leaving me with
more questions than answers.

The next day Mary Frances marched into the quarters.

"I've come to see my grandson." That's the way she was. Cut
her some slack and she usually came around. She cradled him in
her arms and kissed his forehead. "Would you look at that? He
smiled at me."

"It was just gas, MeMaw," Rosey told her, now an expert in all
things related to newborns. I let Mary Frances have a chance to

get to know Willie by slipping into the office to do some book work.

Again that evening she paid a visit, so while she fussed over Willie, I went out front and sat on the steps. The lights of Mayhaw flickered on one by one, the view reminding me that I was connected to the town, to the world of gossip and laughter, to the people who made this the only place on earth I wanted to live. When I sat on the back steps, my soul stirred with loftier thoughts—the world beyond our tiny burg, the bayou meandering through the cypress, draining eventually into the Mississippi, how God kept an eye on all of it and, even more amazing, how He kept it all straight.

I turned and looked up at the Stardust sending its light to the heavens. The lump in my throat matched the knot between my shoulder blades. *A haven.* That's what I wanted to provide for the world's strangers. But it was more like a revolving door. And for my trouble I got a tightness in my neck and shoulders. Dirt under my fingernails. Sweaty armpits. All for people who would be here a day or two, maybe a week. The reality of it was both humbling and satisfying.

I didn't see Peter until he dropped on the steps beside me, one half of his face bathed in neon blue, the other a sunburned orange color. Comical, really. All he needed was a star on his forehead.

He slipped his fingers through mine. "Whatcha thinking?"

"Not much. Just wondering."

"Sounds dangerous."

"It's got me into plenty of fixes before. Sonny Bolander says I need to do less wondering and more paying attention."

"So what are you wondering?"

I couldn't gather a suitable answer into words, so I listened to the rumble of cars on the highway, a cricket in the spirea beside the porch, the scruffy sandpaper sound of Peter's hand as he rubbed it over his chin.

Finally, I looked at him. "You first. What are you thinking?"

"That it's high time you got to practicing for the talent show. My buddies at the mill say it's the highlight of the Mayhaw Festival."

"Not sure I'll even enter this year. Not with four kids to take care of. Why don't you enter? You're the best on the guitar I've ever heard."

"I'm not as pretty as you."

"Get outta here." I rolled my shoulders, the earlier tension now gone. "Tell you what. I will if you will."

"Trouble is, my guitar pickin' would sound better with a certain redhead I know prettying up the stage."

I didn't have to think twice. "You got it. The Pearl triplets never can play in my key."

"Who in the devil are the Pearl triplets?"

"You'll find out soon enough."

The porch light came on, and Roscy stuck her head out. "MeMaw wants to know how much Carnation milk to put in the bottle."

I shrugged and looked at Peter. "So much for the fantasy. Guess I'd better get in there and pay attention to my real business."

"How about we shoot for a jam session tomorrow? Same place?"

"It's a date."

✦

True to his word, Peter brought over his guitar for jam sessions. The girls joined in, while Mary Frances cooed and spent time with Willie. I was afraid my mother-in-law's heart would be broken again when Mrs. Benning came, but I saw no reason for her not to enjoy the time she had.

Ludi and Merciful helped with the cottages and the kids in the daytime. With summer bearing down, it was easier and cooler to cook outdoors, so most evenings we picnicked with whoever wanted to come.

On the Fourth of July, Malcolm cut up a snapping turtle the size of a hubcap and cooked the meat from its legs along with the day's catch. He wangled Ludi and her kids into joining us. Ludi sent Merciful for a quick trip to Zion to get a mess of 'maters from her garden.

As she bit into a thick, juicy tomato, she smacked her lips. "Next week there'll be cantaloupe and string beans."

I shook my head. "Ludi, how do you have time to keep up the garden and do your job here?"

"The garden ain't no burden. It's the place I watch the sun come up ever' mornin' and do my confessin' to the Lord Jesus. The 'maters and melons is His way of saying He be listenin' to me and mindin' what we need."

Malcolm offered her another helping of the fried turtle legs. "You're one of a kind, Miss Ludi, but I know what you mean. I feel the same about the bayou. Even this danged snapping turtle. Some might think it's an ornery nuisance, but I see it as a gift from the muddy waters." He had a gentle way with Ludi and Mary Frances that made me warm inside. He served the rest of us, then lifted his head in greeting as Mr. Sweeney came from his cottage.

Malcolm motioned him over. "Hey, there, you look like a fella who needs to put some meat on his bones. How about some of the best fried turtle you ever tasted?"

Mr. Sweeney laughed. "You can't imagine how many of those ugly buggers I've eaten in my day. We got creeks in Tennessee, you know. Thanks, but no, I've already eaten a fine meal."

Malcolm winked at me. "You know, if I didn't know better, I'd say old Van's falling for that aunt of yours. Second night in a row she had him over for dinner."

A familiar twinge pinched my insides. Aunt Cora always had a good eye for refined men. "Is that so? I thought you might have gone to the jelly tasting downtown."

Mr. Sweeney laughed. "I might've, but I met Cora at the planning meeting a couple days ago. I can't remember when I've seen such dedication to a worthy cause."

"How are the fund-raiser plans coming?"

"This is going to be one of the finest shows I've done. The enthusiasm from Bobby Carl, Mayor Sheldon, and your aunt has been inspiring." His voice flowed with sincerity, a deep passion, and I could see why Aunt Cora was interested in him.

He walked over to Catfish and stooped down. "What you doing there, son?"

Catfish held up the cypress knee he was carving on. "Just messing around. This one's gon' be a snapping turtle." He nodded toward Malcolm, who'd taken his usual spot beside Mary Frances. "For him."

"You have a fine gift there." He lowered himself to the grass and watched as Catfish whittled.

The girls played tag in the grass while Sebastian raced after them. Mary Frances bounced the baby on her lap. Peter sat with his back against a tree and pulled me down to sit by him. The trees hummed with cicadas as twilight fell, hypnotizing us all with its murmuring blue haze. Peter slipped his arm around me and nuzzled me on the neck. As I was imagining what the sweet taste of his lips might be like, headlights flashed between the cottages, breaking the spell.

Half dizzy with the bliss around me, I hurried toward the office.

An unfamiliar car jerked to a stop, and a woman peered through her open driver's side window. "This the Stardust Inn?"

"Yes, ma'am."

"Your name Georgia?"

"Yes." The half-dizzy feeling turned into a swarming nest of wasps in my stomach.

An ample woman dressed in a plain shirtwaist emerged from the car. She pulled a hankie from her bosom and dotted her forehead. "I've come for the Callahan children."

CHAPTER 33

Peter steadied me, his arm encircling my waist, but still my voice quavered when I spoke. "You must be—"

"Theodora Benning."

"Aunt Teddy."

Her eyes widened as if I'd startled her. "Please, call me Theodora." Other than the accent, which had a backwoods sound to it, the woman before me looked reasonable. Clean. A late-model car. Sensible lace-up shoes with a heel.

I offered my hand. "Please, won't you come in?"

When she leaned in to shake my hand, I detected the scent of cloves on her breath and remembered Bonnie said her aunt smelled like Christmas. Sweet. Pleasant. As I ushered Mrs. Benning in, it wasn't Christmas cheer I felt, but something deep and painful. Like someone was getting ready to sever my leg.

The bell above the door jangled when Peter opened the door, and Theodora's lips curved into an anxious smile. "Where is my sweet girl? I've not seen her in a month of Sundays. And a boy I've yet to lay eyes on. I must say, it all came as a surprise."

Peter offered to fetch Bonnie, and I was suddenly aware that I must look a fright and probably smelled like wood smoke. I ran

"I'm Bonnie's aunt, come to take her home with me until her mother gets well."

Rosey nailed me with a look. "Did you tell her, Momma? About the iron lung and Willie? How Bonnie is sad and we make her feel better?"

"Yes, she knows, but sometimes people leave, sweetheart. Not because they want to, but because they have to. Bonnie needs to be with her family."

Mrs. Benning was growing tired of explanations, I knew, and while I was comforting Rosey, Mary Frances came in with Willie, followed by Peter carrying Avril.

Mrs. Benning looked at Mary Frances. "Who the devil are you? And where's the boy? Fiona's kid."

Mary Frances smiled. "Right here. The sweetest thing you ever seen. You must be Bonnie's aunt."

I was so proud of Mary Frances I could've cried. Although I knew it was ripping her apart, she handed the baby over. Or tried to.

Mrs. Benning flinched. "Is this a joke? That can't be Rusty's boy. That's a baby. I assumed Fiona was carrying him when Rusty died serving our country eighteen months ago, and the last time I checked, a pregnancy only took nine months."

Mary Frances and I traded wary looks, but I spoke. "Mrs. Benning. Perhaps you misunderstood. My aunt is the March of Dimes spokesperson who called you. She said you were under a lot of stress with your husband's surgery. No one has tried to fool you into thinking otherwise. The fact is, we're not certain who Willie's father is, only that Fiona gave birth to him after she contracted polio."

Mrs. Benning bolted from the chair and knocked on the girls' door. "Bonnie Fay, come on now. It's getting late." She turned to those of us in the room. "You can find someone else for the boy. Bonnie and I are leaving."

The bedroom door remained closed. I chewed my lip and tried to think of an excuse to delay their leaving.

Peter, ever quiet and observant as he was, wrapped his arms around me. I elbowed him in the ribs. I hated to be comforted when I was frustrated and needed time to think.

He winced, then cleared his throat. "Mrs. Benning, there's no sense in rushing things. Before we get hasty, let's give it a day. Never hurts to sleep on an important matter."

Mrs. Benning slumped back into the chair. "I never expected so much confusion." She waved her hand in front of her face. "I only wanted to help and take care of Rusty's girl. The poor thing needs a stable home, the kind Elmer and I can provide."

Peter went to her. "Your concern is appreciated. I think Georgia can set you up in one of the cottages."

Mrs. Benning pursed her lips. "It looks like I have no choice."

Time. We'd bought some time. I hoped it was enough to come up with another plan.

CHAPTER 34

Willie woke for his night feeding at three o'clock. I put the water on to heat his bottle, then changed him while it was warming. He was such a good baby. Even when he was hungry, he only fussed, clenching his egg-size fists and waving them at me to hurry. Already he had a scowl that reminded me of O'Dell and Avril. I took him to the rocking chair in the office and held him close as he slurped the bottle. I'd always loved the girls' nighttime feedings, when it was only the two of us as the rest of the world slept.

Was it the money Mrs. Benning was after, or was she really trying to help? My gut told me she hoped the profit outweighed the inconvenience of raising a child. And either way, it meant Bonnie and Willie would be separated.

Hopefully, Aunt Cora would start the ball rolling on finding Inez. She'd been having her bedtime chamomile when I'd called and told her things weren't going well with Mrs. Benning. She assured me she hadn't mentioned the trust, only that the polio foundation sometimes assisted with family finances in hardship cases. Mrs. Benning had read more into Aunt Cora's call than she should have.

From my chair, I could see the neon of the Stardust sign through the front window. Nothing worth having was easy, and for a moment, I was glad for the hard work we'd all done. I closed my eyes and rocked and cuddled Willie. When he fell asleep, I tucked him into the portable crib and patted his back until he was sound asleep.

An urge to check on the girls came. I yawned and wanted to crawl back in bed, but I knew I would never sleep until I'd had a peek. I turned the knob and hoped the squeaky hinge didn't disturb them. I tiptoed to Rosey's bed and patted the spot where she should be. The bed was empty.

My heart inched up a notch as I turned to see if she'd crawled in with the Avril and Bonnie, but she hadn't. Their bed was just as empty.

Panic rose in my chest, my face tingling, my arms and legs numb.

Calm down. They have to be somewhere in the house.

I flipped on the light and scanned the room quickly, looking in the closet and wardrobe Doreen had left. I wasn't even sure I was breathing. A slight movement caught my attention. The muslin curtains hung limp at the window, riffling ever so slightly. The sash had been raised as high as it would go and the screen unlatched. My heart was in my throat, electric fear racing through me.

I leaned out the window and saw nothing in the neon haze. The highway beyond was eerily void of sound and cars.

Mrs. Benning. She took the girls.

My temples throbbed as I flew from the front door and looked toward the cottage I'd given her for the night. Her car still sat in the spot where she'd moved it only hours before. I ran around to the bedroom window, hoping for a clue. I spotted something in the grass near the shrubbery. A cypress knee. The frog Catfish had made for Bonnie. She slept with it like it was a baby doll. Why would she drop it unless she was in a hurry...or someone was forcing her away?

Maybe they went to see Mary Frances and hide from Mrs. Benning. That seemed logical. My feet slapped the sidewalk as I ran toward Mary Frances's cottage. I pounded on the door. No light came from her window, so I pounded again. She was a heavy sleeper, but if the girls had gone to her, the light would be on.

Mary Frances appeared, her hair in pin curls, her eyes heavy with sleep. "For heaven's sake, what's wrong?"

I gave her a quick explanation. "Get dressed. We have to hunt for them."

"How could they be lost?"

"I don't know. Either someone has taken them or they've run away. Bonnie's afraid of Mrs. Benning, that's all I know. Hurry. I'm going to get Peter."

His door opened before I got there. "What's going on? I heard you yell."

My breath came out in huffs as I explained once again. "Quick. Get Sebastian. Maybe he can help us find the girls."

He looked from side to side on his stoop. "Sebastian. Come here, boy." When the dog didn't appear, he whistled. Nothing. "I bet he's with the girls. Hang on, I'll get a flashlight and some shoes."

Malcolm Overstreet had now joined us, along with Mary Frances. I glanced at the office, not sure I wanted to leave Willie alone. "Mary Frances, would you go to the quarters and keep an eye on Willie? And call Sheriff Bolander. Tell him to hurry."

Bayou sounds echoed as we searched around the fireplace and trees in back. A screech owl squawked and flapped its wings above us. Bullfrogs that usually sang a comforting chorus now bellowed in a frenzy. Fear roared like a lion in my stomach.

Another thought came. The washhouse.

I motioned for Peter to follow me. "You check the shed and the lean-to while I look in the washhouse."

The door was locked, so I fetched the key from the flowerpot next to it, knowing it was fruitless. The room was dark, nothing disturbed. All the linens stacked neatly on the shelves, the cupboards stocked. But no girls.

Slumping to the floor, I put my hands over my face and let the tears flow. *What if they'd gone to the highway and tried to catch a ride?* Fear worked its way up my spine. With it being the Fourth, there was no telling how many strangers were in town. They could be halfway to Dallas by now.

That's insane. No one would pick up three small girls *and* a big dog and drive off, especially in the middle of the night. They would deliver them to the sheriff's office. Having Sebastian with them was a comfort at least. But where were they?

A momentary thought tried to take root, but Peter's shadow came over me. He offered me a hand and pulled me up, then held out his arms to hold me.

"Don't touch me. We have to find the girls."

"We will. We just have to stay calm."

"How can we be calm when they could be in danger? They could be hurt. Or lost. Or—"

"We can't be sure of anything. The sheriff will know how to approach the situation. In the meantime, we'll just pray they're all right." He clasped his hands before him and closed his eyes.

I bit my lip and prayed. "Lord, help us find them. Please." Fear knotted my throat as my silent pleas continued. After what seemed an interminable time, we heard a car and the crunch of gravel.

I sailed out the door, Peter right behind me.

Sonny had already heard the gist of it from Mary Frances when she called. "Has anyone questioned Mrs. Benning?"

We all looked at each other and shook our heads. The lights in her cottage hadn't come on, so I assumed she was asleep.

Sonny hitched up his britches. "I'll talk to her, but first, Georgia, show me the window where they disappeared."

We looked from the inside, then the outside. He shone his high-powered flashlight on the grass. "This has been trampled on so much, there's no way to see which way the footprints go. You should've called me sooner. Did you hear anything from inside? A car speeding off or one of the girls crying?" He pointed the light in my face like I was under interrogation.

"No. Nothing." Then I held up the cypress knee I still carried. "This. It's Bonnie's favorite possession. I found it out here under the window."

"I'll take it, although there's no chance of getting fingerprints now that you've handled it. Have they done this before?"

Another no.

"Any reason they might have run off? Were they in trouble for something and afraid you would punish them?"

"Good heavens, no. You know me, and you know them. They're sweet girls, and they weren't in trouble. But Bonnie was afraid to go with Mrs. Benning."

He went to Mrs. Benning's cottage and woke her up. I followed to see what she had to say. She was groggy but fully clothed. She'd either slept in her clothes or dressed in a hurry. I suspected the former.

She squinted at the light from Sonny's flashlight. "What's wrong?" She glared at me. "Why are you waking me up? Is something on fire?"

The sheriff explained what had happened. "We thought you might know something."

"Me? Why me?"

"I understand the girl wasn't too keen on going with you."

Mrs. Benning stepped forward. "Bonnie's a shy child. It had been awhile since I'd seen her." She looked around Sonny at me. "You know what's more likely is that this woman's children coerced her for some reason. If the circus I saw in there tonight is any indication, there's no telling what they're capable of. A man living with a woman he's not married to. It's a den of iniquity. Not something I want my niece exposed to."

Sonny looked at me, then Peter. "Is that right? You've invited your handyman to move in? Your aunt Cora will—"

My face flamed, my insides ready to explode. "Sonny, you know me better than that. I'm tired of your accusations, and we've veered way off the point. Three girls are missing. We need to find them. Now."

Sonny turned back to Mrs. Benning. "You're coming with me. Bein' a stranger in town, we'll want to check your vehicle and ask you some questions."

Mrs. Benning drew up her shoulders. "You're arresting me? Because I came to do my family duty and provide a home for an orphan?"

"You're not under arrest. Only in custody for questioning." He turned to me. "If Mrs. Benning had nothing to do with it—and I will find out—then we could be looking at an abduction."

My blood ran cold. "What?"

"Georgia, you know people in this town are scared, and this whole polio outbreak started right here at the Stardust. Could be someone's gone off the deep end and wants to get back at you. We'll want to question all your customers."

"Mr. Sweeney's the only other one. He's next to Malcolm Overstreet." I pointed toward the place. The roadster he drove was gone.

[CHAPTER 35]

I didn't think Van Sweeney was a kidnapper any more than I could fly. Yet he'd never come around to our backyard suppers until last night. He'd seemed friendly and easygoing, talking with Catfish. A guest in our town. Anticipated. Invited.

But he was a stranger.

Odd, too, that a professional had chosen Bobby Carl to be his agent. I shuddered. Was Bobby Carl the one who'd gone off the deep end? Wanting to get back at me for not returning his feelings of admiration?

All of this and more zipped through my head. Sonny shook my arm. "What the Sam Hill is wrong with you?"

"Mr. Sweeney's car is gone. He was here last night when Mrs. Benning arrived."

"What do you know about him?"

"Not much. Only that he's the celebrity entertainer for the March of Dimes fund-raiser. Bobby Carl Applegate's his agent."

"That blows the case wide open. Anyone fool enough to have Bobby Carl for an agent ain't smart enough to kidnap three girls. Peculiar, though, since his car's missing."

Malcolm, who'd stepped out on the porch for a smoke, walked

up. "Sorry, couldn't help overhearing. You were talking about Sweeney?"

Sonny scratched his head. "Yeah, he a friend of yours?"

"Matter of fact, I hadn't seen him in years until he showed up here. We've been getting reacquainted ever since."

"Do you happen to know where he is now?"

Malcolm started to say something, then stopped. "Personal business, I believe. He's not your fella, though. And I'm sure he'd be glad to come to the station tomorrow and answer any questions."

"So you're planning on seeing him?"

"Shore 'nuf. We're going fishing at first light."

"I'd give a million bucks right now to join you, but I've got other things to do. Personal business, you say? What kind of a man has personal business in Mayhaw at four in the morning?"

Malcolm shrugged. "Some do, I guess."

A wisp of an idea went through my head, something that wouldn't quite come to me.

Calm down. Think.

Sonny jerked my arm. "I need you to stay by the phone. I'll call the mayor and tell him to get a search party rounded up. Guess the dispatcher will have to sit with Mrs. Benning down at the county office while we start combing the streets of Mayhaw. Mind if I use your phone?"

"Help yourself."

When he'd made the calls, he held the back door to his car open for Mrs. Benning.

She turned to Peter and me. "If so much as a hair on that sweet child's head is harmed, I will sue you for neglect."

Sonny told her to get in. Before he turned onto the highway, the red light was spinning on top of his car.

Peter guided me inside. The stale air of the office was suffocating, and my arms and legs trembled. I collapsed into the rocking chair and leaned back. Ludi's voice came into my head. "You gotta stop your strivin'. Let the Lord do the strivin' for you."

I hadn't been striving when Mrs. Benning showed up. Worried, yes, about what to do with Fiona's children. And I was still worried that Bonnie would be neglected by the Bennings. But something about Van Sweeney wasn't right, either. He'd been to supper at Aunt Cora's. Had she invited him back for some late-night *conversation,* as she always put it? She was a grown woman and didn't owe me explanations about her private life. But still...

The childhood insecurities skated along my bones. *Give it up. The girls are what matter now.*

I couldn't, though. Theodora Benning and Aunt Cora corkscrewed through my thoughts like a whirlwind.

Quit your strivin'.

A blanket of calm swooped over me. *Ludi. Why hadn't I thought of her first?* Between Sonny's accusations and all the commotion, I obviously hadn't been thinking clearly.

I inhaled deeply and looked at Peter. "I know where the girls are."

CHAPTER 36

Zion. They'd gone to Ludi for help. I was sure of it, and Peter agreed it was plausible.

My body wouldn't stop shaking as I went into the quarters and told Mary Frances and Malcolm that we believed the girls were trying to help Bonnie so she wouldn't have to leave with Mrs. Benning.

Mary Frances nodded. "I had a bad feeling about her. I only hope the girls are all right."

I gave her a hug. "We all do. Can you stay here and listen for the phone in case we're wrong and the sheriff finds them somewhere else?"

Malcolm told Peter how to get to Zion, the quickest way being across the field and into the trees. "I think, though, you'd be better off taking the road. In the darkness, you don't want to take a wrong turn and find yourselves knee-deep in the bayou."

All of Malcolm's summers in Mayhaw and his knowing every fishing spot for miles around gave us confidence he knew what he was talking about.

He told Peter, "When the dirt road ends, you'll have to leave your car and walk. There's a crook in the bayou heading off to the right, so you want to take a sharp left through the trees. Don't worry, there's a good path. You'll come to a break in the trees. You'll know you're in the right spot if you smell the jasmine."

My mind was trying to remember the directions, but the jasmine stopped me. "I thought jasmine bloomed earlier in the year."

"It does. But the blooms fall to the ground, giving a couple hundred feet of the path an intoxicating smell you can't miss. Walking on it releases the scent."

I wanted to know how he knew this, but anxiety over finding the girls skated along my bones. Peter ran to get his car, and as I got in, Malcolm hollered that he'd take care of Mary Frances. Somehow that made me smile.

Ten minutes later, we turned onto a blacktop road then took two other turns. At the dead end, we got out of Peter's car and followed Malcolm's directions along the path. There was no mistaking the jasmine when we came to it. It was a heavenly scent that reminded me of Ludi and the day I first met her.

A sudden terror gripped me. "Peter, what if someone thinks we're intruders? Do you think this is safe?"

"I've got it covered. Catfish and I have a secret whistle we use when we go fishing."

Voices filtered through the trees on our right. "I think it's time to whistle." My heart pounded, partly out of fear for the girls, but also because I'd never stepped foot in Zion.

Peter whistled the first two lines of "Don't Sit Under the Apple Tree," then stopped and listened.

"Really? That's the secret whistle? An Andrews Sisters' song?"

"Catfish thought it was catchy. Caught on right away to the echo part to whistle back at me." Peter repeated the whistle. And like a boomerang, the echo came back.

Five seconds later, Catfish ran up. My eyes had adjusted to the dark and enough light came from Zion behind him that I could see the whites of his eyes like twin moons on his dark face.

"Mister Peter. Miz Georgie. Come quick. Momma be having a conniption. Don' know what to do. The girls and yo' dog, Mister Peter, they just showed up."

I pulled Catfish into a bear hug. "They're here! Oh, I had a feeling."

"The girls be scared out of their wits. They say a terrible woman be chasin' them."

Peter clapped Catfish on the shoulder. "It's not exactly like that, but Bonnie was frightened. We've come to fetch them."

We followed Catfish, and from the edge of the clearing, Zion looked like a cluster of cabins, but as we drew nearer, it became apparent they were nothing more than huts. Some appeared to be wood, others solid black. The phrase *tarpaper shack* popped into my head, and with it, an ache in my heart. How could this be? A village so poor at my back doorstep? Shame, like angry gnats, bit at my soul.

Catfish opened a crude screen door and held out his arm. "This way." From behind us he yelled, "Momma, don't be afraid. It's Mr. Peter and Miz Georgie." We stepped inside. A kerosene lantern graced a wooden table in what appeared to be the main room. Bonnie and Rosey shared a bench and jerked their heads up.

Ludi lumbered from another room, working her apron in her hands. "Lordamercy, I didn't know what to do. The girls came skippin' through the trees, that big, ugly dog with 'em, runnin' like the boogeyman was after 'em."

Bonnie jumped from the bench and ran to me. "I'm sorry. I was a scaredy-cat. Rosey said Ludi can hide us so I don't have to go with Aunt Teddy."

I looked at Rosey. "I'm so mad at you, I could strangle you. What you did was dangerous. And how you even thought of it is beyond me."

She bent her head and looked up at me. "I know, Momma. And you can give me twenty-five whippings. I don't care. That woman was mean to Bonnie."

"She didn't do anything to her. What are you talking about?"

"Bonnie told us one time the woman locked her in the broom closet when she didn't eat her supper. And the man, he pretended he was nice, but he wasn't."

"Bonnie, are these things true?"

Tears filled her eyes, and her chin quivered. "Momma said they're bad. Don't make me go..." Sobs racked her shoulders, and she buried her face in the folds of my skirt.

I picked her up. "Shhh. It's all right. You don't have to go anywhere right now. And I'm not mad at you, but I was afraid because we couldn't find you."

Rosey pointed at the floor. "We had Sebastian. He wouldn't let nothing bad happen."

We all relaxed, and Ludi told us Avril had fallen asleep in the other room. She asked us to sit down and pointed to a couch with a spring sticking out and a picture of Jesus hanging over it. Peter and I sat down, Bonnie on my lap, Rosey on his.

Ludi asked if we'd like some apple cider.

I laughed. "That would be wonderful."

She padded away on bare feet as wide as snowshoes and returned with two mason jars for Peter and me and smaller glasses for the girls. She smiled and folded her hands over her bosom. "Welcome to our home."

The apple cider, rich with flavor and as warm as the friend who served it, slid down my throat like fine wine.

I thanked Ludi and said, "We should go and tell everyone the girls are safe. I'm curious, though, has your husband already left for work?"

"Eli and the other menfolk sleeps over to the lumber camp during the week. He only comes home on the weekends to bring our Sunday service. What we got here is a whole passel of women and kids, but we make do. Yes'm, we make do."

"How many people live here in Zion?"

"Last count we had thirty-one, countin' the baby what was birthed last month. Good thing Mr. Malcolm stopped in. Them breech birthin's is the worst."

An odd feeling came in my chest. "Mr. Malcolm? What did he do?"

"Why, he be the only doctor we got in Zion. Only he don't allow us to call him doctor. Says that's for them people back at his clinic in Texarkana."

"Malcolm Overstreet? The one who's staying at the Stardust?"

"Yes'm. He's been comin' every summer for as long as I can remember. Spends the weekends fishin' the bayou and doctorin' folks here. We ain't never let on bein's we can't pay him much. He says it ain't for the money anyway."

"So that's how he knew how we could find you. And you never let on when you're up at the Stardust. How come?"

"Mr. Malcolm say it's between us."

"I'll be doggone. Can you get Avril for us?"

Peter rose, still holding Rosey, who'd fallen asleep on his lap. "We'd better get back and tell the sheriff to call off the search."

Ludi started wringing her apron again. "You ain't gon' tell him where you found 'em, are you? He might think we coaxed 'em here."

I shook my head. "No, we won't tell him. And for the record, you worry too much about the sheriff. He has a good heart, and we'll just tell him Sebastian led us to the girls."

Ludi shuffled off and came back in with Avril. "Lordamercy, this girl's burnin' plumb up!" She handed her to me. Avril's body was limp with sleep, but her face was hot as fire.

Traipsing through the open field to Ludi's in the night air might have brought on a fever, but another thought plowed into my brain.

Swoosh. Clank. Wheeze. Sounds of the respiratory ward roared in my head.

No, dear Lord. No!

Even in the lantern glow, I saw the flush on her cheeks.

The same look Fiona Callahan had the night polio struck.

CHAPTER 37

Peter drove as fast as he could over the narrow roads. When he turned onto the main highway, Avril stirred and mumbled, "My head hurts."

"It's okay, sugar. We're going to take care of you."

We dropped Rosey and Bonnie off at the Stardust, and I asked Peter to run in and give Mary Frances and Malcolm a quick explanation and to have them call the sheriff and tell him the girls were safe.

Two of them, anyway. God only knew about Avril.

Although my insides churned and frothed with worry, I tried to force the sounds and smells from the polio ward from my thoughts. But they sneaked in anyway. The discordant rhythms of the iron lungs wheezing, groaning. The cries from those confined in the life-sustaining machines.

From inside Peter's car, the first rays of morning gave a peach glow to the horizon, illuminating Avril's face, her discomfort evident in the pucker of her brows, the protruding bottom lip. I kissed the top of her head and tightened the hold of my arms around her.

Time took on a new dimension as we rushed to the hospital,

through the emergency doors, and into a curtained cubicle. As Doc Kelley conducted his exam, I wanted him to be done, to tell us it was only the flu, a bad case of too much night air, or a bad dream. But then he called the nurse and asked for a spinal tray. He positioned Avril in a fetal position and asked me to hold her. He pulled on gloves and worked behind her, talking gently.

"You'll feel a stick when I put this magic medicine in to numb you. Now, I want you to hold still as a mouse. You'll feel pressure in your back while I take a sample of your spinal fluid."

He took a long needle from a tray and asked the nurse if she was ready. She held up a clear tube and nodded. When he poised the needle, I turned away, my fingers digging into the chubby flesh of my daughter.

"It's okay, sweetie. You're going to be okay." I repeated the words over and over, the mantra for myself as well as Avril.

She screamed when the needle pierced her spine, and it seemed to pierce my heart as well.

Doc talked quietly to the nurse, but I closed off my mind and begged God to have mercy, to touch Avril's body, to take the sickness from her. Behind me, I felt a firm but gentle hand on my shoulder and heard Aunt Cora whisper, "It's all right, Georgia. I'm praying, sugar."

Relief, like a cleansing rain, came over me, and I was glad for whoever had called her. Tears slid down my cheeks and pooled in the bend of my elbow.

When he was finished, Doc patted Avril's cheek and told her she'd done well. He looked at me and sighed. "We'll know before long if we're dealing with infantile paralysis. She'll have to lie flat on her back for a few hours now to keep her from getting a headache."

I nodded. It seemed ironic since she already had one when we came in.

As he walked out the door, he muttered, "This is no way to start the morning."

When we got to her room, Peter said he'd better go and straighten things out with the sheriff and would check on us later. Aunt Cora assured him she'd stay until he got back. Avril slept in fits and starts, trying to turn onto her side. I hovered over her, rubbing her arms and legs with the back of my finger to keep her still. It seemed an eternity before a nurse came and told me she'd sit with Avril, that Doc wanted to speak to Aunt Cora and me in the hall.

Aunt Cora took my hand in hers and led me through the door.

The lines in Doc's face looked deeper than ever, but his eyebrows rose slightly at the sight of us. "I have good news. We saw no abnormalities in the spinal fluid. Whatever we're dealing with is not polio."

My body went limp, every hope and prayer I'd clung to now holding me up. My teeth chattered from the quivers in my jaws. "Oh, my. Are you sure?"

"Nearly positive. I think she has a virus of some sort, but it's not polio. Her throat is pink, but her tonsils aren't swollen. The stiffness in her neck is most likely the flu. All of her reflexes are normal, with no pain in any of her joints. If I were guessing, I'd say it's an upper respiratory condition."

We thanked him. Shook his hand. Then Aunt Cora and I embraced and clung to each other until we were both crying and laughing at the same time.

Doc wanted Avril to stay a couple more hours as a precaution, but he thought she'd be right as rain in a few days.

It was all I'd prayed for and more.

Aunt Cora insisted that Avril and I come home with her. "It's quieter there, and she needs rest. From what I've heard, y'all were up half the night."

Doc agreed that being closer to the hospital in case we had other concerns was a good idea. Peter returned as we were fixing to leave.

"Mrs. Benning's gone back to Arkansas. The sheriff told her she would have to apply for guardianship with the state of Texas before he would let her take Bonnie. She wasn't happy and thought she should at least get a reimbursement for her wasted trip."

I blew out the breath I didn't realize I'd been holding. "What a relief. It makes me wonder if I even want them to look for this Inez woman."

Aunt Cora frowned. "Who's Inez?"

"The woman I told you about. Fiona's sister. Bonnie talked about *Aunt Eyes,* but we couldn't figure out she meant Inez. At least Mrs. Benning provided us with that information, so all is not lost."

Peter smiled. "I have some good news there."

My stomach somersaulted. "They found her?"

"I told Sheriff Bolander about her since Cora was busy here with you and couldn't start the process with the March of Dimes people. He made some calls, and it turns out a woman named Inez Lombardy lives next door to one of the police officers in Kilgore. She's been worried about her sister. They're going to talk to her this evening."

"What if she's as horrible as Mrs. Benning?"

"The officer said she and her husband are good citizens from what he can tell. Her husband's the manager of the Piggly Wiggly."

"Did he know the husband's name?"

"No. Why?"

"Bonnie mentioned a man named Uncle Mitch. I think it might be Inez's husband."

"Shouldn't be too hard to find out. I'm thinking of driving

over there Monday if it's the right people. It's going to be a shock when they find this out."

"Don't you have to work?"

"I called the mill, told them what was going on. They said to take all the time I need."

"You don't have to do this."

"I know. But I said I'd see you through this, and that's what I aim to do."

"How can I ever thank you?"

"Don't worry, I'll think of something." His eyes danced, and it was all I could do not to throw my arms around his neck and kiss him, but with Aunt Cora looking on, I refrained.

Aunt Cora picked Avril up and said, "Let's go home."

✳

Avril still had a slight fever and didn't argue when I told her she needed to lie down. I settled her in the bedroom that had been mine growing up. Little had changed. The same yellowed lace curtains hung at the windows. The pink organza bedspread with the ink stain. When I pulled the spread up and looked at the irregular-shaped mark, a memory stirred.

I'd been sitting in the middle of my bed writing a letter to O'Dell to tell him I'd decided not to marry him after all. If he was unfaithful before we married, I could only imagine what my life would be like afterward.

I'd just refilled my pen from the ink bottle, anxious to get the words down while I had the courage. *I'll go away and give the baby up for adoption. It's best for all of us.* Tears streaked down my face and fell onto the paper, smearing the words. I gripped the pen. It wasn't that I didn't want to be a mother. I did. But I wanted a husband who loved me and would be true. A child deserved two parents—two devoted parents—who wouldn't decide one day to dump the child with a relative.

Aunt Cora knocked and came in before I'd finished. "Oh, goodness, what's wrong?"

I told her about O'Dell and my decision to call off the wedding.

"Oh, for heaven's sake. He's just sowing his wild oats. Be thankful he's getting it out of his system. Come on. You're going to be a beautiful bride." She'd leaned over to give me a hug and bumped the ink bottle. The stopper wasn't in tight, and ink poured out like the shame I carried in my womb.

"What if he doesn't get it out of his system? What would I do then?"

"The same thing women have always done. Hold your head up and smile. It's uncomely to air your dirty laundry in public. In your condition, you should be thanking your lucky stars he's willing to marry you." She gave me a hug. "I came up to tell you the irises look too much like funeral flowers, so I'm going to see if we can find peonies instead. Besides, they have such a lovely scent."

The irises might have been the better choice, and I could have protested. I could have packed my bags and gone. I might have, but when Aunt Cora left my room that day, I was lying on my bed running my finger around the ink blob when a strange stirring came in my abdomen. As soft as the breath of a butterfly but as quick as a firefly on a June evening, it came again. I *could* decide not to marry O'Dell Peyton. But in that moment, I knew the one thing I could never do was give up the life growing inside me. My sweet Rosey. Two weeks later, I stood in the gazebo behind Mara Lee and said "I do."

Now, Avril stirred under the sheet, her lips quirked in a slumbering smile. I felt her forehead, which was almost cool. The aspirin had helped, and I knew I'd made the right choice that day seven years ago. O'Dell had been a good father when he was around. It was just all the other times keeping my chin up that my heart felt shattered.

Downstairs, the phone rang for the third time since we'd been home. The weariness of the past twenty-four hours caught up with me, and I let my head relax into the pillow. As I was drifting off, I thought I heard Mr. Sweeney's voice downstairs. I smiled. Aunt Cora and her suitors. At least I liked this one. When I woke up, I was surprised that the moon shone through the lace at the window.

Aunt Cora peeked around the door. "Still doing okay?"

I nodded and went out in the hall with her. "Your phone's been awfully busy."

"We're getting down to the wire with the charity event. People are still worried with the new cases last week, but they also want to fight back. I think we'll have a good turnout."

I sat on the top step of the staircase. "I'm looking forward to it being a busy weekend at the Stardust, too, although most of the rooms are spoken for by Mr. Sweeney and his musicians."

"I suppose they have to stay somewhere. By the way, Peter stopped by and dropped off a bag for you. He said Rosey packed you some things."

"That should be interesting."

"Your young man is nice."

"Peter?"

"Who else would I be talking about?"

"He gets a lot of credit for getting the Stardust remodeled."

She waved away the remark. "You know how I feel about that place. I only mentioned Peter because he seems a decent sort, and it gives me some consolation that, with him there, you're not quite as vulnerable to tramps or criminals darkening your door."

"Your fears are ungrounded. All of the people who've come to

the Stardust have been nice. One man says he's been every summer for thirty years."

"Someone I know?"

"Malcolm Overstreet."

"It sounds familiar, but I can't place him."

"The funny thing is, he remembered Mr. Sweeney. Said they
both stayed there years ago."

"You sure know a lot about your customers."

"Yep, we're one big happy family. And get this, Malcolm is
sweet on Mary Frances. She's started fixing herself up, putting
color on her cheeks. She even painted her toenails and started
wearing stylish clothes."

"Get out of here. Your Mary Frances?"

"Yep. The change in her has been miraculous."

"You've changed, too. I like your hair. Did Twila Flynn cut it
for you?"

"No. Ludi did."

"Your colored woman? You let her cut your hair?"

When I nodded, Aunt Cora shook her head. "I can't believe
you trusted a colored woman."

"She's my friend and has more talents in her little finger than
I'll ever have. I wish I'd cut it ages ago."

"Why didn't you?"

"O'Dell liked it long. Not that it kept him home, but I'm getting past that. As a matter of fact, I've decided facing the truth of
our relationship is for the best."

Aunt Cora picked at the polish on her fingernail. "There's still
a place for being discreet."

"Maybe so, but when it affects others, it's senseless to keep up
the charade. It wasn't Bonnie's fault her mother had an affair with
O'Dell. I saw how haunted the poor thing was, not knowing if

her mother had abandoned her, or if she was even alive. That's why I took her to Tyler when I went to get Willie. I wanted her to see her mother, even if it wasn't under the best of conditions."

"She's awfully young to be taken onto a polio ward."

"The people at the hospital didn't think so, and I was shocked at her resilience. She saw her mother in the iron lung and didn't even flinch. Climbed up on a stool and caressed her mother's face. It was precious."

"I hope she's not scarred for life."

"I think not knowing would have left a bigger scar."

"I don't know where you've gotten all these ideas, Georgia. I've simply never understood you."

"You tried. I know you did. I do wish you'd told me my parents had problems and weren't coming back. It would've saved us both a lot of grief."

"You were too young to handle the information."

"You might have been surprised."

She drew her lips tight, her body rigid beside me. Funny, but I no longer felt anger toward her as I had in the past. A bit sad and melancholy, but perhaps I was simply unable to wring out any other emotion after the stress of the past two days.

She turned to me. "Why does the name Malcolm Overstreet sound so familiar?"

Either she hadn't heard a word I said or she was ignoring me. "Perhaps he was one of the men who sneaked in the back door to entertain you."

My skin prickled with a million tiny needles. The words had just slipped out. The moment I said it, I wished I hadn't. No matter what my beef with Aunt Cora, I had never accused her in such a way. And she'd been a pillar for me with Avril.

She laughed. "Whatever are you talking about? Men at the

back door? I swan, Georgia, I think you're the one with a fever."
Her voice was tinny, hollow.

"I'm sorry. I shouldn't have said that."

"You're right, you shouldn't have. But I'm flabbergasted, absolutely stymied by where you came up with such a statement." Her
voice had returned to normal, and like truth massaged over time,
I believed she did think she was innocent. That my child's eye
hadn't seen the men who came and went. That my young imagination wasn't capable of figuring out Aunt Cora was nothing
more than a courtesan in her own home.

Avril touched me on the shoulder. "Mommy, I'm hungry."

"Oh, sweetie, you must be feeling better." I touched her forehead. As cool as a spring breeze.

Aunt Cora rose and scooped Avril up. "So tell me. Are you
really, really hungry? Hungry enough to eat a bear? Or only hungry enough for some of Auntie's special tomato soup?"

She giggled. "I want a Popsicle. My throat hurts."

Avril had two Popsicles while Aunt Cora fixed tomato soup for
herself and me. In her usual fashion, she didn't mention our earlier
conversation until I was ready to tuck Avril into bed.

"I remember Malcolm Overstreet. You know, maybe it's time
we had the talk you've been pestering me about for twenty years."
She patted me on the cheek. "Someday soon."

Either Aunt Cora, too, had decided to quit striving or her iron
will had finally cracked. And something about that made my own
foundation feel it was about to shatter.

CHAPTER 38

Avril woke up with a stuffy nose, a low-grade fever, and enough energy to power a fishing boat through the bayou. Aunt Cora agreed to drop us off at the Stardust before she headed to church. She refused my invitation to come in but promised she'd call later to check on us.

Mary Frances met us with open arms. "You've no idea how glad I am to see you. I am worn plumb down to the nubs. I haven't slept a wink in two nights, the girls had to fix their own breakfast, and I have blisters on my feet from these blasted high heels."

"Whoa. Let's start from the top, okay? First of all, why don't you get some comfortable shoes? And Rosey's old enough to help out, so that's no problem. How was Willie?"

"Oh, he's been an angel. You know, O'Dell was the same way. The best baby on earth."

"I'm sure he was. Why don't you take a break and put your feet up for a while? And take Avril with you."

The two of them were gone before I could snap my fingers. The office was a mess. Cookie crumbs and crayons scattered on the floor. Stray coffee cups. But it was good to be home, and I hummed as I went to work.

After clearing most of the mess, I turned my attention to a stack of mail. Bills. And more bills. I set them aside and picked up the next envelope. A letter with an Oklahoma postmark and Doreen Palmer's return address.

I ripped it open and read through her news. A new great-nephew. A niece's wedding. And she'd found a house to buy one block off Main Street. She asked how we were doing and how business was.

On the third page, I read a long paragraph. Then read it again. My heart hammered at the cryptic words.

By now, I'm sure you've settled into a routine. I wasn't completely honest with you about the reason Paddy wanted you to have the Stardust. It is true you've always been dear to us, but you don't look like Paddy's grandmother or any of the Palmer and Tickle clan we know of. You used to sit on the steps of the Stardust and watch the cars that went by, always looking for the one that would bring your folks. Of course, they never came. It nearly broke our hearts watching you. We wanted to tell you the truth about your parents, but Paddy had given his word and then spent every day of his life wishing he hadn't.

Paddy and Doreen knew and they didn't tell me? I bit my lip and turned the page over.

The answer is at the Stardust.
One other thing. Give Malcolm Overstreet my regards. He has a few secrets of his own and might shed some light on your situation.
Give my love to the girls.

Doreen Palmer

My head swam with thoughts. First, Aunt Cora told me it was time I learned the truth. Well, almost time. Whenever *she* deemed it time. But Paddy and Doreen knew? Who else? And the answer was at the Stardust? Where? There were ten cottages, an office with quarters, a washhouse, and five acres of land. I would be old and gray before I found the answer.

A part of me no longer wanted to know. I'd made new friends, seen my mother-in-law transformed before my eyes, and come face-to-face with O'Dell's mistress. I'd had enough drama to last a lifetime. Not to mention having to still decide what to do with Fiona's children.

Why had Doreen written now? Had she been giving me enough time to get acquainted with Malcolm Overstreet in hopes he would tell me? It seemed chancy at best. What if we hadn't hit it off? Or what if this was the year he found another fishing hole? His secret, of course, was the aid he rendered to Zion. She knew he'd come to doctor the folks who had no other means of medical support. It all seemed far-fetched that I would connect the dots. It had to be something else.

Willie's cries brought me back to the present. I put Doreen's letter in the ledger that I hadn't gotten to and put it and the unpaid bills in the drawer. There was too much to do to worry over my own personal demons.

*

As tired as I was, I didn't sleep well. When Willie woke up for his feeding, I went over Doreen's letter again, trying to read between the lines. *The answer is at the Stardust.* A challenge. Was that Doreen's intent—to spur me into action?

When morning came and I heard Ludi singing across the meadow, I met her and Merciful in the washhouse.

"Morning, Miz Georgie. How's Miss Avril?"

I handed her a cup of coffee, strong the way she liked it. "Avril couldn't be better. How are you?"

"Can't complain about a thing."

Merciful asked if she could see the girls, and I told her they'd saved her a biscuit. She skipped off as Ludi gathered the cleaning supplies.

"You gon' spoil my child."

"That's the plan."

She sipped the coffee. "You didn't need to come prancin' out here the minute I showed up to bring me no coffee. I say you must got somethin' else on your mind."

"Is it that obvious?"

"Hmmm?"

"I got a letter from Doreen Palmer yesterday, but something she wrote puzzles me."

"How is Do-reen?"

"She sounded fine. Going to a wedding. Someone had a new baby."

"She comin' back for a visit?"

"Not that she said. But she did mention there was something she thought I should have found by now. It was mysterious almost, and she didn't say exactly what it was. I thought you might know if she had a special box or hidey-hole I haven't discovered."

Ludi held the coffee cup in both hands, brought it to her face, and inhaled like the scent might jiggle her memory. But the only thing that jiggled was her double chin when she swallowed. "No, ma'am. Can't say as I recall any such place out here in the wash-house. I wouldn't be knowing about over yonder, though." She nodded toward the quarters. "I guess you been over it by now."

"Not yet. I thought you might know of someplace."

"What you be looking for?"

"I'm not sure. A letter maybe. A photo. Could even be something from a newspaper."

Ludi drained her coffee cup and held it out to me. "Thank you, Miz Georgie. Let me know if you happen on it."

While Merciful played with the girls, I searched the office. One cabinet had paperwork I'd been through before, but not thoroughly. I dug in and went through it piece by piece. Nothing but old receipts, a few recipes. I shoved the box back under the counter and went through the three drawers where I kept the ledger and money tray, extra brochures, and miscellaneous items. Still nothing.

Frustrated, I gave up and had just started on the pile of bills when the office bell jangled.

"Hey, Bobby Carl. What can I do for you today?"

"What's going on, Georgia?" I wondered if something had blown in his eyes the way he kept squinting.

"What do you mean?"

"Your hair. Something's different."

"I got it cut, but it's been awhile. Guess you didn't notice when you brought Mr. Sweeney to register."

"Guess not. I liked it better long."

Another good reason to cut it, but I just shrugged. "Matter of taste, I guess. It's definitely cooler. Anything in particular you wanted?"

"Oh, yeah. I came to ask what's going on with your aunt Cora?"

"Nothing that I know of. Why do you ask?"

"Rumor has it she and Van Sweeney are having creative differences. Man, I hope this isn't going to put a damper on the charity concert." He leaned on the desk, close enough that I could smell the Brylcreem on his hair.

"I was with her yesterday. She didn't say anything."

"I think it just happened. She met with Sweeney before our committee's breakfast meeting today. When we all got together, the tension was as thick as fog on the bayou."

"Maybe she was tired. She's had a lot on her mind lately, and it wouldn't surprise me if you read something else into it. What did she say?"

"It was the mayor's secretary who overheard her conversation with Sweeney. I don't know the whole thing, but she said she'd never give her consent. Made us wonder if they're arguing over how to use the funds they raise. Not that it matters to me as long as I get my cut."

"Has anyone ever told you you're a busybody?" I started straightening brochures, hoping he'd get the hint that I didn't want to talk.

"Gee, Georgia, I can't help it. When you've been a radio reporter for six years, you can't just turn off the instinct, you know."

"So maybe you should go back on the radio."

"I'm considering it. Sweeney hasn't been as plum a deal as I thought. He's only interested in these small-town, low-paying gigs. Wouldn't even hear of me trying to book him in the clubs I had lined up in Memphis and Shreveport."

"Sorry. He seems like a nice man."

"Something screwy's going on." He crossed his arms and huffed out his frustration.

"Don't get yourself worked up."

"You'd think since I'm his manager, Sweeney would keep me informed."

"I can't help you there. But I do need to go check on the kids. See you at the festival."

"That sounds promising."

I left it at that. I had too many other things to worry about besides resisting Bobby Carl's wiles.

＊

After supper, Peter's car pulled up in the drive. I knew Inez Lombardy was Fiona's sister the minute they stepped through the door of the Stardust. She had the same pale eyes as Fiona and Bonnie. The same translucent skin, but her hair was dark and curled softly around her face. Following them was a lean man with a crew cut and a cautious expression.

Peter made the introductions: Inez Lombardy and her husband, Mitch.

I extended my hand, all the while sizing them up, trying to assess their adequacy and intent. And whether I could hand over the two children I'd come to love as my own.

Inez had a low but mellow voice. "Peter's told me how attached you've become to my niece and nephew. It was terribly nice for him to come to us in person."

"He's been a big help, and I'm glad to finally meet you."

Awkwardness filled the room. I had a million questions about Fiona. Did they know she'd stolen my husband? That she'd given him the son he always wanted? If they were close, why hadn't they looked for Fiona? Would they care for my girls' half brother?

Peter, bless him, smoothed the way. "Inez and Mitch have had a rough time. They only found out yesterday about Fiona's illness. We went to Tyler so Inez could see her sister."

Inez crossed her arms and rubbed her pale skin. "It's a miracle she's even alive. And the nurse said it could be months before we know what the future holds." She frowned, then leveled her gaze at me. "I feel partially to blame for this. Fiona was so lonely after Rusty was killed. I was the one who suggested she go to work. I even offered to watch Bonnie while she waited tables at the café."

A picture formed in my mind. An attractive woman serving coffee, pocketing tips, thinking of her child at home and a husband she'd never see again. I could nearly taste the hunger for companionship Fiona must've had.

I shrugged. "Don't blame yourself. You couldn't have known what would happen. Polio has a way of lurking in the shadows, choosing its victims. It might've happened anyway."

"The polio, yes." Inez stopped and chose her words carefully. "It wasn't the polio I was thinking of. It was O'Dell. When Fiona told me she'd met someone, she began to live again. Her face glowed, and she giggled when she told me things he said. Their friendship progressed rather quickly. Too fast, I thought, but I tried to stay out of it, and it never once occurred to me he was married."

Another image flashed. O'Dell, tired from a day of knocking on doors, making one or two sales, maybe none. He had to eat. Why wouldn't he chat with the waitress?

Her eyes pleaded with me as though she had to convince me Fiona wasn't a floozy. "I don't think Fiona knew about you, either, Georgia. When she found out she was having a baby, they talked about marriage, but he kept stalling. Then he disappeared. She thought he was scared because of the baby, but she was determined to find him." Her face darkened, and I could tell it hurt her to continue.

"We argued. I told her she was foolish, that if it was meant to be he would come back. She'd heard him talk about his mother in Mayhaw, had even mailed a birthday card to her for him, so she knew where he was from. She'd been feeling poorly for several days, and I wanted her to go to the doctor. All she could think of was finding O'Dell. Finally, I told her to go on. I was tired of arguing. She told me not to worry, that if things worked out, she would let me know. But I never heard from her. Not one word."

Mitch Lombardy stepped forward and took Inez's arm. "It's okay, doll. Things have worked out. Just not like we expected."

Inez chewed her bottom lip and looked at me. "Can we see the children?"

The moment I'd dreaded. *Bonnie.* How would she react to Inez and Mitch? I glanced at Peter, looking for some sign. Assurance shone in his eyes.

I stepped toward the quarters. "I'm so sorry. I've completely forgotten my manners. Let's go in and let me fix you an iced tea or a cup of coffee. Which would you prefer?"

They exchanged glances, and in their silent conversation, I saw their own doubts and hesitation. Mitch spoke softly. "Iced tea would be nice."

Peter said, "I'm going to pass this time. I'll see you later."

I mouthed *thank you* to him and motioned for the Lombardys to follow me.

CHAPTER 39

I gathered my perkiest voice and opened the connecting door to our quarters. "Knock, knock. We have company."

Mary Frances sat on the sofa between Rosey and Bonnie and held Avril on her lap. Bonnie, still shy from her traumatic experience with her aunt Teddy, looked up, wary, but in an instant her face lit up and she squealed, "Aunt Eyes!" She ran into the outstretched arms of Inez and hugged her neck. "Where's Mommy? Did she come?"

"No. Your mommy is still sick, but here's the kiss she wanted me to give you." She put a loud smacking kiss on Bonnie's cheek, and in an instant, I knew all would be well.

The feeling was short-lived. Mary Frances put her hand to her mouth and closed her eyes. My insides twisted. The Lombardys would cherish Bonnie and her brother, but for Mary Frances, losing baby Willie had to be torture.

Rosey crossed her arms. "Does this mean Bonnie is leaving? What about Willie? He's just as much our baby as hers." My spine tingled. She was right, but I'd not told her the truth of it. I knew her childish logic didn't put it all together, but by telling her, I would be tarnishing O'Dell's name. I swore I'd never do it. And yet, she should know Willie was her half brother.

Mary Frances rose from the divan. "I think it's time the Lombardys met Willie, don't you, Rosey? You can help me change him, okay?"

When they came back, Mary Frances placed Willie in Inez's arms. "We're going to let y'all get acquainted for a while. We'll be outside." She jerked her head toward the office for us to follow.

Once outside, Mary Frances pulled her cigarette case from her pocket and lit up. "You girls sit down." She looked at me. "I think you need to tell them the truth."

Rosey, even sitting on the steps, managed to look prissy. "You should always tell the truth. That's what the Bible says."

I squeezed between the girls and pulled them close. "You're right. There's something you should know."

In simple words I told them how much they were loved, that once their daddy loved me, but then he'd fallen in love with Fiona. "She's a nice lady who didn't know your daddy had another family. I didn't want you to stop loving your daddy, so I didn't tell you."

Rosey sighed. "Is that why the kids at school called Daddy a cheat?"

I was taken aback. She knew this already, the same way I'd known about Aunt Cora's gentlemen friends without her telling me. I gave her an extra hug. "That's what some people call it, but it doesn't mean he was a terrible man, just that he made a mistake."

"What does this have to do with anything?"

"The other lady your daddy loved was Mrs. Callahan—Bonnie and Willie's mom. I think God let them find us so we would know you had a brother...baby Willie."

"If Willie's our brother, is Bonnie our sister?"

"No, she had a different daddy who was a soldier. But you both had daddies who died, so you're sisters in a way. But Willie is both your brother and Bonnie's."

Avril tugged on my arm.

"Wait a minute, sweetie. Let me finish. When Bonnie's mother gets better, she will want Bonnie and Willie to be together, the way you and Avril are together."

Mary Frances finished her smoke and ground it out with her shoe. "Willie's lucky. He's going to have two families, and we'll go and visit him. Maybe he can even come here when he's older."

Rosey crossed her arms. "Bigger, like a boy, you mean? I don't really like boys."

Mary Frances laughed as Avril tugged harder on my arm.

"Do you have a question, Avie?"

"Yes. May I please have a Popsicle?"

It was the escape I needed. I knew there would be more questions, but the gate had been kicked open. I ruffled Avril's hair and said, "I think that's a splendid idea."

I passed out Popsicles to the girls, and after we'd discussed the guardianship papers, I invited Inez and Mitch to stay overnight. They said Peter had suggested they pack a bag. Bonnie asked to stay with "Aunt Eyes," so we fixed a rollaway bed for her.

The next morning I showed Inez how to make Willie's formula with Carnation milk and corn syrup. The good-byes were tearful, and I almost broke down when Mary Frances kissed Willie on the forehead and passed him over to Inez. She'd already exchanged addresses with the Lombardys and accepted an invitation to go to Kilgore over Labor Day.

Ludi and the kids came, and Catfish presented baby Willie with his own cypress knee—one with a hollow spot in one end for Willie to hold like a baby rattle.

My own hollow spot that had longed for the truth about my

parents no longer seemed as important. Maybe the truth I was meant to find at the Stardust was contentment and purpose. And there was a heap of work to do before the Mayhaw Festival and a talent show to get ready for.

Peter returned to work at the mill that morning, but when he'd picked up his lunch, he asked me if I could get Mary Frances to watch the girls that evening. When I asked why, he said Van Sweeney wanted to take the two of us to dinner and discuss a proposition. When I asked what, he said he was running late and would see me later.

What Mr. Sweeney wanted to discuss was a mystery. Unless, of course, it had something to do with the concert on Friday and his supposed disagreement with Aunt Cora. I thought of calling her, but then I'd be as pathetic a gossip as Bobby Carl.

CHAPTER 40

I spent extra time with my hair and makeup and slipped on the tangerine dress Aunt Cora said went with my complexion. Spending an evening without children or an emergency to clear up made me giddy in anticipation. When the office bell jangled, I kissed the girls and thanked Mary Frances for being a dear, then went out to greet Peter. He smelled divine and had on dress slacks and a pale blue shirt the same shade as his eyes.

"Ready?"

"Yes, but nervous since you've not told me what's going on."

"You look nice. Makes me wish we could dump Sweeney and find us a place to go dancing."

"What's stopping us?"

"You'll see."

We rode in Mr. Sweeney's car to the Cypress Lodge on the Longview highway. Sally had told me it was one of her favorite places to eat and had promised we'd go to lunch there one day. One day had never come, and I made a note to call her, to ask if we could get together since things had settled down.

Mr. Sweeney asked for a quiet table, and the waiter led us to one overlooking a small pond where ducks swam happily in circles.

The setting sun gave a golden glow to the water. Peter sat to my right, Mr. Sweeney across from me.

After we'd ordered and had sweet tea to sip, Mr. Sweeney cleared his throat. "I'm sorry for all the intrigue. I've wanted to talk to you for several days."

"My life's been rather complicated lately." I hoped Malcolm hadn't told him I suspected him of kidnapping the girls, but he'd been friendly and hadn't mentioned it the few times I'd seen him.

"You're charming, you know. As is the Stardust." He toyed with his tea glass. "I should probably confess something to you before we begin."

The waiter brought salads and set them before us, but my hand shook when I picked up my fork. "There's a lot of that going around."

"What do you mean?"

"Nothing. Just an observation." And I was certain he didn't want to know about my dramas with Mary Frances and the girls. "What are you confessing?"

"I didn't mean to make it sound alarming. It's about your friend Applegate."

"What's he been up to now? Sorry, I know he's your agent, but he gets carried away sometimes."

"So I noticed. My confession, though, is for something I did. When I answered Applegate's ad in the Nashville paper look-ing for new clients, it was the Mayhaw address that captured my attention. When he agreed to meet me, I found him to be earnest and thought I would encourage him by signing on with him. The truth is I've made a lot of money in investments and hardly a plug nickel in the music business." He took a bite and chewed slowly, seeming oblivious to the knot growing in my stomach.

A knot that told me to be careful.

"I told Applegate from the beginning I only performed occasionally and mostly for charities, but he got the impression I wanted to revive my career, maybe sign a recording contract. I was ready to tell him no when he mentioned the Mayhaw Festival. I remembered coming to it years ago when I was with a touring group. We had a vaudeville act with comedy, a few singers. I did a solo segment with a top hat and a cane I twirled around. The girls in the audience loved it."

"Is that what you're doing for the benefit?" Maybe he didn't have enough material and needed Peter and me to help out. Bobby Carl had no doubt exaggerated my experience and talent.

He laughed. "Not too enticing, is it?"

"I don't know. People like sentimental shows. And it sounds fun; I'm looking forward to hearing you."

"I've updated the act, of course. Added some jazz tunes and a nice band. All that to tell you that one of the things I'm most interested in is finding places where I can put my investments to work for another of my passions."

"So music isn't your passion?"

"It's only one of them. My sister in North Carolina contracted polio seven years ago. Thankfully, she survived but remains in a wheelchair."

"I'm so sorry. It's a dreadful disease." The waiter came and removed our empty salad plates. "So you signed up with Bobby Carl because of the polio benefit here? I'm still not sure what Mayhaw itself has to do with it."

"I've become aware of the need for families of polio victims to have a place to get away for a week or two and spend leisure time with their families in a pastoral setting. Often they're confined for long periods of time in nursing centers as they recover. These provide a great service but don't afford much in the way of atmosphere or privacy."

"I thought FDR built a place like that in Georgia."

"Yes, Warm Springs, and it's a wonderful place. Unfortunately, it's not always possible for families to travel there, so my dream is to see retreat centers built on a smaller scale in other regions. I think the Stardust would be an ideal location."

I appreciated Mr. Sweeney's enthusiasm, but something eluded me. Some detail I knew was missing.

The waiter brought out steaming plates with our entrées and placed them before us. Steaks for Peter and Mr. Sweeney. Spaghetti and meatballs for me. We ate for a few minutes in silence, and I agreed with Sally—the food was superb.

Peter asked how my dinner was, and I licked my lips and told him it sure beat the pants off turtle legs.

Mr. Sweeney laughed. "I knew from the minute I saw you that I was going to like you. I've talked to your pal Peter here and want to propose something that involves both of you."

Peter's eyebrows raised, but I had a feeling I was the only one in the dark, that they'd already had this conversation. He winked at me. "Remember you owe me one."

"When did I say *that*?"

"When you said you didn't know how to thank me. I told you I'd think of something. Only Sweeney's the brain behind this. I hope you'll give him a fair shake."

I looked at Mr. Sweeney. "Okay, I have the feeling I'm fixing to be railroaded, and it has something to do with me being the owner of the Stardust. I'm all ears, but before we get too far into the conversation, you need to know one thing. The Stardust is not for sale. It's part of the terms of Paddy Palmer's will. I have to run the Stardust for five years before I can do anything with it." A niggle came into my brain. Was the five years to give me time to find out the secret lurking there? Hmmmm.

Mr. Sweeney made an O with his mouth. "That's even better.

We weren't sure what the terms were. You see, Peter and I have come up with a rough plan."

Peter pulled a piece of notepaper from his pocket. "I've drawn some preliminary sketches. Van thinks we could expand the Stardust in the back as you and I had originally discussed. With help from the investors, we could add a swimming pool, a playground, a couple of units outfitted for the special needs of polio victims, and a small multipurpose building with a kitchen and space for families to gather."

"Goodness, you've certainly been busy, planning all this behind my back. What happens to my regular customers? The vision I have?" The dream I had of the Stardust being a beacon for weary travelers now seemed small, like wishing for an ice-cream cone when I could have the whole ice-cream parlor.

Mr. Sweeney reached across and patted my hand. "We're not trying to take away your dream. And there would be no cost to you for the improvements. We would hire Peter to be the foreman of the building projects and then give him a salary to make improvements and do the maintenance. In turn, your cottages would be perfect for families of polio victims. Mothers, fathers, aunts and uncles, cousins. They would be your regular customers. Recovering patients are no longer contagious, and the rental income would be more steady as reservations would be made ahead of time. It would only expand your original plans."

"What about Ludi and her kids? I can barely afford to pay her. Who would pay for additional help?"

"We would. Some details have to be worked out, but for now, we want to know if you are interested in letting us pursue this."

"It sounds exciting, but it's a lot to take in. I'd have to talk to my attorney."

Mr. Sweeney rubbed the back of his neck. "There's one other thing."

Ah. Something about his hesitancy made me wince. I twirled spaghetti on my fork and waited.

"It's your aunt Cora. She's not keen on the idea."

"No great surprise there. She's never been crazy about me running the Stardust. And I'm sure Peter's noticed she never comes around."

Mr. Sweeney frowned. "Has she ever said why?"

"A family disagreement, I think. Paddy Palmer, who left me the Stardust, is a distant relative. No one even remembers what the fuss was about, but Aunt Cora won't budge. Why do you need her approval?"

"I don't *have* to have it to proceed with the plans. But I wanted to announce it at the benefit, and she won't hear of it."

Bobby Carl's conversation now made sense. "And you want me to talk to her?"

He nodded. "Having her approval would mean a lot."

"She's not an easy woman to persuade. Once her mind is made up..."

"It's one of the delights I'm discovering about Cora."

"Delights? That's an odd way to put it."

Peter leaned over and whispered to me. "Van Sweeney has a crush on your aunt."

This time, Mr. Sweeney's neck reddened all the way up to his eyebrows. "Peter's right. When I walked into the first committee meeting and saw her, I nearly passed out. She's hardly aged a day since I met her all those years ago."

"You met her before?"

"She was one of those girls on the front row. We did three shows, and she came to every one of them. I figured she'd be married and matronly by now."

"If she heard you say matronly, she'd never speak to you again. And married? There's not a man alive who's ever suited her, so if you're the first, I'll be the one who's shocked. Maybe you should've invited her to this dinner."

"I did."

"And what was her reason for declining?"

"She had to shampoo her hair." He laughed. "Yeah, I know, it's the oldest excuse in the book."

"I'll talk to her and see what her objections are. Since she's so dedicated to finding a cure for polio, maybe she's looking at it from a different angle."

"Thanks, that's all I can ask."

The waiter cleared our empty plates. "May I offer you dessert? We have fresh peach cobbler tonight."

"Not for me," Peter and Mr. Sweeney said in unison.

I smiled and said, "No cobbler, but I'd love a dish of ice cream."

CHAPTER 41

Mary Frances and Malcolm sat at the kitchen table playing cribbage when we returned from dinner. I'd asked both Peter and Mr. Sweeney to come in for coffee, but only Peter had accepted.

Mary Frances played a double run of three and counted out loud as she moved her pin along the board to win the game.

Malcolm threw down his cards. "I can't beat you no matter what." He grinned at us. "I've never seen anyone so lucky."

Mary Frances rolled her eyes. "Lucky? It's pure skill." She put the pins in the compartment on the back of the cribbage board. We chatted about the dinner while the coffee perked, and Malcolm told Mary Frances they'd have to try the Cypress Lodge some night when she wasn't on duty.

Doreen's letter again flashed through my mind. *Malcolm might shed some light on your situation.* It looked like the only thing Malcolm was capable of was flirting with my mother-in-law.

I pulled coffee mugs from the cupboard. "Coffee, anyone?"

Malcolm yawned. "None for me, thanks. I've got an early morning engagement with a fishing pole."

Mary Frances gathered her things and said she was ready to turn in, too.

My skin itched to say something, but whatever Malcolm knew might be so insignificant he didn't remember. I took a chance. "Say, Malcolm, I got a letter from Doreen Palmer today."

His face brightened. "How is the old girl?"

"She sounded fine. Said to tell you hello."

"She and Paddy were two of the finest people I've ever known. They were crazy about you."

"You must've thought it strange for a child to be visiting old people."

"Paddy said you were a relative, if I recall. Guess I never gave it much thought."

He picked up the cribbage board and offered his arm to Mary Frances. Halfway out the door, Malcolm turned around. "Sure do miss swapping fishing stories with Paddy."

"He was a character all right." I thanked them for watching the girls and held the door for them.

Peter handed me a steaming cup of coffee and invited me to sit by him on the divan. We talked briefly about Van Sweeney and his plans for a retreat. Then Peter surprised me by asking what my aunt Cora was like.

"It depends. As a volunteer, she's dedicated and tenacious. Nothing stops her once her mind is made up."

"Sounds like someone else I know."

"You mean Mr. Sweeney? He seems more diplomatic—"

Peter looked at me, his eyes full of laughter. "No, I meant you. You're one determined girl...a lot like your aunt, I'd say."

"We are nothing alike. Trust me, I've always been her cross to bear."

"I doubt that. So tell me, how old were you when you came to live with her?"

"It's a long story."

"I've got all night."

"Well, it all started when Grandfather Tickle died..."

I told him about being abandoned and the frustration of never knowing why my parents left. I then showed him Doreen's letter, which he read with a scowl on his face.

"The answer is here at the Stardust?"

"Apparently. I'm not sure I even want to know anymore, and now it seems that Doreen and Paddy knew all along. I trusted them, and they didn't tell me. I've gone through most of my life thinking I'm flawed in some way and that's why people leave me."

He draped his arm around my shoulder and nuzzled my neck. "If it's any consolation, you'd still be the same beautiful woman whether you know why your parents left or not."

"In my head, I know you're right—not necessarily beautiful— although it's sweet of you to say so. I think it's more that I always thought it was my fault." My hand toyed with the front of his shirt and through the cotton I felt his muscles ripple, taut against ribs.

"You were a child. And no one leaves a child without a good reason."

"That's what puzzles me. Aunt Cora has chosen to not tell me, an action Paddy and Doreen condoned. It makes me think they must've had something to do with it."

In the crook of his arm and with my face against his chest, I could feel his heart beat steady and strong. I lifted my chin and wrinkled my nose. "I'm starting to sound like an echo, saying the same things over and over."

"I like to hear you talk, but if it's bothering you, I have a fix for it." His free hand cradled my face as his lips found mine and grazed them ever so gently.

My breath caught, and I knew I wanted nothing more than for Peter to kiss me again and again. He must've read my mind, for his lips were sweet and tender, then full on mine, and for the moment, nothing else in all the world mattered.

✦

The following morning, the girls were teaching Merciful how to play Go Fish, so I grabbed a second cup of coffee and went to the office to give Aunt Cora a call.

She asked me about Avril and then said, "I've been expecting you to call."

"Why's that?"

"Because of the absurd idea Van Sweeney's got up his sleeve."

"You mean expanding the Stardust into a retreat center?"

She sniffed. "I'm not opposed to the general idea, but he needs to think twice about the Stardust."

"The setting is ideal with the cottages we already have."

"It would only disrupt your lives further. You and the girls don't need that."

"Is it because of the Stardust or Mr. Sweeney himself?"

"We know nothing about Van except he appeared out of thin air with a grandiose plan."

"He's familiar with Mayhaw and the Stardust. He's been open about saying he'd been here before and has fond memories. I didn't know until last night, though, that you'd met him before."

"It was ages ago. I wasn't even in the tenth grade."

"You must've made quite an impression for him to remember you."

"We were a bunch of silly girls, giggling because he winked at us from the stage."

"You're not a silly girl now. And last night, I got the distinct impression Mr. Sweeney is still interested in you."

"What he's interested in doesn't concern me in the least. With my schedule, if Cary Grant walked in the front door right now, I'd have to tell him to come back next week."

"I know you're busy, so I'll get back to the point. Would you—and the March of Dimes—be willing to support the retreat center if I agreed to it? I think it would be wonderful for people like Fiona, her sister Inez, and the kids."

"You don't even know if Fiona will make it out of the iron lung. Some don't, you know."

"Sadly, that's true. I was only using them as hypothetical examples. And I would want to discuss it with Hugh Salazar before I give a definite answer."

"It's obvious Van has you convinced."

A commotion broke out in the quarters, and Avril ran into the office. "Rosey said come get you. We can't get the drawer unsticked in our room."

I put my hand over the mouthpiece. "I'm talking to Aunt Cora. Go try again."

She stuck out her lower lip. "I want the fish Catfish maked for me, and the drawer won't open. Please." She batted her lashes and lowered her chin, and I knew tears would follow.

"Aunt Cora, I need to go. Won't you think about what it would mean for families?"

"I'm trying to, Georgia. Give the girls a hug."

Avril pulled on my hand and took me to their room. It was a drawer in the wardrobe that was stuck. The hulking piece of furniture Doreen left behind still smelled of mothballs when it rained, so I didn't let the girls keep their clothes in it. It had come in handy for all their other belongings. The drawer in question would only open an inch, with all the coloring pages and assorted junk jamming it.

"Are you sure your fish is in here?" I looped my finger in, trying to find it.

"Yes. I put it there when MeMaw made us clean our rooms."

Rosey looked in the dark depths of the drawer. "I can see it."

"I'll get a coat hanger and see if I can hook it."

Avril started laughing. "You're funny, Mommy. You're going to hook my fish."

"I'm going to try. And you're right, that is funny." I worked the hanger around and thought I had it, so with a firm hold, I wiggled the drawer, trying to dislodge the cypress fish. The drawer popped open with a crack of wood splintering. I handed the prized possession to Avril and looked to see what I'd broken.

The bottom of the drawer had split, but something seemed odd. I removed the contents of the drawer and discovered that the shattered wood concealed a shallow compartment.

My neck veins throbbed, the pressure like a noose tugging at my jaw. Doreen had left the wardrobe hoping I would discover its secret. My lungs had run out of air, leaving a half-dizzy, half-silly bubbling in my head. My fingers worked to remove the rest of the splintered bits, but already I could see the edges of a photograph and a paper with blurred ink.

Scooping up the items in my hand, I stumbled back to Rosey's bed and sat down. Either I had found some long-forgotten relic that meant nothing or I had struck gold.

I prayed it wasn't fool's gold.

CHAPTER 42

"Mommy, what's wrong?" Rosey's voice was far away, like she was shouting through water.

I thought I was drowning myself. That my arms and legs couldn't get the oxygen to continue splashing. My lungs burned as I stared glassy-eyed at the paper in my hand.

My birth certificate. At least the date of my birth was correct. *May 1, 1927.* And my first and middle names. *Georgia Lee.*

My stomach heaved.

Birth mother: Cora Tickle
Age of mother: 16
Birth father: Unknown

Rosey stood close, her body warm next to my shivering one. She waved a photograph in front of my face. "Momma, why's there a picture of me when I was little?"

"Why?" That was the question. *Why? Oh Lord Jesus, why?*

"I don't know, Rosey...it's not you. Look, you've never had a dress like that. It's not you." My voice was sharp. No one else was in the picture, only me standing beside the car of my childhood dreams. I took the picture from her, rage bubbling up from the depths.

Aunt Cora. *My mother. This time she would give me the answers.*
Now. Before I lost my nerve. And my breakfast.

"Rosey, go find Ludi and tell her I have to run an errand. You girls mind what she tells you."

I didn't wait for her response, just grabbed my purse, my birth certificate, and the photograph. My hands grew numb from gripping the steering wheel, and I don't remember the drive over to State Street and Mara Lee. Quivering legs carried me to the back door. I flung it open and saw something hurtling through the air toward me.

Glass shattered against the doorjamb. Aunt Cora stood wide-eyed and poised with another one of Grandma Tickle's china plates.

"I told you—" Her jaw dropped, her mouth trying to form words. She blinked, let her hand with the plate drop to her side, and winced. "Sorry. I thought you were that miserable Van Sweeney sneaking back in."

"What's gotten into you, Aunt Cora? Or maybe I should be saying Momma." I waved the birth certificate through the air.

"Oh, my." Her face turned white. "He's already told you. How? He left here not three minutes ago. What were you doing? Listening at the keyholes again?" She laughed, a tinny cackle. "You were good at that when you were younger."

She looked at the plate in her hand, reared back, and hurled it, too—not at me, but at the open door. It shattered on the porch railing, the china bits like a wind chime ruffled by a sudden breeze.

"I was not listening at the keyhole." My nostrils flared as I breathed through them. "And why are you breaking Grandma Tickle's dishes?"

She pressed the back of her hand against her mouth, her face contorted. "I'm sorry. I'm so sorry."

"How could you? You had a million opportunities to tell me you were my mother, and you never let on. Not once. I'm sorry for the trouble I've caused you. All this time, I thought it was my parents who were ashamed or hated me. Now I see you must have despised waking up every day and having to face whatever shame I'd brought to you."

My breaths came out in huffs. "Don't worry. You won't have to endure my presence any longer. I will disappear from your life. I'll give up the Stardust and take the girls somewhere else."

"No. Please. Let me explain—"

"You had your chance."

I turned to go, my heart leaden, questions still slamming against my skull like the steel balls in a pinball machine.

Aunt Cora grabbed my arm, her fingers biting into my flesh. "You're right. I had a chance to give you up. As a matter of fact, my father thought I did. But I couldn't. It didn't matter that I was sixteen years old and your father didn't even know you existed. I couldn't do it. Never. Please. Hear me out."

This wasn't the poised, always-in-perfect-control Aunt Cora I knew. Her veneer had cracked, and I saw a tired, desperate shell of a woman.

I removed her hand from my arm and through clenched teeth said, "Only because I would regret it forever if I didn't hear the story, I'll listen."

"Come. I'll fix us a cup of tea."

"Don't bother, but I would like to sit down."

We sat facing each other at the breakfast table. Two half-empty cups sat on the table, the remnant of Van Sweeney's visit and the cause of Aunt Cora's outburst. I knew he must be the unknown father, but I had to hear it from her own lips. An unnatural calm spread over me; I was ready to hear what she had to say.

She folded her hands on the table. "You had to have known my father to understand. He was harsh, controlling, and ruled our home with an iron fist. My poor mother endured his rants with grace, and I believe now it was an act of mercy that God allowed her to pass from this earth when I was twelve years old. My sister, Justine, took her death hard and started standing up to Father. They went round and round until he kicked her out and told her he never wanted to see her again. She left home when she was seventeen and married Gordon Mackey. They lived in Kipling, but Justine would still visit her friends in Mayhaw once in a while. She was wild and daring, not always in a good way.

"I was left to handle Father. The summer I was fifteen, I wanted to go with my friends to see the touring vaudeville act, but Father wouldn't let me. As luck would have it, he was called to Shreveport on business, so I went anyway. Three nights in a row. The last night, my friends heard of a party at the Stardust, and I was afraid to go because Uncle Paddy might see me. But when Van Sweeney, the one I had my eye on, asked me to come, I did.

"Some of the guys brought liquor. I'd never had a drink in my life, but that night I did. It felt so liberating. At first we were all just laughing and dancing, but then people started pairing off. I started feeling sick and went to the bathroom in one of the cottages. When I came out, Van was waiting for me. He'd been drinking, too, and..." Tears brimmed in her eyes.

I leaned back, my own memory of O'Dell flashing like a marquee in my head. "You don't have to explain that part. I know what you mean."

She smiled, the first since I'd come to her house. "I guess you do. And I now realize I pushed you into marrying O'Dell because you at least had a man who offered. Not that Father would have allowed me to marry Van. By the time I found out I was expecting, Van was long gone. I went to the Stardust to ask Paddy and Doreen for his address so I could write and tell him the news. They suspected something was wrong and had seen me that night even though I thought they hadn't. They didn't have his address but forced me to tell Father about the baby."

It didn't sound like the Doreen and Paddy I knew, but they probably thought they were helping. "Is that why you didn't like them?"

"No, they ended up helping me. Father sent me to an unwed mother's home in Tyler and made it clear I had to give you up. He told people I had a nervous breakdown. I wrote Paddy and Doreen and begged them to help me. They're the ones who arranged for Justine and Gordon to take you. Paddy offered to pay them for their trouble. Justine took advantage of them and threatened to spill the beans if Paddy didn't give them more money. Blackmail, really.

"When Father died, they brought you to the funeral. Paddy told them he was through giving them money, so they left you with me. I was thrilled and gladly gave them their half of Father's bank account with the promise they wouldn't come back. Or tell. I knew I'd never find a husband if word got out that I'd had a baby out of wedlock."

I laughed, but it was harsh. "Guess that didn't pan out so well, huh?"

"I know. You reap what you sow, and I wanted to tell you the truth, but when you got older, I just couldn't."

"That still doesn't explain why you didn't get along with Paddy and Doreen. You owed them a lot."

"I regret so many things. They're one of them. They thought I should tell you the truth, but I'd already made up my mind. We argued, and I refused to see them. I was mortified when you started going out there. I was afraid they'd tell you."

"I guess that's what Doreen meant by saying they'd given their word."

Alarm flashed in Aunt Cora's eyes. "Doreen is here? She gave you the birth certificate?"

"No." I told her she'd written and how I'd found it in the wardrobe. "Funny. I was just trying to help Avril get the cypress knee Catfish carved for her."

"Who in heaven's name is Catfish?"

"Ludi's son. He has the most amazing talent for carving. He told us the legend about cypress knees, how they connect the trees up and down the bayou. He compared them to people, that we're all connected even when it doesn't seem like we are."

"Uncle Paddy used to tell me that story. I'd forgotten." Tears glistened in her eyes.

A lull fell between us. It didn't change the years of lies Aunt Cora told me. How could I ever get used to thinking of her as the woman who gave me birth, then lied for twenty-five years? The coil wrapped around my heart tightened.

Aunt Cora placed her hands on her cheeks and rubbed them. "I don't know what happens now. I guess it's your call. I'm too old to care about my reputation, and with Van coming back, I'm in more of a tizzy than ever."

"I think he cares for you. And you must've told him about me. I guess that's what you were shouting about. Why did you tell him when you wouldn't even tell me?"

"I didn't tell him. He figured it out. He said you look just like his sister. He and Malcolm Overstreet started comparing notes, I think. Malcolm was at the Stardust that night. Not part of the vaudeville act, but he partied with us. What a mess."

"It's a mess you created. I think you should untangle it. Maybe it's time you told the truth for a change."

"I didn't expect you to be so bitter."

"I guess that's one thing you did teach me." My mouth tasted sour—the same way it did every time O'Dell cheated on me again. I hated the dirty way I felt, raw inside. I gathered up my birth certificate, the photograph, and my purse. "One other thing. How did your mother die?"

"I thought you knew. She had polio."

CHAPTER 43

I'd never felt so alone as I did when I left Mara Lee. Yearn-ing most of my life to know the truth, and now it was like an ocean wave, swelling over my head, slapping me in the face. I had to remind myself to breathe. The logical thing would be to turn O'Dell's Ford around, go back to Mara Lee, break some more of Grandma Tickle's china, and scream at Aunt Cora to get it out of my system.

I had always said I could deal with the truth. What I'd never gotten beyond was how exactly I would do that. It sounded so much more logical in my head. The people in my imagination who I would have to absolve were Justine and Gordon. Never had I imagined it was Aunt Cora. Stupid of me!

All the signs were there. The big deal she made of my birthday every year. Ha! A day I'm sure she could never forget. Her protec-tiveness of me... of the girls. Of course. I had that fierce mother-ing complex, too. I would die before I let something happen to one of my girls.

A horn blasted through my rolled-down window. I looked up in time to see I was driving in the wrong lane and cars were swerving to avoid me. Someone hollered "Watch out!" from the sidewalk.

I jerked into the right-hand lane, gunned the engine, and drove until I found a spot where it was safe to pull over. My hands ached from gripping the steering wheel. I flexed my fingers to work the pain out, then leaned back and closed my eyes. Tears trickled down my cheeks, slowly at first, then in a steady stream as my chest heaved with sobs.

Pressing the back of my fist against my lips, I tried to gain control. Bitterness nestled into the hollow spot I'd reserved for my parents, but it had Aunt Cora's name on it. *My mother.*

Tears welled up again. Would my life have turned out different if I'd grown up knowing she was my mother? Would I have confided in her and taken a different path with O'Dell? I shuddered. My "mistake" with O'Dell was no different than Aunt Cora's. And while I should be ensuring that my girls didn't make the same mistakes we did, I wasted my energy lamenting O'Dell and his unfaithfulness and despising Aunt Cora for not telling me the truth about my parents.

The truth was there now. I could stay mad at Aunt Cora, deny Van Sweeney was my father, and harbor resentment toward O'Dell till the earth stopped spinning. And if I did, it would rot my soul.

I wanted the shackles gone. All of them.

Digging through my purse for a hankie, I came up with the photo of me beside Justine and Gordon's car. I did look like Rosey, wild curls and all. But I was frowning, sadness in my eyes. It dawned on me that I couldn't remember anything about my childhood before the day we came to the Stardust. Surely, there had been birthday parties and Christmas, but I didn't have a single memory. It was like that part of my life hadn't existed...that it all began the day I came to live with Aunt Cora.

Live. That's what I wanted to do. Live happily. Freely. Without hanging on to remorse. Without passing on to my girls a bucket of mistruths and resentment.

I found the hankie and wiped my nose, then turned the car around. I couldn't wait to tell Aunt Cora that I forgave her. And loved her. And wanted her to be my mother.

✳

After supper, Mary Frances and Malcolm took the girls for ice cream so Peter and I could talk. When I'd gone back to see Aunt Cora, we cried in each other's arms and talked about the future. We agreed that we would talk to Van together and proceed from there. Neither of us knew if he would even stick around for the benefit. She had a meeting to attend, and I had been gone longer than I intended, so I went home and kept up the pretense. A few more days wouldn't hurt, but my soul-searching had also revealed that I no longer wanted to hang on to the bitterness I had toward O'Dell, so I'd come up with a plan.

Peter thought we were going to rehearse for the talent show, so he'd brought along his guitar. And Sebastian. He seemed surprised when I hooked my arm in his and led him around to the back steps of the quarters. Catfish waited on the steps as I'd asked him to. He was hunched over like he wanted his body to swallow his head.

"It's okay, Catfish. I need for you to show me something."

"What, Miz Georgie?"

"The place where you found Mr. O'Dell's body washed up. Think you could do that?"

Both he and Peter looked at me as if I'd lost my mind.

"Come on now. It'll be dusk soon, and I want to see it."

Peter stowed his guitar in the washhouse and told Sebastian to stay. The dog lay down with his paws over his face and pouted, but he stayed.

Catfish led the way, his steps heavy at first, looking back every dozen yards to see if we were still behind him. I'd worn sturdy shoes, and a dress with pockets for what I wanted to carry. Tickle grass brushed against my legs as we went across the meadow. I inhaled the deep scent of the outdoors, and as we neared the trees, the bayou smells crept toward us. Rich. Moist. Fish and pine smells melting together, thick in the back of my throat.

When we reached the trees, our feet padded on the spongy needled floor as curtains of Spanish moss waved us through. We passed the clearing where jasmine branches reached for the sun, their blossoms gone but their scent rising like dew from the earth. Catfish darted fawn-like between the trees then came to an abrupt stop.

"This is the place." He pointed at the murky water with shades of green and brown shifting in the shadows. "Right here. It got stuck in the cypress knees."

It. Not he. Or Mr. O'Dell. I hated to make Catfish revisit the terrible memory, but I wanted him to know, too, that nothing was his fault.

I pointed to the spot. "There?"

He nodded and stepped back.

I stepped closer and tried to picture O'Dell's body. Not the bloated mess I knew it was, but the way he was in life. Loving to his daughters. Content on the bayou. Stillness rose up from the waters, and a tern upstream squawked. I tried to think of what O'Dell must've felt that day. Torn over what to do with the mess of his life? Regret, perhaps, that he'd gotten himself into a situation that had no easy solution? I thought he was so deep in despair, he didn't notice the water rising, roiling, speeding him toward eternity.

My hand slid into my pocket, my fingers curled around the rose petals I'd plucked earlier. I didn't throw them but tossed them out like I was feeding chickens, scattering them here and there, watching as they floated, clumped together, drifted, then became one with the lazy water.

My eyes misted as my heart released O'Dell to his beloved bayou.

I turned and took a small dark hand in mine. "Thank you, Catfish. You're a brave boy. I'm lucky to know you."

Tears tracked like raindrops down his cheeks. He didn't answer but gave my hand a squeeze. His free hand swiped across his eyes.

Night had settled in the woods, a hint of campfire in the air. I gave Catfish a hug and swatted his bottom. "Run on home now. Your momma's probably got supper ready. See you tomorrow." I didn't have to tell him twice.

When we reached the open meadow, Peter stopped and put his arm around me. "I've no idea what that was all about, but I have to say, I felt something back there. It was either a swamp ghost or the presence of the Almighty."

"I felt it, too. Before you think I'm prone to insanity, I should explain. Today I realized my obsession with O'Dell and all the wrongs he did to me would last forever if I didn't release them. I have two girls I would die for and a mother-in-law who's part of the family whether her son is alive or not. Without O'Dell, none of that would have been possible. I had to go to the bayou tonight and let go of my bitterness."

Peter squeezed my shoulder. "I know it's tough. I'm honored you chose me to go with you."

"I was afraid if we came upon a water moccasin or something I'd need you to protect me."

"Ah, so now I know the real reason."

"I needed you to myself for another reason. It may take me

awhile to get it all out. Please be patient." I reached in the other pocket of my dress and pulled out a wad of tissues. "I'll probably need these and don't want to cry all over your shirt."

We took a different route home, following the cypress line along the bayou. I told Peter what I'd discovered in the wardrobe and about my visit with Aunt Cora. That Van Sweeney was my father. And she was my birth mother.

My mother. A flood of tears came, and I had to stop and blow my nose. A crescent moon had risen above the bayou, its points tilted upward. I sniffed and pointed to it. "My lucky day. The moon's smiling."

Peter drew me in and kissed me long and hard. "Every day with you's my lucky day." He held me close for a long time, then relaxed his hold and kissed my forehead. "I believe you were in the middle of telling me something."

"The intermission was nice. Now, where was I? I remember. The tough part. When I left Aunt Cora's, I honestly didn't know if I could ever forgive her."

"It's a lot to take in, I admit. How do you forgive something like that?"

"I wrestled with it, but in the end it wasn't as hard as I thought. God has a way of bringing us to our knees, doesn't he? Aunt Cora has devoted her life to fighting polio and gave up a lot to raise me. Granted, we didn't see eye to eye most of the time, and I know there are repercussions to our actions, but she was loving and devoted and generous. She made an immature choice once, but she did what she honestly thought was the best for me. And whether it was or not doesn't matter."

"So you've talked to her?"

"I went back to her house after storming off. This is new territory for both of us, so there were a few tears. Van Sweeney doesn't know what drama he's been swept into. I just hope he stays through the benefit on Friday night."

"I bet you won't have to worry there. Besides, it seems to me he's the center of the drama, as you call it."

"We hope to talk to him together...if he's willing."

We came through the sycamore grove behind the Stardust and rounded the corner of the end cottage. Peter stopped. "Here's your chance. Look who just drove up."

My heart went into overdrive. "I think I'm going to faint."

"Faint? You said you wanted to talk to them."

"I do. That's not why I'm light-headed. Aunt Cora once told me the governor would dance at her wedding before she stepped foot in the Stardust. Do you think it's a sign?"

"More like a sign that you're a goose. Come on, you have company."

Since Mary Frances and Malcolm were back from getting ice cream with the girls, Peter offered to go in and let me talk with Aunt Cora and Mr. Sweeney alone. A gentle glow from the Stardust sign lit our way as we strolled through the flower garden the Magnolias had brought to life. Aunt Cora stopped by a rosebush and plucked a newly opened bloom.

"Van insisted we come here instead of you coming to my place."

I chuckled. "I didn't know you hated the Stardust because it held so many bad memories."

"They weren't bad. As a matter of fact, I loved this place once like you did, sweetie. But it also held my secrets. It's lovely what you've done with it." She held the rose to her face and inhaled.

"I had a lot of help, and I'm glad you came." My underarms grew damp with the thought of talking to my dad—such a strange thought still.

Mr. Sweeney started us off, though, by clearing his throat. "I know I'm the newcomer here, and it's been a heckuva week. Before I came, I dreamed that Cora would remember me, but I knew my chances were slim. Imagine my delight to find her involved in the one thing that's been my passion. Not to mention renewing our...uh...friendship." He took her hand and raised it to his lips, grazing the back of it.

He turned to me. "And I've found someone I didn't even know was missing. Georgia, I know what a shock this is to you, but from the minute I saw you, I knew you were my daughter. Dragging the truth out of Cora was harder than you can imagine."

"I can imagine, all right. You had more success in ten days than I had in almost twenty years. But you're right, it has been a shock." My legs trembled, and I crossed my arms, rubbing the goose bumps on my bare flesh.

Aunt Cora pulled me into her arms. "I know I can never make this up to you. I've robbed you of a mother—"

"—and cheated me out of a daughter." Mr. Sweeney's voice interrupted, but his tone was light.

Aunt Cora put her hands on her hips and looked up at him. "I didn't even know where you were. If you'd have come back, I might've—"

"No more of what might have been, Cora." Mr. Sweeney pulled her into the crook of one arm and held out the other for me.

I leaned into him, his body warm with a sweet pine scent. Fatherly. Strong. He kissed the top of my head. "I do want to inform you, it's going to be much harder to get rid of me this time. I plan to stick around Mayhaw and see if your mother can stand me."

Your mother. "She deserves someone nice, and I'm glad it's you."

Aunt Cora—my mother—said, "If it's all right with you, Georgia, I'd like to be the one to tell the girls they now have two grandmothers."

My throat clogged, and I bit my lower lip. "Are you sure?"

"I have a lot to make up for, and I'd like to start by telling them the truth."

"The truth is good. And yes, we'll tell them...together."

The three of us linked arms to face our new beginning.

CHAPTER 44

The next few days were a whirlwind. Rosey latched on to the news that Aunt Cora was her grandmother and used it to her advantage, starting with Aunt Cora's offering to take us all shopping for new outfits for the Mayhaw Festival. Avril was oblivious, and I hoped that, like me, she wouldn't remember her early years and would grow up thinking our new order of things was normal. Where Aunt Cora and Van Sweeney were headed was anyone's guess, but I predicted wedding bells in their future.

Ludi shook her head and did a hallelujah dance until her feet gave out. I made her let me make a pattern of her foot and take her measurements. While Aunt Cora shopped with the girls, I picked out new shoes for Ludi—extrawide—and two new dresses. Ludi nearly cried when I presented them to her, but clutched them to her chest like they were purest linen.

Hugh Salazar called and said Aunt Cora had been to see him. "The woman looks ten years younger."

"Maybe if you'd told me the truth, you'd look ten years younger, too."

"You always were a handful, Georgia. Now get your pretty

little self down here so we can discuss this deal Sweeney's cooked up."

The night of the concert, spirits ran high, both at the Stardust and in town. Polio had taken its toll on too many people. Aunt Cora left the master of ceremony's duties to Bobby Carl, who looked like a penguin in his tuxedo, but I had to admit, he had a certain verve in front of an audience. Especially when he introduced Aunt Cora as the First Lady of the war against polio.

Van Sweeney was a natural on the stage as his baritone voice belted out "Hard-Hearted Hannah, the Vamp of Savannah" and "Play a Simple Melody" where one of his band members did the countermelody. He glided from ragtime to minstrel music into jazz as easy as a catfish slipped between the cypress knees on a lazy bayou. The audience sang along, clapped, and gave him a standing ovation that led to two encores. He ended with "God Bless America" and thanked everyone for being generous and giving to the March of Dimes.

"Together we can stamp out polio." The flag above the town square stood as proud as our hearts that night.

Aunt Cora closed the show by asking Mr. Sweeney and me to join her on the stage for the announcement of the Stardust retreat center.

After a brief summary of what we had planned, she thanked everyone for doing their part. "Polio is a battle we will fight until we find the cure. I pray that tomorrow might be that day."

A loud cheer went up. She waved and shouted above the roar, "Don't forget that tomorrow is the talent show. God bless you."

✦

Peter and I didn't win the talent show. Rosey did. She surprised us all by asking the Pearl sisters to play "Swing Low, Sweet Chariot."

Her version had all the heart and soul of Ludi's rendition, but with actions. Rosey strutted and swooned and tapped her foot, never missing a lick.

Later, as Rosey lapped up being the center of attention and showing off her trophy, my friend Sally Cotton came up to me. "There's no doubt, she gets her talent from you."

"I don't know about that, but I do know she comes by it naturally." My eyes drifted to the circle around Rosey where Van—who insisted I stop calling him Mr. Sweeney—had his arm around Aunt Cora and looked up to make eye contact with me. He smiled and winked.

Sally noticed. "What's going on? Is there something I'm missing?"

"You've missed a lot, but if you're free next week, let's have coffee and catch up."

"Sounds divine. By the way, where's that honey of yours?"

"If you mean Peter, he's supposed to be fetching us some lemonade."

One of the Magnolias waved at Sally so she bustled off, and as I stood there taking it all in, my heart swelled with warmth. Friends. Family. A brighter future. Tears wet my eyes, and I felt a hand go around my waist. Aunt Cora.

"Georgia, sweetie, what's wrong?"

"Nothing. I was just thinking how lucky I am to have you and the girls. And Peter and Van, too."

"I know."

"There is one thing. I saw Hugh Salazar awhile ago, and it reminded me. All those men who came in the back door of Mara Lee when I was a kid. What were they doing? Or maybe I should say, what were *you* doing?"

"I must admit, I had no idea what you were talking about when you brought it up. Then I realized who you saw was Hugh, Mr.

Wilkins from the bank, a few men from out of town who were investors. My sister wasn't happy with only half of the Tickle fortune. She bled me for every penny she could. It took all those men to juggle the oil royalties and property investments I had so we could keep our head above water during the Depression. Even then, you know how run-down Mara Lee got."

"But if you'd told the truth, Justine wouldn't have had a hold over you."

"I don't know. Because of her, I was able to keep you. It was a small price to pay. Besides, she was family, and nothing was ever easy for Justine."

I almost asked if she knew where Justine was now, but I was afraid it would spoil a perfect evening. Instead, I kissed Aunt Cora's cheek. "By the way, what do you want me to call you?"

"I think plain old Cora would be nice."

"You got it, but there's nothing plain or old about you." I linked my arm in hers. "Come on, let's find Peter and see what's taking so long with that lemonade."

We met him halfway to the lemonade stand. He had a sheepish look as he handed over the chilled cup. "Sorry, I got distracted."

"I hope she was pretty." I wrinkled my nose at him. Cora waved at Hazel Morton from church and excused herself.

Peter cocked his head. "Funny, I never thought of Bobby Carl Applegate as pretty."

"So what's up with our favorite promoter?"

"He liked my number in the talent show, the solo I sang. He thinks I've got a shot at the big time in Nashville."

"Oh, really?"

"Took me twenty minutes to convince him that the Georgia I was singing about was you and not the state." He lifted his glass. "To you, ma'am. And many more happy memories at the Stardust."

"How many times do I have to tell you not to call me ma'am?"

"Guess that depends on how long you let me stick around."

"How about forever?"

"That sounds like a proposal to me."

I sipped my lemonade and looked into his clear blue eyes. What I saw there was a lifetime of picnics and kids squealing as they ran through the grass. I saw hot summer days and cypress knees connecting God's creation. I saw straw hats and long, slender fingers strumming an old sweet song. And I saw two people growing old under the neon glow of the Stardust.

A small hand tugged my dress. I stooped to look into Avril's face.

"Yes, sugar, what is it?"

"Can I have a Popsicle?"

1. The Stardust Tourist Cottages held Georgia's earliest memories of her parents. What is your earliest memory? Can you picture where it took place? Have you ever revisited it or the home where you lived as a child?

2. Georgia always longed to know why her parents left her. Was it right for Aunt Cora to withhold the truth from her? What part did society's pressures play in Cora Tickle's actions? Is it the same or different today in regard to having children out of wedlock? In what ways?

3. O'Dell had a wandering eye even before Georgia married him, but her aunt insisted she go through with the wedding. Was this good advice? How much of it came from Cora's past experience? Have you ever felt forced to make a decision in order to please someone else? What were the results?

4. Georgia clung to her dream to keep the Stardust open even when adversity came. Why do you think she was so determined? Have you ever clung to a dream even when it seemed illogical? Did your persistence pay off?

5. Polio (infantile paralysis) played a major role in *Stardust*. Were you familiar with the fear and hysteria it caused in the

first half of the twentieth century? Have you known anyone who had polio? Can you think of any illnesses or threats to society today that people fear? Has public hysteria or media attention caused you to fear things you normally wouldn't?

6. The Stardust symbolized open arms for those who needed a haven. How was this an extension of Georgia's hospitality toward others? If you have the gift of hospitality, how do you exemplify it in your own life?

7. Georgia felt responsible for her mother-in-law, Mary Frances. Her obedience in doing the right thing led to a positive change in Mary Frances. Can you think of a time when you did something out of obedience and saw good come from it? If nothing happened, would you still say you'd done the right thing?

8. Peter Reese came to the Stardust in need of work and a place to stay. What qualities did Georgia see in him to make her trust him? How do first impressions affect your decisions? What if Georgia had been wrong about Peter's honesty and work ethic? How might this book have turned out differently?

9. Did the setting add to your interest in the story? What settings intrigue you? Small town or city? Southern, international, or seaside?

10. The cypress knees symbolize being connected in mysterious ways. Sometimes God brings people into our lives for reasons we don't understand. Can you think of a time when someone came into your life unexpectedly? Did the person you connected with come for a short season of your life or become a lifelong friend?

11. Segregation, poverty, and illiteracy marked the community of Zion. Do you think prejudice and poverty still exist in

America today? Has anyone ever shown prejudice against you because of your race or your circumstances?

12. In spite of her circumstances, Ludi Harper had strong faith. How did she show this in her everyday life? What effect did this have on the people around her? When you are faced with difficulties, does your faith stand firm or waver?

13. Malcolm Overstreet secretly provided medical services to the people of Zion. Do you think he kept it private out of modesty or fear of repercussion from the white community? What are some ways you use your talents to give back to your community?

14. When Ludi brought Fiona to the Stardust, no one knew who she was or how disruptive her presence would be to their lives. How might Georgia have reacted if she'd known this was the woman O'Dell left her for? How did Fiona and her children help Georgia embrace O'Dell's infidelity?

15. When faced with bitter truths, Georgia seemed to have a forgiving heart. How did this mesh with the rest of her personality? Why is it harder for some people to forgive than others? Have you ever had to forgive someone for a great injustice? How does faith play a role in seeking and bestowing forgiveness?

16. Cora had a passion for the March of Dimes since her mother died of polio. Georgia took in Fiona's children because she knew the feeling of abandonment. Do your passions in life spring from personal experience? What passions would you sacrifice or die for?

If you liked *Stardust,*
be sure to pick up Carla Stewart's
award-winning first novel,
Chasing Lilacs

"Stewart writes about powerful and basic emotions with a restraint that suggests depth and
authenticity...Coming-of-age stories are a fiction
staple, but well-done ones much rarer. This emotionally acute novel is
one of the rare ones."   —*Publishers Weekly*, starred review

Sammie Tucker has plenty of questions about her mother's
"nerve" problems. About shock treatments. About whether her
mother loves her.

As her life careens out of control, Sammie has to choose whom
to trust with her deepest fears: her best friend who has an opinion
about everything, the mysterious boy from out of town whose
own troubles plague him, her round-faced neighbor with gentle advice and strong shoulders to cry on, or the elderly widower
who seems nice but has his own dark past.

Trusting is one thing, but accepting the truth may be the hard-
est thing Sammie has ever done.

"*Chasing Lilacs* is the kind of coming-of-age story that sticks to you
beyond the last page. Unforgettable characters, surprising plot twists,
and a setting so Southern you'll fall in love with Texas. Carla Stewart
is a new talent to watch!"

                              —Mary E. DeMuth, author of *Daisy Chain* and *A Slow Burn*

You may also enjoy
Broken Wings

"A memorable story, beautifully written. Set against the backdrop of Tulsa's intriguing jazz culture, Carla Stewart's *Broken Wings* is a captivating intergenerational tale of friendship, love, and music that surpasses the boundaries of age and time."

—Tina Ann Forkner, author of *Ruby Among Us* and *Rose House*

Onstage, the singing duo of Gabe and Mitzi Steiner captured America's heart for more than two decades. Offstage, their own hearts have throbbed as one for sixty years. Only now, Gabe has retreated into the tangles of Alzheimer's, leaving Mitzi to ponder her future alone.

In another world, everyone believes Brooke Woodson has found the perfect man—a handsome lawyer with sights on becoming the city's next District Attorney. If only Brooke felt more sure. If only her fiancé could control his anger. If only his love didn't come with so many scars.

An accident lands Brooke in the hospital where Mitzi volunteers, and the two women quickly develop an unlikely friendship. And with Mitzi's help, kindness, and insight, Brooke learns how to pick up the broken pieces of her life.